## AN EMPTY CHAIR IN
## THE OVAL OFFICE

It was exactly three o'clock when the truth of the matter became known to anyone beyond the President's wife, Mrs. Stanley, Harry Brownell, the President's secretary, and two Secret Service men. At that hour the members of the Cabinet assembled in the library on the second floor. They talked in low tones, as if in the presence of death.

When the door opened, they jerked about to face it. Mrs. Stanley entered, and those seated rose. She seemed out of breath, her hair was untidy, and she had put her hand on the back of the chair as if she needed it there. She said, "I have had a problem, gentlemen. I can keep it for my own no longer; it is yours and the country's. The President has been kidnapped."

Bantam Books by Rex Stout
Ask your bookseller for the books you have missed

BAD FOR BUSINESS
BLACK ORCHIDS
THE BROKEN VASE
THE LEAGUE OF FRIGHTENED MEN
THE MOTHER HUNT
THE MOUNTAIN CAT MURDERS
NOT QUITE DEAD ENOUGH
PLOT IT YOURSELF
THE PRESIDENT VANISHES
THE RED BOX
RED THREADS
THE RUBBER BAND
SOME BURIED CAESAR
TOO MANY CLIENTS

# The President Vanishes

Rex Stout

**BANTAM BOOKS**
TORONTO · NEW YORK · LONDON · SYDNEY

THE PRESIDENT VANISHES

*A Bantam Book / published by arrangement with the author*

*PRINTING HISTORY*

*Farrar and Rinehart edition published 1943*
*Bantam edition / November 1982*

ISBN 0-553-22665-7

*Published simultaneously in the United States and Canada*

---

*Bantam Books are published by Bantam Books, Inc. Its trademark, consisting of the words "Bantam Books" and the portrayal of a rooster, is Registered in U.S. Patent and Trademark Office and in other countries, Marca Registrada. Bantam Books, Inc., 666 Fifth Avenue, New York, New York 10103.*

---

PRINTED IN THE UNITED STATES OF AMERICA

O      0 9 8 7 6 5 4 3 2 1

# Contents

MONDAY—PANORAMA                 1

TUESDAY—ANTICLIMAX             37

WEDNESDAY—CONFUSION            49

THURSDAY—STALEMATE           117

FRIDAY—CURTAIN               163

# MONDAY—PANORAMA

# 1

The radiator, when Chick Moffat put his hand on it as one of his last gestures before going out a little after eight o'clock that Monday evening, was cold. Not that it mattered particularly, since it was the end of April and that meant, in Washington, that Spring's local errands were done and it was leaving for appointments farther north. Hardier boys were diving into the Potomac, the petals of the famous cherry blossoms were browning into oblivion on the green lawn, and working whites were outdoor uniform at the Navy Yard.

Chick Moffat put his hand on the radiator through force of habit, scarcely aware of its cold response. That didn't matter. The things that did matter had already been attended to; he had just spent three hours at it. He stood by the window and moved his head in a slow half-circle for an approving inspection of the ordinary but pleasant room. There was no doubt of it being comfortable. The furniture was his own: in this, the living-room, as well as in the small bedroom through the door at the right, with bath adjoining, and in the kitchen at the rear where he often prepared and ate his own meals. The chairs were yellow wicker, with blue pads of imitation leather, the rug, plain brown and spotless, was large enough to leave only a narrow strip of flooring visible along the walls, and the four or five pictures hung at eye-level were, with one exception, colored prints of landscapes in silvered frames. The exception, above the desk which stood against the wall across from the entrance door, was a large autographed photograph of the President of the United States.

Chick muttered half aloud, "Nothing to be ashamed of, if you ask me."

He had lived here six years, having rented the place and bought the furniture on the occasion of his promotion to Special Duty in the State Department, and having stubbornly hung on to it when three years later he had been picked to fill a vacancy in the White House squad. The Chief of the Bureau had hinted pointedly that a White House man might reasonably be expected to inhabit more respectable and accessible quarters than a rummy third-floor flat a good mile southeast of decency, but Chick had let the hint bounce off his nose. He hated furnished rooms of any degree of respectability whatever, and would if necessary have informed the Chief himself that rather than live in one he would move to Alexandria, wear overalls, chew tobacco, and keep chickens.

That had been three years ago. He still lived here, and was still on the White House squad.

His head completed the slow half-circle. Everything was in order. But before he could go, and go he must soon, there was a thing to be done. He had put it off until eight o'clock, but now it must be done. He sighed, crossed the room to the desk, picked up the telephone and put the receiver to his ear, and gave a number. He sat on the edge of the desk and his toe was nervously tapping the floor.

A voice said hello.

"Hello yourself. Listen, Alma. . . . Of course, don't you know my voice? Listen, Alma, I can't come."

He wanted to kick himself. So damn blunt. It always fussed him so just to hear her voice. Ass.

Her voice was saying, "No? I'm sorry."

"Are you?"

"Are I what?"

"Sorry."

"Of course. Not desolated beyond hope, but sorry—certainly. Particularly since this seems to be the wildest night Washington has known in a century, with rumors like snowflakes in a blizzard, and I had hoped you would be indiscreet. The distaff side has had a dull day."

Chick Moffat, the receiver tight against his ear, was frowning at a corner of the desk. "Well, I haven't. Nor a dull night either—that is, who will? I mean . . . listen, Alma. Of course I can't talk, damn it, I never can to you. I can't come. I've got to go on duty."

"Oh. I thought you were on duty today."

"I was. But I've got . . . well, I can't come. I thought maybe I could manage to stop in for an hour, if you'd let me do that, instead of going to a movie, but I can't make it. You know how when a soldier goes to war he gives his sweetheart something to keep? I thought maybe I'd bring you my favorite necktie—"

"Chick!" Her voice was thin with excitement. "Is it war?"

"No. How do I know? Nobody knows. Who ever tells a watchdog anything except to shut up when he barks? Nobody

3

knows but the President, and maybe he doesn't. Can I send my necktie to you parcel post?"

"Save it for your sweetheart. Tell me, Chick, is it war?"

Chick scowled at the watch on his wrist. "Alma, please. Listen, Alma, I've got to go—"

"All right. I'll sit and knit. Good-bye."

The click was in his ear. Still scowling, he hung up the receiver and put the phone on the desk. He stared at it a moment, and sighed. Then he opened a drawer of the desk and took from it an automatic pistol which he stuck in his pocket. Across the room, when he went to take his hat from the rack on the wall, he fumbled and the hat fell to the floor.

He muttered furiously, "Go ahead and get nervous, my hero," snatched up the hat and jammed it on his head, and went out.

# 2

At the moment that Chick Moffat was moving his head in a half-circle to inspect his living-room Sally Voorman was saying to Mrs. William Robert Brown:

"Could you imagine such rotten luck? Could you even imagine it? I *would* round out the season, wouldn't I? With my well-known flair. On account of it's being so late, nearly May, I took every precaution. One ambassador, and I got the Jap. Three of the best Senators, and I got them. The only general in Washington that can laugh without getting red in the face. Sam Agnew, and that alone was a triumph since the golf season has started and no poker could be expected. And so on. I tell you it could not have been better done. And look, just look around and see what I've got—did you ever see such a mess? I've been begging—would you believe it, begging?—into the phone for two hours trying to fill out, and there is the best I could do! That old fool Blanchard, for instance. I'll tell you what, Mabel, I am firmly convinced that the President decided to go before Congress with his war message on Tuesday the twenty-ninth only because he knew my dinner was Monday and that was the only thing on earth that could ruin it. Why, I ask you, why couldn't he—"

Mrs. Brown had the voice for interrupting and when so minded could use it. She said, "Sally. You say war message?"

The other, slim and pretty, stared at her with blue eyes. "Of course. Isn't it?"

"I don't know. Do you?"

"Well—it's about war. That's what I meant."

"Oh." Mrs. Brown's lips tightened, but she opened them again. "Yes, about war. I hope, against it. I hope that with all my heart and soul. I trust you do."

Sally Voorman's shoulders lifted and dropped. "I would, I suppose, if I knew anything about it. I know, Mabel, you have a serious mind, but the only hopes I've had room for today have been concentrated on this dinner, and look what has come of them! I'm out of politics, in fact I've never been in."

"War isn't politics, my dear. It is indeed the only human activity that is rottener than politics."

"Goodness!" Sally smiled at her, and patted her shoulder. "Then I'd better stay out of that too.—But it's eight-twenty, Lord help me, and this merry crew must be fed. Here comes your man. Pray for me, do."

She glided off.

Three hours later Sally Voorman stood in the spacious entrance hall of her home, smiling up at a man much taller than herself. This Senator, the only one of the "three of the best" who had not failed her, with brown hair nearly gray and the furrowed face of a veteran but minor statesman, looked down at her with exhausted brown eyes that wanted to return her smile. Some of the guests had departed; those who remained were divided between desultory dancing in the drawing-room and bridge tables upstairs. They were alone in the hall.

"I had wanted to talk to you." The blue eyes were unfalteringly up to him.

The Senator did in fact smile; heavy, but a smile. "My dear child! Thank you for that, and the dinner. It was a nice dinner."

"It was not. It was terrible. Such talk, and such tempers! For a while I thought the war would start then and there, and I would have to ask Barton to serve revolvers instead of salad forks."

He nodded. "We're all jumpy, and no wonder. You're too young, my dear. You don't realize."

"Perhaps. But tell me, is it war?"

"I wish to God I knew."

Sally insisted. "I mean the President. Wasn't that the phone call? What is he going to say?"

"I don't know. The phone call was...well, a meeting. That's where I'm going."

She nodded. "I know. At Senator Allen's. And between here and there you'll have to make up your mind which side you're on."

"Ah." The exhausted brown eyes blinked heavily; the effort at a smile had been abandoned. "The meeting has got into gossip then."

"I don't know. Does it matter?" Sally Voorman's nice smooth fingers took the lapel of the Senator's black topcoat to pull it straight, and hung onto it. Her blue eyes were straight up at his, with purpose in them. "But it does matter, of course, that you can carry that meeting if you want to. That's what I wanted to talk to you about. Maybe I'm a numbskull, as Mabel Brown says, but if so I'm with the majority at least; there are a lot of us, and we know which side we're on. We hate war, of course, but we know there are a few things that are even more hateful. That's the way we feel about it, we numbskulls, and the only thing that makes us the least bit doubtful is when we see one of the leaders, a real able proven leader,—well, when we see him hesitate. Aren't you ashamed, really now aren't you ashamed, to make us numbskulls doubtful?" Gently the nice white fingers shook the lapel. "Aren't you now?"

The Senator was looking down at her, his lips pushed together and out, his big old shapely head moving perceptibly from side to side. He grunted. "So. My dear child. Blue-eyed jingo."

"Nonsense." She was scornful. "We shouldn't call names, should we?"

"No." He dragged the word out, gave it length. Suddenly he said "No!" again, shorter and louder, and then muttering something about being late, backed away freeing the lapel from her hand, and turned and started for the door. But halfway to it he turned again. His voice was low but explosive. "Listen, Mrs. Voorman. This is a dirty business, let it alone. For God's sake keep out of it. Here's a message for your husband, I suppose he's still upstairs playing bridge. Playing bridge! Tell him this is my opinion of him for dragging you into this, tell him of all the filthy—"

The Senator sputtered to a stop. He stood looking at Sally, his lips working without words. After a moment he muttered, "God bless me, what am I saying?" He moved to get his hand on the doorknob, paused and said loudly and oratorically, "My dear child!" and opened the door and left.

# 3

Around nine o'clock, at about the time Sally Voorman's guests were choosing weapons for the roast guinea hen, a man stood in an automobile, a small roadster, somewhat battered, with the top down, and yelled at the top of his voice. This was at the corner of Tenth and C Streets, Southeast, not more than a mile from the Capitol itself. Another man sat behind the steering wheel, his foot poised in readiness over the starter button and his head twisting ceaselessly about as his eyes searched the half-darkness of the sidewalks and pavements under the street lights. The crowd that had collected to listen was not large, and it stood at a distance, shifting uneasily, taking and losing shape as this one and that one pushed their way out and newcomers floated to the edge. The orator was screaming:

"It's the workers' blood they're after! It's you and me will have to bleed! So! It's the Congress we voted for. It's the guys we elected to sit there in the Capitol that are going to put it over on us. And the President. Yes, the President! Oh, you can mutter, the whole damn country can mutter and then go out and get shot! Sure, I know the President would like to be a nice guy, and he would be a nice guy at a tea party, but this is not a tea party! This is war—do you understand that, you saps, war! Tomorrow noon, in fifteen hours now, the President goes to Congress. He says it's a damn shame, but we've got to fight. Or maybe he don't. Say he don't. I think he will, but say he don't! What then?"

The orator stopped and coughed, hard. At a tug on his coat he stooped to his companion at the steering wheel, listened to words in his ear, nodded, straightened up, and screamed again:

"What then? I'll tell you what then! Congress will tell him to go to hell and they'll go on and protect our honor. My honor and your honor. Hell! My blood and your blood. They're mixing up a new cocktail in Europe. They've been at it for over a year. *Crème de sang*, they call it. That's French. Cream of blood. Creamy blood! German blood, and English blood, Italian, French, Russian, Jap, Polish, the whole damn works. They're filling the rivers and oceans with it! Now they want ours to go with it, and Congress meets at noon tomorrow, and no matter what the President says, in spite of all hell, they're going to vote us in. Do you realize that? Us, the workers. You and me! Creamy blood! Red cream, that's us!

"But maybe not if we make hell hot enough. Maybe not, comrades! All right, sneer, you! Sure I'm a Communist! I'm from Boston, Massachusetts, and I guess that's America. There's nearly a thousand of us come to this town, and we're all Communists, and we're all workers, and we've got rights and we've got blood! And we don't want to lose them. Do you? That's a fair question, do you? If you don't, come with us! Come tomorrow noon, to the Capitol, that's where we're bound for, and let those babies know we're alive and we'd just as soon stay that way. But don't wait till noon. Come early! No rough stuff! Come and let them take a look at us. They're yellow. If there's enough of us it'll turn their stomachs just to look at us. Comrades! Come with us, start—"

A sharp tug at the orator's sleeve yanked him down; the starter groaned at its task, and the engine roared. The driver called a sharp warning to a couple of loiterers in front and blew the horn. A low growl went through the crowd, "Cop, beat it, cop," and it began to break up and move.

But at that instant, before the car's wheels started to roll and while the cop, approaching in his stride, was still thirty paces off, a speedier and more violent interference took command. From across the street, from nowhere apparently by its swiftness, there was a rush of forms, men running, half a dozen or more, straight at the roadster, shouting as they ran one word for a battlecry, "Union!" They kept on shouting it as they pulled the driver from the car, knocked him down and kicked him around. The cop came trotting, blowing his whistle. The orator stood up grasping a two-foot piece of iron pipe, but his first blow went wild and before he could manage

8

a second one he was pulled down from behind and he stopped scratching and trying to bite when a kick in the groin doubled him up and he dropped. By that time the cop was down too, asleep by his own nightstick. One of the men had climbed into the roadster and was pulling at the gear lever, but another called to him, "Out of that, you damn fool! Come on! Union!" The man leaped from the car and they sped away, running low, together. Even in the dim light they looked alike, for they were all coatless and their shirts were of one color, gray. They disappeared into an alley as approaching whistles were heard from two directions. On the pavement, the orator was twisting and groaning, but the cop and the driver were silent and did not move.

The crowd, which had begun to move with surly slowness at the approach of the cop, had vanished as if on wings at the first sound of the battlecry from across the street. Two of its members, old friends in adversity, seated with doughnuts at the counter of a lunchwagon many blocks away, showed no particular desire to discuss the affair, though one of them did mutter a little above a whisper:

"Anyhow, the Gray Shirts really did that guy a favor, now maybe he won't have to go to war."

# 4

"Absolutely no sense in it at all," the gray-haired man declared. "I might as well have stayed in New York and slept in my own bed."

The younger man, standing, looked embarrassed and crestfallen. "I'm sorry," he said. "I had no idea he would refuse to see you."

There were four men in the room, and though they were all in their several ways sufficiently striking in appearance, the room itself had its own position to maintain and it triumphantly succeeded. It was large, heavy with elegance, and solidly assured. Books behind glass, in modern sliding panels, were in recesses, the walls were dark with old wood, bronzes were tastefully on the mantel and the brown leather chairs satisfactorily continued the tone. Two of the men, one middle-aged with a pointed nose and a bald head, the other old and white, were seated at an end of the large Maura table looking at the title-page of an old quarto; the gray-haired one, comfortable in a chair near a window with a tall drink at hand on a taboret, was massive but not untidy; the younger one, not really young, soft and handsome, stood before him deferentially.

"I'm sorry," the younger man repeated. "But, if I may have an opinion, it was worth your making the trip. I thought you could see the President and swing him over, and I'm astonished he wouldn't see you. Rollins told me on the phone at noon it could positively be arranged. But maybe it couldn't have been done; I don't know; perhaps the President is hopeless; for two months I've kept my editorial writers busy branding him a straddler. You've seen that, I suppose?"

The gray-haired man grunted, "I don't read newspapers."

"Oh. Quite right. I don't blame you. I have to, since I publish one. But the point is this, Stanley must be ignored. Our dependence, God help us, must be upon that herd of subnormals we call our Congress. Whatever Stanley says tomorrow, they must say war. That's why I say it was worth your making the trip. Corcoran's coming here to see you, I bullied him into it, he's due in an hour. And just the word getting around that you're in Washington will do a lot of good." He grinned; his grin was also soft. "I'm glad you don't read newspapers. My leader in the morning is a repudiation of the influence of international bankers. I should hate to have you read it in my own house."

An old thin malignant voice came from the end of the table. "So you bullied Corcoran, did you? Is he, then, senile like me?"

The gray-haired massive man, who had been sipping his drink, put down his glass to chuckle. 'Ha! You senile, Geroge? You will skip that. I wouldn't be surprised if you should skip death itself.—But see here, Grinnell. What's this about Corcoran?"

"He's coming here to see you, that's all. At ten o'clock. He balked, but I insisted."

"Would you mind telling me what for?"

"What for? What for, sir?" The publisher, Grinnell, was flustered.

The massive man sighed with disgust. "Damn it, what for, yes. There must be one or two things you're aware of, I don't see how you could help it. You're dragging Corcoran here. Of the nine men that run the Senate, there are three that can't be touched. I respect them for it and wish them no worse than a decent burial. Tilney is a sentimental ass but dangerous. The other five men are definitely committed, tied up. You didn't know that? I suppose not. Corcoran's job tonight is with Tilney, not with me, and you drag him off. If you know what for, tell me."

Grinnell, flushing, said, "Tilney is at a dinner at Sally Voorman's."

"Sally who?"

"D. L. Voorman's wife. The Allentown man with the Steel League. Tilney likes her."

"Is Corcoran there?"

"No. He was at the White House at six, for half an hour. He'll see Tilney, of course, at the meeting at Allen's office, around eleven."

The massive man picked up his glass and shook it to the tinkle of ice on crystal. He sipped at its contents, grimaced, and then slowly drank it empty and replaced it on the taboret. Instead of reaching for a handkerchief, he let his upper lip slide over the lower, and then reversed the process.

He said, "Drivel. Not you, Grinnell, good God, no, just all the talk. Drivel. The President is out of it, has been for a week. I knew it then, you know it now, he will know it tomorrow. Whatever he may say, in spite of his Y. M. C. A. popularity, the House will go for war five to one. They can't wiggle out of it. The Senate is just as sure, by a smaller margin. Sure, so far as one permits sureness to enter into practical calculations. At any rate, there is nothing I can do or care to do. My persuasions have been administered. Don't think, Grinnell, don't think that I came to Washington to coax your damned Congressmen."

He got up from his chair, breathed, and shook himself. "But I did come. Eh? Yes, I came." He crossed, big steps with his big feet, to the end of the Maura table where the other two men were turning leaves of the quartos. He said in a new tone, quieter and more even but with more vibration beneath it, "I came to Washington to see you, George. I'm glad Grinnell told me you were here, since but for that I wouldn't have come. Are you having a pleasant visit with your son-in-law?"

The old white man looked up from the quarto. His old eyes

were nearly lost in the wrinkled folds of the lids. "Thank you, Martin. Quite pleasant. Now you can go back."

The massive man chuckled. "I'm invited for the night. Is that a good book you've got there?"

"Moderately good." The old man closed the quarto, carefully, and carefully laid it on the table and slid it back from the edge. "You want to talk, Martin? It's a moderately good book. Somewhat better—" He swallowed. "Somewhat better than the conversation I've been listening to."

"You didn't like it?"

"My remark was not based on my preferences. Rather on an objective analysis. We need not discuss it. You do not need to be told how stupid you are; you know it and you successfully ignore it. That is your only strength."

Martin Drew seemed about to chuckle again at that, but something stopped it; he stared a moment and said, "Not as stupid as you are, George. So I understand. Maybe you are senile." He wheeled around. "Grinnell. There's a room I suppose where your father-in-law and I could have a little talk?"

"Of course." The publisher was eager. "We'll leave you here. By all means." He turned to the bald-headed man with the pointed nose. "You won't mind, Tom."

"Sure." The bald-headed man rose from his chair. He hesitated. "However, there is a thing I wanted to ask Mr. Drew . . . tell him would be better . . ."

Martin Drew said, "Well? If it's brief."

The bald-headed man looked at him. Suddenly, for no apparent reason whatever, he smiled as if really amused at something, shook his head, and turned to go. "Never mind," he said. "Useless."

When the door had closed behind the two departing, Martin Drew took the chair one had left vacant, wheeled it around, and sat down. He took out a cigar.

The other spoke. "That man with a nose like an ant is an idealist, and yet he knows more about eighteenth century quartos than I do." Whatever the old white man said, his voice was the same: precise, thin, and shockingly malignant. "Another of nature's asinine tricks."

Martin Drew, having lit his cigar, said, "George. Whose money besides yours is behind the Gray Shirts?"

The wrinkled folded lids buried any gleam. The thin voice said, "Yours, perhaps?"

"Hell. Senator Corcoran will be here in twenty minutes. Subtlety can wait. Whose?"

"You do not appear to be wearing one."

"Are you?"

"Bah. Gray Shirts? A ferment in the dregs, a snatch at recovery in the garment trades."

"Yes?" Martin Drew blew out smoke. "There were riots today in Atlanta, Boston, and Cleveland. Peace demonstrations were broken up in a dozen cities. Four women were killed in Dayton. In all cases, Gray Shirts; in some just a scattering, in others considerable numbers. Their leader, the man who calls himself Lincoln Lee, is in Washington. The Communists approaching Washington today were attacked on the outskirts; all the police got was the wounded ones."

"Well, Martin. I thought you didn't read newspapers."

"I don't."

"If that man, Lee, is in Washington, why don't the police arrest him?"

"They would if you would tell them where he is."

"Bah." There was a faint amusement in the thin voice. "I tell you, ferment of the dregs."

"Yes? Would you tell me what you are doing in Washington?"

"There is no necessity, Martin. You have already mentioned it. I am having a pleasant visit with my son-in-law."

Martin Drew blew clouds of smoke, and made no concession of courtesy when the other waved a skinny white hand in front of his face to get air. Martin Drew spoke. "Look here, George. You said I was stupid. Keep that label for yourself. I tell you that, and I came here alone, but I'm not alone. We had a little talk this noon in New York. You know who the group would be, but others were called in too. I doubt if even you should ignore them. We agreed pretty well on everything. I don't need to tell you that we've got to go in the war damn quick, right now, you're not that stupid and you know the situation in Europe and Siberia as well as I do. I know you were against the Russian loans in the first place and maybe you were right, but now we've got to see them through, Soviets or not. Anyway that's only a fraction of it, and Japan would be worse. We declare war this week, or God help us. Tomorrow's the day, and it can be done and will be done. Stanley's out of it, but Congress is sure. There are only one or two things that could possibly interfere, and one of them might be the Gray Shirts trying to scare people that

13

don't need scaring. Damn it, don't you see the psychology of it? Congress is patriotic, thank God. They don't need scaring, not any more. Let a few Reds stand around and yell tomorrow, what's the difference? I told you I come from a group, and I bring the decision of a group. Tomorrow, and Wednesday, and Thursday—until war is voted—there are to be no Gray Shirts on the streets of Washington, and damn few anywhere else. Is there anything wrong with that?"

The white head was nodding, the eyes looked closed. Martin Drew almost shouted, "Goddam it, are you asleep?"

The thin voice sounded, "Of course not, Martin. I am laughing."

Drew glared. "You damn old pirate."

"Thank you, Martin." The eyes could now be seen to be open. "But don't misunderstand me. I am not laughing at the Gray Shirts; I would not make that mistake, as certain persons in Germany once made the mistake of laughing at the brown ones. I'm laughing at you and your group. You overlook so many things."

Drew blew out smoke. "For instance?"

"Well. I hardly know where to begin. Most important, perhaps, President Stanley's enormous popularity, and the fact that he is an extremely persuasive talker."

"He's lost it. Enough of it."

"Possibly. What if tomorrow noon he persuades Congress to delay, and in the evening takes to the radio? Would you like to listen in? I believe that is the phrase."

Drew shook his head. "He can't swing it."

"Possibly. But he is also ingenious. What if he calls for war, but asks—giving reasons, there are quite a few good ones—that it be limited to the Pacific front?"

Drew stared, and then abruptly got up. He said, "Good God."

"Stupid?" The thin voice was thinner from ferocity. "You and your group. That had not occurred to you? You grossly underrate President Stanley. Don't forget he is a mongrel—the Mediterranean in at the night-window.—Ha! That movement betrays you; your squeamish sentimental backing off from facts. Of course he's a mongrel, and mongrels are never completely calculable. They cannot be trusted. They are often beggars and bums, but infrequently they are geniuses, and you can't trust them. They will submit to incredible degradations, or—and here I believe is where President

14

Stanley may possibly belong—they will have visions or lightning strokes of insight too swift for you. For you, Martin, far too swift."

Drew sat down again. He had crushed his cigar into a tray. He said, "What else?"

"Well . . . do you want more?"

"No. What good are your Gray Shirts against that?"

"Relinquish that assumption, Martin. It will simplify things. Whatever I may be ready to tell you will be told. But nothing from me will ever be for your group of idiots. Understand that. Cut loose and we'll see."

"I wonder." Drew frowned. "I wonder if you're not a damned old idiot yourself."

"I am George Milton." The thin voice was a blade in the air. "You asked me what I am doing in Washington. I am here, that is all. I have been here for a week. I have been occupied. After all, it is the Congress that votes. But, as a commentary on your childish assumption that the program has been definitely arranged and that the tunes will follow in proper order, let me say that I am waiting on each hour to decide the following one. But proceed, by all means, you and your group; you will possibly do more good than harm. We are all after the same fish, but I have preferences as to tackle and bait—and my companions."

"Have you seen Stanley?"

"No. There is no use, till he can be disarmed."

"Will he try to talk us off tomorrow?"

"I don't know. Long odds, yes."

"If he does, how sure is Congress?"

"The House, short of a stampede, well in hand. The Senate, probable, but at bottom incalculable. Nothing will tell but the vote. If it is against us, the proper diversion at the proper moment might bring reconsideration. The night will tell us something, the morning more. I have a telephone at my bedside. Ask me at breakfast."

Drew took out another cigar and cut off its tip. He was frowning. After a moment he opened his lips to speak, but the sound of the door opening stopped him. Grinnell, standing on the threshold, hesitated a moment before he spoke:

"Senator Corcoran is here."

Drew looked a question at George Milton. The old white head wagged faintly, and Drew nodded to Grinnell.

"Bring him in here."

Mrs. Burton, with her widespread palm, patted at the cavern
of her open mouth. "Oh dearie me," she said, and yawned
again. "I suppose if I stayed up till eleven o'clock every night
I'd soon get used to it, but I couldn't do that anyway with
Harry's breakfast at half-past six in the morning. Excuse me,
Mrs. Brenner. Yes, no doubt about it, you're certainly right,
if Japan wins the war the next thing we know they'll be taking
California and Nebraska and that is where our food supply
comes from. I may say that I know something about that,
since my husband is a grocer. You'd be surprised at all the
names of places on the boxes and cartons, it's astonishing.
You can't help but agree to that, Marion; at least we've got to
protect our food supply."

Marion Vawter snorted. "Nonsense. I guess we'll manage
somehow to get something to eat. I say we should keep out of
the war. That's all I say."

"Oh, forget it." This was a new voice. "That's what Charles
says when the children come from high school and begin on
the war. He says forget it. He says they won't fail to let us
know when we're in it and what's the use of talking about it.
That sounds sensible to me. You know, Charles was an
election inspector when we lived in Richmond. Anyway, I
certainly don't come to these meetings to talk about war. Is
this a Mothers' Club or what is it?"

Leadership spoke next; leadership reposing, as it had for
five years in the Acker Street Mothers' Club, in the person of
Viola Delling, the wife of Delling the druggist. There was a
persistent half-belief throughout the membership that their
president was a D. A. R., though none had ever had the
effrontery to get her down to a yes or no on that.

"But my dear Kitty." However authoritative Viola Delling
might find it necessary to become, there was always understanding and friendliness in her voice. "Shouldn't we talk
about it, after all? Don't you suppose Betsy Ross ever mentioned
war to her friends as she sat sewing our flag, our first Stars
and Stripes? Don't you suppose Martha Washington discussed
the activities of her husband, the Father of Our Country,

when she entertained gentleladies at Mount Vernon? I imagine, too, that Mrs. Abraham Lincoln—"

There was a giggle on the outskirts, and a shrill younger voice: "That would be fun, let's discuss the activities of our husbands, selling real estate and wrapping up groceries and mixing prescriptions..."

A general titter ran around, but no open laughing. They did respect their leader, and had no clear idea of the reasons for their invariable and immediate response to Harriet Green's deviltries.

Viola Delling smiled tolerantly. "Well, Harriet, no one expects you to be serious. But war is serious, very serious. Of course we must enter it, our duty and mission are plain." She sighed. "It is too bad that our President is reluctant in the face of duty."

But that was perhaps too strong; almost, indeed, a major error in tactics. A swift storm assailed her:

"He's not reluctant!"

"President Stanley's all right! He knows what he's doing."

"Why don't you wait and see what he says?"

"He's got a right, hasn't he? It's his business to do what he thinks—"

"Viola! You criticizing the President!"

"Maybe if there was enough reluctant like him—"

And so on. Viola Delling got her smile set and rode the storm with it, but nodding to show that there was really no argument. At the right moment she put up a hand palm out. "My dears! Certainly. Certainly! The President is the arbiter of our destinies. I have every confidence in him. Whoever attacks the President attacks our country, and I imagine you know how likely I am to do that. I imagine I don't need to defend myself. You girls have all seen my home on many delightful occasions; you have seen the Stars and Stripes draped in its place of honor above my bed. But what confronts us is war!" Her voice took on vibrancy. "Our duty and our mission and the defense of our homes! We cannot leave that to others, other mothers and other sons!"

A mutter came from Marion Vawter: "When they get somewhere near our homes it will be time enough to defend them."

"Ah!" The leader smiled at her. "Then it will be too late."

"You're right, Viola." An oldish plump woman was nodding approvingly. "Some of you are too young to remember the

17

last war. I'm not. I remember it only too well—the papers and the pictures and the things—my younger brother went—he lives in Norfolk now. What the Germans did! And what they would have done if we had let them win. That war showed us what the Germans are. Beasts! They would do to us exactly what they did in Belgium if they got a chance. I saw a picture—"

"Of course—" Viola Delling was trying to head her off. She said "Of course" three times, making it louder each time, but the plump woman was wound up:

"I saw a picture nobody was supposed to see, the cashier at the bank showed it to me one day when I went to make a deposit, we made a deposit every day when we had the hardware store. It was some German soldiers and a baby and two children, and the soldiers were holding up some pieces—hey, what are you pinching me for?"

Viola Delling dived into the opening. "Gertrude. Yes, that was terrible. But of course this time the Germans are on our side—that is, the attacks on our commerce, the insults to our government—our allies will be those whose ideals measure up to our own. I'm sure the Germans have nothing but remorse for the past, and it is blessed to forgive."

Nods agreed with her; a few snorts, the loud one from Harriet Green, were disregarded. The plump woman got new breath:

"I don't care, I won't trust the Germans. The rest of you can do as you like, but I won't trust them. Look at their new king, Hitler. I saw a picture of him. Well! But anyway, whatever happens, I'm behind the President. Whatever happens, mind you!" She looked defiance at the leader. "I'm in a better position than the rest of you to know what kind of a man he is. My son, Val, delivers groceries to the White House every morning with Callahan's truck. He used to have a better job, but I tell him there's no disgrace in any kind of work so long as it's honest. He goes to the White House every morning, and many times he's seen the President walking there in the grounds. He often smiles at Val. Several times he spoke to him. You ought to hear Val describe his voice and the way he looks! Well, as you see, I've got good reasons for what I say. I'm behind the President whether I trust the Germans or not."

The Acker Street Mothers' Club nodded politely but were not impressed. They had heard of Val Orcutt and the President before. Mrs. Brenner, who had previously been worried about the food supply, got the floor:

"Look here. What I don't understand is like this: the war has been going on over a year. England and France and Germany and Russia and all of them are fighting and killing, but they can't hurt us any because they're too busy. Why can't we just send our army to California and when a Jap pops up anywhere just simply shoot him? It seems to me that's the menace. Why do we have to go declaring war against everybody at once?"

There were several approving nods. Harriet Green said, "Now that's an idea."

But Viola Delling smiled tolerantly. "I'll tell you why, Freda. It wouldn't be honorable. We must assume our share of the burden, the bitter along with the sweet. I guess we all know what that means, all mothers know. Who of us would be willing to sacrifice honor for happiness? Then can we without remonstrance see our President—that is, well, our country's honor should be as precious to us as our own. More so. Do you girls think, does one of you think—"

There was a double interruption. A bell rang somewhere, and simultaneously a dark-haired skinny woman who had been sitting motionless and silent on the edge jumped up from her chair and leaned forward, toward the leader, as far as she could get over the intervening chairs. Her eyes were blazing, and as she began to speak she also began to tremble.

"You make me sick! Do you hear that? Viola Delling, do you hear that? You're a dirty old pig! You talk about our honor and our sons, I'd hate to be a son of yours! I've sat here and listened to you and kept my mouth shut, and I kept thinking I ought to go home . . ."

Hands were pulling at her. The bell rang again, and Mrs. Burton, muttering something about answering the door, edged her way out of the room. Viola Delling maintained great control:

"Mrs. Tice. I'm sorry. We know you lost two sons in the World War, and we know about the one you have left, and we're sorry. I personally am also sorry that you think it necessary to dye your hair, since nothing is lovelier or more honorable than the white hair of a grief such as yours. No greater service could be rendered—"

The dark-haired woman shook herself loose and screamed at the top of her lungs, "Shut up!" Then all at once she stood up straight and was silent. A shiver ran over her, then another one, and she turned to go. Harriet Green got up from her chair to follow her. At the door leading to the hall they had to squeeze past Mrs. Burton and the newcomer who had rung the bell.

Before any comments could become vocal Mrs. Burton was back in the room. Beside her was a young man, tall, red-faced and awkward, but with a good pair of eyes. He stood with his hat in his hand, his jaw set not to grin.

Mrs. Orcutt, the plump woman who was behind the president, arose from her chair and called to him, "Well, Val! You're late enough. I said ten-thirty." She informed the Acker Street Mothers' Club, "Val always comes to take his mother home." They knew that.

Val Orcutt nodded. "I know, I couldn't help it." He added as if an apology were needed, "I didn't want to come in. Mrs. Burton made me."

Mrs. Burton, after finishing a yawn, explained, "I thought he might give us the latest news of the riots."

Most of them were up from their chairs. A chorus invited the young man, "Yes, do!"

"There's no riots." Val looked annoyed. "There's been a few fights around. The cops won't let you stand still anywhere. Nothing much."

Viola Delling got her smile on him. "But isn't it true that Washington, our capital city, is overrun with Communists?"

"I don't know. They didn't run over me."

The leader was for pressing on with it, but she knew when an audience was through. Some of the members were cross, and all of them were sleepy and ready to go home. So Viola Delling kept her leadership by heading the file to the bedroom where they had left their wraps.

On the sidewalk, strolling homeward with her arm through that of her son, Mrs. Orcutt asked, "Why were you late, Val?"

Val Orcutt coughed. Though he was twenty-six, and quite healthy and alive, and really not a fool, it was true that he had never, in any important respect, told his mother a lie in all his life. "Oh—why—nothing interesting. Well, interesting maybe. Listen here, mawm. You know I always know what I'm doing. Now just don't ask any questions."

# 6

This library, though it happened to be in Pittsburgh, might have been almost anywhere—that is, in any large American city. It definitely lacked the touch of genuine culture which, in the Grinnell library in Washington, had been supplied by the daughter of old George Milton as a successful covering—like a layer of cream on Grade A milk—for the vulgar source of its existence. This library, though anything but niggardly, was raw and unassimilated. First the interior decorator, not too well chosen, had done his worst, and then the owner had failed to restrain his independence. Green tapestry cushions, a gift from someone, were scattered on a red leather couch. An immense chromium humidor was against one side of the fireplace from an eighteenth century French château. Tooling on the backbones of the books made it appear likely that literary classics were indeed worth their weight in gold. On the massive table of a pinkish wood from the Brazilian forests, among a miscellany of papers and accessories, stood four telephones of different colors. The white one was a private line to Washington, the blue one, private to the executive offices of the Federal Steel Corporation, the brown one, private to the Penn Trust Company. The black one was just a telephone.

The forceful-looking, firm-jawed, middle-aged man who was in a chair pulled back from the fireplace, and who surely would have been taken on sight for a member of the high staff of big industry, was the pastor of the First Presbyterian Church. The one seated at the desk, not much older but considerably more worn, with the appearance of an evangelist at a revival meeting, the fire of rapture deep in his gray eyes but still burning, was the Chairman of the Board of the Federal Steel Corporation. His secretary, the third man, was standing at the end of the desk talking into the black telephone, but all he was saying was the word "Yes," repeating it at intervals.

At length he returned the receiver to its rack and faced his employer. "It's all right," he said. "He read it all to me. It's not a masterpiece, but it's all right."

21

The steel man nodded. The pastor smiled, amused, and observed, "So much for freedom of the press."

"Huh?" The steel man was hoarse. "I suppose you know that my bank owns that paper."

"I knew it in a way, yes. *A priori*. Not empirically."

"Oh. See here, Prewitt. Don't imagine you're imposing on me. I have great respect for you, but not because you use words that I wouldn't bother with." He turned to his secretary. "What's the matter with you? You're as white as a bride. Go and sit down." He pushed a button in a row on his desk.

The secretary murmured, "I'm all right."

"The hell you are. Look at you. Sit down." To the pastor: "Kilbourn and I have had a day of it." He glanced at the electric clock on the wall. "Past midnight! It will soon be over—begun rather." He twisted his head to the opening of a door. A man stood there. "Ferris, bring some port for Mr. Kilbourn, and I'll have a glass of milk. You, Prewitt?"

"I might help with the milk."

"A pitcher and two glasses. Bring the port first. Damn it, Ben, why don't you sit down?"

Ben Kilbourn was standing close to the desk, leaning against it, steadying himself with his hand on its edge. The blood had gone from his face to leave it white, and his eyes were fixed on his employer as if through a fear that should they once get off they would not be able to find the focus again. He opened his mouth to speak, but got only a futile gasp instead of words. The second attempt was more successful.

"Mr. Cullen, I wanted to say, I'm resigning. I'm quitting my job."

"The hell you are. Sit down first and resign afterwards." The steel man was on his feet, grasping his secretary by the arm and turning him. "Come on, do you want me to carry you? Prewitt, kick that chair around."

The secretary's protests were feeble. They got him into a chair, and with his muscles relaxed he began to tremble. The man arrived with the wine, and Cullen took the bottle and glass and poured it himself. With a grunt of command he held the glass to Kilbourn's lips and persevered until it was drained. "As soon as you show me some color you can have another one," he promised. "Then you'd better go to bed and get some sleep. You can resign tomorrow, no hurry." He turned to the pastor. "He was shell-shocked in the last war.

22

This last week I've pushed him pretty hard and it's got on his nerves."

The pastor said, "It isn't eminently Christian to work a man into a breakdown."

"Huh? I'm not a Christian."

"Now, Cullen. Don't forget I'm onto you."

The steel man backed off. "That's your bluff. I like it in you, Prewitt. I'm about as Christian as a bald eagle, but if you think that worries me any... Feeling better, Ben?"

"Much." Kilbourn was swallowing to keep the port down. The blood was sneaking into his cheeks and his eyes looked better. "I knew this was coming. I'll take another shot of that."

Cullen filled the glass and handed it to him.

"Thanks." He gulped it, with no respect for the years it had taken to arrive at its label. "You've certainly got spots of decency, no doubt about it."

Cullen never grinned, but the fire, the concentration in his eyes, could relax for humor. "On resigning you give me a recommendation, huh?"

Kilbourn nodded. "Put it that way. I won't ask you for any. I'm no good."

"You go to bed and go to sleep. Sleep all day tomorrow. We're finished with this. If you want—"

"Finished?" The secretary laughed, one sharp high-pitched cackle. "You mean we've started it. We've helped to start it. I'm sick, I know that. I must be. I'm not naturally soft, I'm as hard as you are. I suppose it's the hangover from that damned shell-shock, anyway I'm sick and no good. It's funny, I didn't realize until tonight what we've been doing. I don't blame you, I don't blame anybody. Go ahead with your newspapers and your movies and your bribes and your radio, persuading the morons to go get their heads shot off to put your steel mills back on three shifts, what the hell? It's your game and what's going to keep you from playing it? I've been helping you with it. Only tonight I've gone sick on it. The vote is tomorrow, and it's all done, absolutely, and I've just realized it. I don't mean the horrors of war, I mean it's just too damned dumb. Maybe I do mean the horrors of war, since I'm sick maybe I don't know what I mean."

He had to stop to swallow, and when he lifted his hand to put it in front of his mouth it was trembling again. He muttered, "Could I have a little more wine?"

23

The steel man, pouring it, observed with real gentleness and sympathy struggling through his hoarseness, "Ben, all you need is plenty of sleep. Here, this is all you get or it will keep you awake—"

A low-toned buzzer sounded from the desk. Kilbourn like an automaton started to rise, but Cullen pushed him back and crossed to the telephones and picked up the white one.

The pastor put his hand on Kilbourn's shoulder, and listened with him.

". . . No, this is Cullen. . . . Voorman? Go ahead. . . . Good. . . . Good. . . . It doesn't surprise me, what do you think we pay you for? . . . Tilney couldn't swing it anyway. . . ."

It went on. After ten minutes the steel man hung up, and as he turned back towards the others the fire in his eyes was up to rapture again.

"God bless our country," Ben Kilbourn said, and gulped the wine.

The pastor's jaws were firmer than ever. "Is it war?"

Cullen nodded. "Tomorrow." He glanced at the clock. "Today."

The pastor breathed deeply. "We are then in need of God." He swallowed, and cleared his throat. "Its time for me to make my oration then, Cullen. I'm afraid it won't be as good as Mr. Kilbourn's, it hasn't the background." His voice, forgetting about resonance, seemed thin.

Cullen said, "You got an oration, Prewitt? Here's our milk sitting here, better drink it first."

"No, thanks. Or—here, I'll take it. I can't very well get into heroics sipping milk. I dropped in this evening to tell you something, I couldn't make it earlier." He drank a third of the milk. "You know, of course, that on the past five Sundays I have preached against war. You know I abhor it."

Cullen nodded. "That's your business. Did it affect my Easter check?"

"No. Some it has. Not yours. You're a good sport, and a man. So am I. That's what I came here to tell you. If war is declared tomorrow—today, I know quite well what the expectations of my congregation will be, including yourself. They expect that next Sunday I will find that God has changed his mind. Well, He hasn't, and neither have I, and I won't. I am against war for good, and I shall say so."

Cullen said, "Huh? We'll kick you out."

"I shall say so."

24

"Maybe. It's six days till Sunday. Nonsense, Prewitt, you'll be committing suicide."

"Of course. But here's my real confession: my difficulty is not a spiritual one, it isn't even emotional, it's intellectual. Mr. Kilbourn said it: it's just too damned dumb. My choice is not between life and death, it is between intellectual suicide and corporeal. I'm against war for good. I wanted to tell you that, Cullen, and I also wanted to warn you that I am not alone. You may be in for trouble that you little suspect. There's a lot of courage around, I have only my own mite, and you may get into trouble."

Cullen stared at him. "That's not courage, it's only cold feet. I like you, Prewitt, but you can't lay down on us. You'd better sleep on it. Come around tomorrow. I'll be busy, but come in for dinner. My wife will phone you." He turned to his secretary. "You need sleep too, Ben. Go on up and tuck yourself in. I'll get along without you tomorrow. You'd better forget about resigning till the war's over.—Come on, Prewitt, I'll see you to the hall. I'm tired."

"There's no use in my coming tomorrow, Cullen. My mind is made up."

"All right, we'll see. Come along. Good night, Ben."

The steel man and the pastor went out, and Ben Kilbourn was left alone. He sat staring at the wineglass in his hand. He noted that his hand was not trembling. He thought that was odd, and waited, watching it, for a long time. Finally it did in fact begin to tremble. He watched it. Suddenly he got up, let his arm go back, and hurled the wineglass at a framed photograph of the Board of Directors of the Federal Steel Corporation on the wall beyond the desk. It hit smack and was fragments.

He looked at his hand to see if it was still trembling and muttered to himself bitterly, "I guess I'm sick."

# 7

The Maryland Avenue Garage was one of the most modern and efficient in the city of Washington. There were four floors, steep curving concrete ramps, an elevator, bright red gasoline pumps on wheels, a neat and business-like office.

Any midnight all four floors were crowded with the gracefully massive powerful beasts on four wheels which drank the gasoline and waited to roar and leap at their masters' bidding. This Monday midnight, like any other, they were there: roadsters, limousines, sedans, and on the first floor the more ponderous and somewhat less graceful vehicles of the city's retail commerce. There stood the three black carriers of elegancies from Pritchard & Treman's, with the name of the firm, snobbish nearly to the point of invisibility, minute in a lower corner; the dozen or so Fords of the City Parcel Service; the larger and more vulgar trucks with *KLEINMAN'S* sprawled the length of each side; and five others, dark red, medium-sized and sturdy, with the legend, *Callahan, Fine Groceries and Meats*, displaying a compromise between the aristocratic murmur of Pritchard & Treman and the annoying shout of Kleinman. Of these five last, one had been backed expertly into its narrow space by Val Orcutt at six o'clock that afternoon, upon completion of his rounds.

At midnight there was still activity. A man entered in a large roadster with the top down, roared up the ramps to the third floor, nodded good night to the floorman, and walked his way back down to the street. A uniformed chauffeur steered through the entrance a dark blue limousine bearing on its door the shield of the Republic of France; this, being an embassy car, went up only one flight. A black sedan, quite ordinary-looking, arrived. It went all the way up. Gliding across the top floor, it sought no niche in the ranks, but continued along the central alley to the front of the building and stopped with its nose against the wall. The driver got out and walked back down the alley to meet the floorman who was approaching. The driver said, not very loud, "Union." The floorman nodded and said, "Union." The driver hastened back to the sedan, opened the rear door, and said, "All right."

Four men got out. Two wore felt hats with turn-down brims, and two caps; all had their coat collars turned up. One led the way a few paces down the alley and then, turning to the right, squeezed between two cars and kept on, sidewise, twisting through the maze. The others followed. Finally they were brought up by a wall. The leader put his hand to it and fumbled around in the dim light, found a button and pushed it. A door opened directly in front of them and a man's face appeared in the crack. The leader said, "Union." The door swung back, and they went in.

There were thirty or more men in the room. All were under middle age; some were scarcely more than boys. Their coats and hats hung on hooks along one wall, and their gray shirts were open at the neck. A few sat around a table near the center of the room; the others stood scattered in groups. An unshaded electric bulb dangled from the ceiling on a cord. The rich dark brown of the walls was thick slabs of insulating cork, and there were rubber strips around the edges of the door to keep the light in.

As the five entered they were greeted with a muttered chorus, "Union!" and everyone stood straight. The man who had led the newcomers, stocky with light brown hair and a clamped mouth with one corner twisted down, took the whole room in with a swift sweep of his eyes. One who had been seated at the table hurried over to him and then turned to the crowd: "Men! Here he is!"

There was a murmur, but the stocky man disregarded it. He walked abruptly to the table, brushing a chair aside, and rapped with his knuckles on the transmitter of a telephone which stood there. "What's this?" he demanded. "A decoration?"

One who stood near him said, "Why—it was put in last week—"

"You don't mean it's connected?"

The other met his eyes and said with a touch of resentment, "Sure."

"Sure what? A sure trap? It is. Take it out tomorrow. No. Not tomorrow. Leave it in, but don't use it. If it rings don't answer it."

The other persisted, "I don't see what—"

"I do. You should. Let's find out." He turned to the room. "Union! Men, you tell him. I say that telephone is dumb and dangerous. You who agree, show your hands." Hands shot up, many of them. The stocky man did not wait for laggards. "You who disagree, show it." There were none. He turned to the culprit. "You're in the ranks, beginning now. We'll choose a man for the place later. Well?"

The other did not hesitate. He lifted his right hand and laid it on his heart, and said firmly and clearly, "Union."

"Good. The Gray Shirts of the Union do not fear danger, they welcome and embrace it, but they will not be betrayed by stupidity." He turned to the room again. "Men! Gather before me."

27

They stepped briskly, with eagerness, not taking their eyes off the stocky man as they moved. Partly the forcefulness of his words, partly the electric crispness of his voice, had galvanized the air for their lungs. They collected into a compact group and stood straight, gazing up at him as he mounted a chair.

He did not raise his voice. "Men, I am Lincoln Lee. A few of you I have met before, in Detroit or Memphis; most of you see me for the first time. This is my first entry into Washington, but it will not be my last. On a not distant day I shall enter it to stay, as Mussolini entered Rome and Hitler entered Berlin. Not that I shall imitate either their ideas or their methods; this is the United States of America, and none but Americans shall guide its destiny, none but Americans shall point the way, none but Americans shall accompany us to the goal. Well, men?"

The chorus was instant, a breath of zeal, "Union!"

"Yes. Union. Union of the blood and the ideals America needs and must have; for all others, contempt and destruction. You know them and I can name them. The dirty whining Jews, the tricky lying Pope-lovers, the Reds, the Anarchists, the filthy Communists; you know the enemy. We are not enemies of the good Americans who have not yet accepted our leadership. We wish only to show them that we are the leaders, *I am the leader*, they are waiting for, and their millions will be in our ranks. I am now hunted and despised. That is my present pride, it is the foot of the ladder on which I shall mount to my future glory, and your glory, and the true grandeur of America. Men, you will mount the ladder with me?"

"Union!"

"Now, America has other enemies who must be destroyed. The yellow men from Japan, not even human, the Britishers who want the earth and will know they're licked at last when we turn their muddy little islands upside down in the ocean, the French frog-eaters who borrowed the last war from us and wouldn't pay it back—common dirty welchers. They are America's enemies and must be destroyed. We've got a sissy in the White House, a weakling with water in his blood and without a spine, but in spite of him America must deal with her enemies, and if he gets himself between the battle lines he'll have to get hurt. We don't squirm at that. We squirm at nothing! There is only one gantlet we force any man to run,

28

but all, from White House to gutter, must pass through that: he who stands in America's way must be destroyed! Neither your brother nor my sister can escape; and no Red, no Jew, no Pope-lover. We are hard, and hardest of all to traitors!"

He paused for the chorus: "Union!"

"We are hard, and we are patient. Those who lack patience will disappear from our ranks, and we shall not salute their graves. In the days ahead, for the destruction of our enemies abroad, we must expect separation and delay. I do not know when I shall see you again. My lieutenants are your commanders; obey them. One who proves himself unworthy of your reliance will pay the penalty swiftly and without fail. Those whom I trust, you may trust. Be patient, time is with us. Wherever you may find yourselves, on the battlefields of Europe, on the front with our allies in Siberia, on the deck of a ship after the yellow men, remember that we are hard, we do not forget, and we want the future only for the glorious day it holds for America."

Lincoln Lee paused. His mouth twisted, a nervous grimace that certainly was not a smile, and he said in a lower tone from which everything was excluded but insane ferocity:

"Men. I talk big. I am big. Union!"

There was no sound or movement; his voice had hypnotized them. They did not even breathe the chorus. He let his eyes move over them, from face to face, seeing each one, and after that was finished he said in a different tone:

"That's all. Don't leave, whether you have your orders for tomorrow or not. Take your coats for pillows and lie on the floor; get some sleep if you can. There may be a change in plans." He got down from the chair, agile and sure on his feet. "Grier! Fallon! Let's look it over. Where are your lists? Put that telephone on the floor; be careful; get some string and tie the hook down."

One man got at the telephone, another came forward with an envelope and began removing papers from it, a third unfolded another paper, quite large, and spread it out on the table, disclosing a map of the city of Washington. Lincoln Lee sat down and bent over the map.

# 8

When Alma Cronin got up to go home it was half-past twelve. On receiving the telephone call from Chick Moffat, at a little after eight, to the effect that he would be unable to keep his appointment with her for a walk and a couple of hours at a movie, she had been, of course, momentarily disappointed but had refused to confess to pique. She had plenty of intelligence and was quite aware that she was far from having Chick Moffat finally and satisfactorily oriented in the pleasant groves and meadows of her emotions. Was it possible—heaven forbid—that there was a bit of jungle there and he had found it?

She had first met him one day a year back, in a corridor of the White House. She had been new there then, and on seeing this hatless man striding along with the assurance of familiarity she had stopped him to inquire:

"If I keep going will I get to the President's office?"

He had smiled with his eyes. "You will, madam, if you make all the right turns and nobody stops you."

"I see. Thank you for the encouragement. Mrs. Stanley asked me to take the President his wrist watch." She dangled it by its strap from her finger. "She says he forgot to put it on, and he's a lost soul without it."

"That's what I was going for." He held out his hand. "Will you entrust it to me? I'm Chick—Charles A. Moffat, Secret Service."

"Thanks. I'm Alma Cronin, Assistant Secretary."

He had half turned, but gone back again. "Don't you want to come along so you'll know the way next time?"

She had gone with him.

That had led to something, a walk or a dinner, and another one, and neither he nor she had seemed to develop an inclination to let the matter drop. Alma knew perfectly well that there could be nothing to it. She was an intellectual, knew all about trends and undercurrents and the social ferments, and was a member of the Women's League for Peace, whereas Chick Moffat—well, he read *Collier's Weekly* and played poker with newspaper men. With so wide a space between the roads their minds were traveling, it seemed odd to her that she should find an increasing pleasure in strolling with him through Rock Creek Park or in letting him, on winter evenings, sit for hours in the only comfortable chair in her room and tell her jokes—until it suddenly occurred to her one day that she was fond of him. That explanation was quite satisfactory and even soothing. But as winter began to retreat before spring, and she found herself becoming indifferent to those of her friends who did not know Chick or regarded him as unimportant, a suspicion sneaked through her defenses that "fond" was hardly the word. There were various little symptoms which alarmed her, for instance catching herself singing one day while making deviled ham and onion sandwiches. She had hurried home from work, buying the ingredients on the way, and the sandwiches were intended for Chick's delight upon their return that evening from a violin recital. With beer. She disliked onions and managed easily without beer. And with onion-tears in her eyes she was singing! She dropped the knife onto the newspaper and went to the bathroom and wiped the tears from her eyes and looked at herself in the mirror. She thought, if these inexorable facts are capable of two interpretations, I'd like to know what the other one is. As sure as God made little apples, I'm teasing a man's stomach to show him what he'd be missing in case. She said aloud, "Alma Cronin, you're compromising yourself, and with onions!"

As she finished the sandwiches, vaguely seeking justification, it occurred to her that Chick was no more enamored of violin music than she was of onions and beer; and he had bought the tickets. But that only made it worse. Both of them frantically clutching at an alien culture, just to show . . . Ha! She decided that the situation provided the only decent excuse for a war that she had ever heard of: Chick Moffat might go away to it, and then this nonsense . . . But the jest gagged her, and there was a sudden definite aching pain low in her breast, so definite and pronounced that she put her hand there without knowing it. It was a different sort of feeling entirely from the fiery indignation which had on occasion been aroused in her at a meeting of the Women's League for Peace. It really scared her; she felt helpless and betrayed, and for the first time since puberty unsure of the next hour and the morrow.

31

But none of the débris of that collapse was left to inform Chick Moffat's eye when he arrived thirty minutes later.

Nothing happened in the following weeks. For one thing, Chick appeared to be stymied at friendship; for another, her sense of humor was stubbornly jealous of its prerogatives; and for still another, the war controversy approached a crisis and Alma was hot in the fight. Her position at the White House was both unofficial and unimportant, since she was merely the secretary of Mrs. Robbins, who was secretary to Mrs. Stanley, who was the wife of the President. But Mrs. Stanley was friendly, democratic, busy, curious, and indiscreet; so Alma learned many things a secretary of a secretary should perhaps be kept in ignorance of. She wrote, at dictation, letters to capitalists' sisters and Congressmen's wives, which, left by catastrophe as the only records of our time for the enlightenment of posterity, would convince future historians that the twentieth century United States of America was a matriarchy. Alma was not concerned with that; she was ready to help with any stab at the threat of war; and since her heart was in it as was her mind, she let the issue of her private crisis wait for a better moment.

So when Chick phoned her that Monday evening that he could not come she refused to admit pique, though she would have liked to be with him that evening, the eve of defeat or victory. She wondered whether his being recalled to the White House after having spent the day there meant any new development since her departure at six o'clock, and then remembered that he hadn't mentioned the White House, but had merely said that he had to go on duty. Elsewhere, perhaps? Possibly the street demonstrations were getting harder to handle; on her way home she had twice seen police breaking up groups and shoving them along, and this was not the part of town where such things were supposed to happen. Frowning, she stood looking out of the window. There was no telling, but she would like to know. She sat down with a book and stuck to it for over an hour; when her restlessness made the prolongation of that gesture not only irksome but silly, she went to the phone and called up the Lindquists. They were at home and said come, please do.

For three hours she sat around at the Lindquists' and drank claret lemonade and listened to people talk. There was always an informal procession at that house: lobbyists with ideals, musicians, a Representative or two, assistant Bureau chiefs,

Russian embassy people. Carl Lindquist, who had inherited a paper mill in Minnesota, was under no necessity to work but did a lot of thinking and had selected Washington as the proper scene for that activity. Alma liked his wife and didn't mind him much.

That evening she stayed late, after midnight. The group had thinned until only four or five were left, sprawled in the comfortable chairs with the highballs et cetera which were their reward for giving Lindquist something to think about. A man whom Alma did not know, whose name she had caught as Birch or Bartsch or something, was off on a bypath of the only road the conversation had traveled that whole evening, the war.

"There are lots of reasons why Stanley can't help it," he was informing them. "If he doesn't go into that war he'll find himself in one anyway, right here at home. I say that not so much on account of the unrest and the scattered rioting of the past few days; that is perhaps merely a fugitive aspect of the immediate question, whether to enter the war now. I say it's a law of physics, it's bound to erupt, and then look out! You have no idea—I myself have only a vague and incomplete one—of the amazing extent to which doctrines of hatred and counsels of destruction have seeped into every stratum of our social and economic structure. Do you know what I heard today, for instance? It's incredible. I was told—and the source, while not unquestionable, was worthy of consideration—I was told that among the White House squad of the Secret Service there are two Gray Shirts. The President's own bodyguard! How's that for a commentary on the state of things?"

Florence Lindquist snorted and said, "Oh well. Now I'll make up one." Her husband had probably acquired plenty of material for thought for one evening, for he chose to take it lightly too. He shook his finger ponderously at Alma. "Anyway, I hope your friend Chick Moffat isn't one of them. I'll wager he is. How do we know you didn't even make his shirt for him? What are you trying to do, bore from within?"

Alma made him some sort of answer. A little later, seeing that it was half-past twelve and feeling both restless and bored, she got up and distributed her good nights and went home. Walking alone the short four blocks through the mild April night, she was irritated and depressed beyond any warrant she could think of. Certainly the nonsense at the

Lindquists' did not deserve it. She wondered if there was any chance that Chick had called up again, or might yet do so. This was the first time he had ever broken an appointment with her.

# 9

At two o'clock in the morning there were still five men left in Senator Allen's office. It was really a room in the Senate Office Building which had been assigned to the committee investigating the munitions propaganda, but since Allen was chairman of the committee the room was in effect, for the time being, his.

The room was filled with stale smoke and was in a good deal of a mess, for forty men had gone in and out that night. The smoke had got into the corners and was settling down to stay. During the past couple of hours Senator Tilney had several times opened a window, but his colleague Wilcox, allowing a minimum interval for courtesy, had each time closed it again. The five left were all Senators: Reid, slim and wiry, almost diminutive, still alert, frowning with disgust, was erect in a committeeman's chair; Corcoran, tall and loose-jointed, wearing the famous Windsor tie with his evening clothes, sat on an edge of the long table and yawned; Tilney stood at a window with his back to the room, the exhausted brown eyes looking, perhaps, in the April night for what they had failed to find in the blue eyes of Sally Voorman, or in the thick smoke dully floating in the committee room, or anywhere else; Allen, big and slick and wary, well-made and well-tailored, wandered around humming to himself; Wilcox, from the West, youngest of the five, who had shown during his first term that he knew how to follow and would not let his shrewd deep eyes show the bitterness of the waiting for his chance to lead, stood in front of Corcoran and appealed to him, but as an equal. Nearly, at least, as an equal, nearly— soon, more!

He said, "For God's sake let's go home."

Corcoran wearily shook his head. "Not till Tilney sends us. We've got to give him all he wants."

"But I tell you we don't need him." Wilcox was snapping. "We need sleep, not him."

Reid spoke from his chair; his voice was as alert as his appearance, without fatigue. "You only tell a man you don't need him when you have to bluff. It isn't necessary to try to bluff Tilney. He knows what we have; you're missing the point." He turned toward the man at the window. "Tilney, you know all the arguments as well as I do. You could brief the case on either side. Will you commit yourself? That's all. You know what the assurance of a united front will mean to us. It will save a dog-fight. Give us your word now. I think you'll be with us on the roll-call anyway, but we want it now. We ask you to give it to us, with no prejudice on any of the issues on which you foresee future disagreement."

Tilney had turned. The exhausted brown eyes were again blinking at the smoke. He walked across the room, and, paying no attention to Reid, stopped in front of Corcoran and said, "Wilcox is right. What we need is sleep. I'm going home. Your war bloc looks good, Jim. I think you've got it."

Corcoran got off of the table. He was well over six feet, inches above Tilney, who was not small. "Come with us, Bronnie." There were three men in Washington who called Bronson Tilney "Bronnie." "Damn it, what is it? Loyalty to Stanley? He's not expecting it. Hatred of war? Maybe you think I love it. Reid does and Wilcox does. Let them. I hate it. During these twenty years in Washington I guess you and I have learned to choke down hate. What is it? Do you think you can stop the tide? Not a chance. What is it?"

"It's just a belly-ache, Jim." Tilney reached up and patted the other's shoulder. "I've got the belly-ache, that's all." He turned and got his eyes around to the other three, Wilcox to Allen to Reid. "Gentlemen. I shall not decide what to say about your war until I have heard the President tomorrow. That's final. I should have made it final two hours ago. At present no one knows what the President will say. If after he has spoken my conscience will permit it, you will find me as ready to swallow bitterness as you are to feast on gall."

Wilcox snapped, "Good. That's that."

Reid said, cold but friendly, "Don't try to fight us, Tilney."

Allen was sarcastic and not friendly at all. "Leave your conscience at home. It's less trouble that way."

Tilney, disregarding them, was muttering something to Corcoran, and the latter was shaking his head. "No," he said when Tilney had finished, "we can't do it. It has to be before adjournment tomorrow. Today. We're committed. Come with us, Bronnie. Take your time. I'll wait here all night for you."

Tilney, not bothering with another no, moved away. "Goodnight, Jim." He nodded vaguely in the general direction of the others, walked slowly and not very steadily across to the door, and went through it, leaving it open behind him.

Wilcox said, "He's dead on his feet."

"He won't be at noon," Reid observed, pushing back his chair and getting up. "Going my way, Jim?"

Corcoran had moved around the table and stopped in front of Allen, looking down wearily at his slickness. There was venom in his tired voice. "If you find yourself smothering some day, buried under Bronson Tilney's conscience, don't yell for me."

Reid said, "Forget it. We're all sitting on the same keg of powder. Let's get some sleep."

# TUESDAY—ANTICLIMAX

# 1

On a day when the President is to appear in person before a joint session of the Congress, Washington on the lazy Potomac assumes outwardly, not without a touch of self-consciousness, a little of the air of a world-capital. This, the least self-made of cities, built by the most violently self-made men in the world, is ordinarily and obviously content with its rôle of celestial rooming-house for the hordes whose heaven is a public office and whose salvation is the national pay-roll; but now and then it arouses itself reluctantly to a half-hearted realization of its position as the nucleus of the most potent and dynamic among the world's half-dozen imperial atoms. The quadrennial Inaugural Day is such an occasion; New Year's Day, for obscure and indefinable reasons, is one; another, in much smaller degree, is a day when the President talks to the Congress. The visible evidences of the difference from any other day are next to imperceptible: more police on Pennsylvania Avenue, more people on the sidewalks, and more costly limousines headed for the Capitol; but the difference is somewhat greater where it really exists, in the psychological tone of the inhabitants. The air is by no means as electric as it is in Cleveland or St. Louis on the opening day of a baseball World Series, but there are sparks and currents which commonly are absent.

This particular Tuesday, though, this day of a President's visit, began early to show promise of more than something a little different—possibly, even, something unique. At ten o'clock in the morning Major General Francis Cunningham stood looking out of a window in the office of the Secretary of War and growled, without turning around, to that official:

"What the hell does this town think it is, Paris changing cabinets?"

The Secretary, reaching for a telephone, made no answer.

The police were still in control. The army, uniformed, trucks, gas-bombs and guns handy, was ready at its base, but it was not yet active. The question was still open. The first clash had taken place shortly after dawn, when a group of Communists five hundred strong, out near the Marine Barracks, had started marching west up Virginia Avenue, and a police captain who had read about Napoleon had disregarded the general orders and had decided that the Reds should wait a while. A few had been hurt, the Communists' orderly march had been turned into a stampede, and the captain had been dressed down. Later, from the top of a building near Garfield Park, bricks and stones had begun to fall on the same Reds; a few had tried throwing them back again, but their leaders urged them out of range and they went, leaving a few comrades in a truck bound for a hospital. Police mounting to the roofs caught three men in gray shirts, all that remained in sight.

Throughout the early morning there were minor skirmishes here and there, mostly southeast, some north of the Union Depot. After an affair on Second Street from which everyone had scattered before the arrival of the police, a Gray Shirt was found stretched on the pavement with the side of his head smashed in like a dropped flower-pot. That was the only fatality reported; they were not really killing yet, only rehearsing for it. All details were being relayed from police headquarters to the office of the Secretary of War, against the moment when the army might have to step in.

When the Secretary turned away from the telephone Major General Cunningham asked him, "Well, what does our good-hearted President say?"

"It's up to me." The Secretary rubbed his ear. "Funny. I'm to decide if and when it's necessary. I didn't get the President, but Brownell said that's final. He's sending it over in writing."

"Well?"

The Secretary shook his head. "Wait till we hear again from Tanner."

Tanner, Chief of Police, in his own office, not so private, was beset. He hated trouble. Burglaries and traffic violations and even an occasional murder were not trouble; they were affairs of business and to be expected; but the Communists and Gray Shirts and that kind, while their activities seemed to him plainly criminal and that was that, had roots that sneaked underground into so many pockets of political subsoil that it was necessary to treat them almost as if they possessed the rights of ordinary citizens. That was confusing and certainly made trouble. And they weren't the only ones. He had just hung up the telephone receiver after talking to a lieutenant who had reported that at the corner of Fourteenth Street and New York Avenue a bunch of women, a hundred or more, were demanding permission to march down Pennsylvania Avenue to the Capitol. They were members of the Women's League for Peace, the lieutenant said; well-dressed, determined, and carrying anti-war banners as big as bedsheets. When the Chief of Police had instructed the lieutenant to tell them to go home, and the lieutenant had replied that it would take a squad to handle them, the Chief had yelled into the transmitter, "All right, let the damn fools march!"

A similar request which arrived around eleven o'clock was too much for him; he told the captain who phoned it in to call up the Secretary of War and report it direct. At the War Office the call was put through to the Secretary himself. Cunningham was still there. The Secretary listened to the captain on the phone, asked a question or two, and then said, "Hold the wire." He turned to the general: "Here's a tale for you. Three hundred Grey Shirts are in an alley down by Twelfth Street and Pennsylvania. Their leader says they're going to march to the Capitol. The police captain says they're not. And how do you like this, the leader shows him a permit signed by Commissioner Forrest!"

Cunningham's eyes opened. "No!"

"Yes."

"It's forged."

"The captain says he knows the signature. Has Forrest a legal right to sign such a permit?"

"I think so. I don't know. Who's the leader? Lincoln Lee?"

"No. A tall man with black hair."

Cunningham snapped, "Arrest him. Chase them."

"Arrest him for what?"

"For not being Lincoln Lee. What's the difference? Any way, don't let them parade. Chase them."

The Secretary hesitated a moment, then spoke into the telephone and gave the order. When he had finished he turned back to the general: "What do you know about Forrest?"

The reply was incisive. "I don't know a single damned thing about a single damned soul. It's a good thing I'm a soldier and not supposed to, it saves me embarrassment."

The focus of the excitement, of course, the center toward which these radii of fervor and fear converged, was the Capitol building. The police, mounted and on foot, kept clear

40

only those spaces which had been roped off. They tried to show forbearance, but now and then a skull got rapped or a horse stepped on a biped's foot. No gray shirts were visible; there were many coat collars turned up, but of course it was legal for even a good citizen to turn up his coat collar. The throng increased in both size and unruliness, and the police got a little rougher. When the Chief of Police arrived on the scene around half-past eleven he was more relieved than alarmed; from the reports he had suspected worse. He even began to think he might finish the day without the army as he got out of his car and started a round of visits to his officers on their various posts at strategic points. Any in his path who did not promptly make way for him were brushed aside with vigor; he was plenty big enough and his contempt was very real. At a quarter to twelve, fifteen minutes before the scheduled time for the arrival of the President, he brought up at the foot of the steps to the west entrance, directly in front of the delegation of the Women's League for Peace. They looked tired, excited, and grim, their banners erect on high poles; more than a hundred of them, surely.

The Chief spoke to one in front, apparently the leader: "You ladies look out of place huddled here."

"We are not huddling!" She was indignant. "We want the President to see us. Is there a better place?"

The Chief shook his head and strode on, toward a spot where a little whirlpool was gathering around a man who had started to make a speech.

# 2

Inside the Capitol, in the House chamber, another mob had gathered. More precisely, three others. There were the visitors' galleries, packed to the last inch; the press gallery, with no absentees; and the floor.

In the first there were wives of Senators and Representatives, embassy men, lobbyists, an ex-President's widow, society bell-cows, an A. F. of L. vice-president, judges' wives, a miscellany of government officials from bureaus, commissions and boards, and a small scattering of those who can, alas, be called merely people. The chatter was deafening, since the

41

session had not yet been called to order; and it was uncommonly high-pitched, for all were taut with expectancy, even those whose sophistication was of the variety that confuses itself with indifference. It was a knowing crowd; it knew the line-up in the House, the Senate war bloc, the spot where the President would stand below the presiding officers; it knew everyone by sight; it knew that Mrs. Stanley had not yet made an appearance; and above all it knew that not only a great nation but an entire world, the whole of an immense tortured civilization, was holding its breath in expectancy of what this knowing crowd's ears would hear and eyes would see before all others.

The occupants of the press gallery, not onlookers but characters in the drama and thoroughly aware of it, moved restlessly about, talking, watching, disappearing below and coming up again. A few scribbled on pads. The bureau heads were there, the stars, and all the irregulars who had been able to get in.

On the floor a majority of the lawmakers and warmakers were in their seats; groups were in the aisles; members drifted in from the cloakrooms and out; pages walked and ran. Among the veterans and leaders, Reid stood by a wall with Representative Morton, listening with a frown, Corcoran talked with a group on the Clerk's platform which included Speaker Horner and the Vice-President, Sterling and Jackman, anti-war champions, conferred where the former sat, Allen and Wilcox were not visible, and Tilney sat motionless with his chin on his chest and his eyes closed. Everyone was nervous and tense, even the lowly of the herd who knew how they had to vote no matter what happened. They, like the supers in a stage spectacle, shared only in the excitement, leaving the glory for their betters, but at least no one could deprive them of that.

At three minutes past noon the Speaker and the Vice-President mounted to their rostrum, the latter banged his gavel, mumbled something and glared, and the session was convened. The vocal clatter died down gradually, members hastened or sauntered to their seats according to temperament, the gavel banged again, and silence began to emerge. The Clerk of the House read something which nobody listened to. A Senator arose halfway back, was recognized, and launched into what was apparently a discussion of the geography of the

United States. Stragglers were wandering in from the cloakrooms.

The discussion continued. The Vice-President was observed to lift himself in his chair and raise his brows at someone; the speaker on the floor hesitated a moment and then went on with the geography. It was twenty past twelve. Up in the gallery Sally Voorman whispered to her husband, "Is the bum working up suspense for his entrance?" There was other whispering; it increased, gradually, to an audible murmur. They had waited for the show long enough; they were in no mood for a late curtain.

At twenty-five minutes to one a page appeared from the side, leaped up the steps, and handed a slip of paper to the Vice-President. There was a rustle throughout the chamber. So; of course, a telephone message that the President was leaving the White House; another quarter of an hour then. But to the surprise of everyone, amazement even on the floor and in the press gallery, the Vice-President, after leaning across to mutter something to the Speaker, rose from his chair, descended from the platform, and left the chamber at the side the page had come from. There was a buzz all over. The Speaker banged the gavel and demanded order. The Senator was still doing geography.

In not more than three minutes the Vice-President returned. Instead of resuming his place, he crossed the floor to the head of an aisle and beckoned to Senator Corcoran, who hurried from his seat to join him. The Vice-President spoke in an undertone; those close enough saw that his face was white and that Corcoran, as he listened, stiffened and set his jaw. The conference, with every eye above and below focused on it, went on for minutes; finally Corcoran turned and went back down the aisle. He stopped to direct a glance at Reid which apparently had a meaning, for Reid nodded in reply, and then returned to his seat.

The Vice-President mounted the rostrum again. The Speaker handed the gavel to him, and he took it. He did not sit down, but stood with his lips tight. The Senator speaking from the floor faltered, left a predicate without an object, and resumed his seat. The Vice-President cleared his throat and spoke to a breathless stillness:

"I have an announcement to make. Information had been received that the President has suffered an indisposition and

43

is unable to come before us. It is therefore necessary to postpone the purpose of this session."

The silence hung in the air an instant, then was broken by a gasp of astonished dismay from floor and galleries. Before the Vice-President had finished Corcoran was on his feet. The Vice-President said, "Senator Corcoran."

"I move we adjourn."

Half the members were up from their seats; a dozen were shouting for recognition, the loudest Senator Allen; one of them was a second for Corcoran. The Vice-President brought the gavel down, shouted a brief sentence into the upturned faces of the joint session of Congress, and left the rostrum, taking the Speaker with him.

All that was left was bedlam: indignation, alarm, bewilderment, chaos.

The man seated next to Bronson Tilney, Collins of Vermont, yelled in his ear, "It's a dirty clever trick, but he'll pay for it." Tilney, his eyes more exhausted than ever, paid no attention to him.

A quarter of an hour later Mrs. Richard Arthur Coulter, homeward bound in her limousine with her friend Diana Freeman, evolved an idea that might have prevented the contretemps, "You know, my dear, I think a President should have an understudy, like an opera singer. Don't you?"

3

Of the reports which circulated through Washington that Tuesday afternoon, it was more than ordinarily difficult to sift the facts from the rumors. For three hours perhaps a hundred thousand citizens thought the President had been assassinated; where that one started was not known, but it traveled all over the city, and beyond. That was what the afternoon was like. President Stanley wanted more time to make up his mind; or he had a nervous breakdown; or he was drunk; or he had been assassinated by a Red or a Gray Shirt or a Jap; or he had put over a fast one on Congress. The odd thing was that these uncertainties were passed around and discussed not only by the common folk who are often permitted to learn only what is supposed to be good for them anyway, but even by persons who were accustomed to expect more prompt and definite information. The Senate and House leaders, the first rank ambassadors, the chiefs of the press bureaus, for all their frantic efforts, were left with nothing better than their choice among the morsels of wild conjecture which were clogging the telephones and telegraph wires of the country.

At half-past three it became known definitely that the Cabinet members had been summoned to the White House. At four, the Secretary of State appeared in the room in the Executive Offices maintained for the representatives of the press, announced brusquely that no information would be given until the Cabinet meeting had ended and he could not tell when that would be, and departed. The press howled at his back.

It was more of a let-down, perhaps, for the groups gathered in the Capitol grounds for the purpose of demonstrating this and that, than it had been for the lawmakers in the chamber. Characteristically not only of them but of the two-footed race they belonged to, they at first regarded it as a low trick designed primarily for their frustration. They howled, and began to look around for a head to crack or somebody to trip up. But the police got earnest, and it soon became evident that the anticlimax and the uncertainty had caused the temper of the demonstrators to deteriorate from sacrificial ardor to plain ill-nature. That was easier to deal with, and they were scattered ignominiously; the grounds were cleared and the streets patrolled with no worse results than a few busted jaws and a broken bone or two.

It was exactly three o'clock when the truth of the matter became known to anyone beyond Mrs. Stanley, Harry Brownell, the President's secretary, and two Secret Service men. At that hour the members of the Cabinet, summoned by Brownell by telephone, had assembled in the room ordinarily used for their meetings during the Stanley administration—the library on the second floor. They were all there, including the Vice-President; Billings, Secretary of Agriculture, called from a conference with the Federal Trade Commission, had been the last to arrive. Some seated, some standing, they were waiting. For the President? They did not know; Brownell had said come. They talked in low tones, as if in the presence of death; their nerves were on edge and there was nothing to say.

When the door opened they jerked about to face it. Mrs.

Stanley entered, and those seated arose. Secretary Brownell followed her and closed the door behind him. Mrs. Stanley came forward, stopped, and looked around as if counting them. She, who always smiled, was not smiling. She seemed out of breath, her hair was untidy, and she had put her hand on the back of a chair as if she needed it there. She said, "Be seated. Please do." Alex Liggett, the urbane Secretary of State, went to manipulate her chair for her. She shook her head, then changed her mind, nodded her thanks and sat down. Secretary Brownell stood beside her; the other men took chairs.

She said, "I have had a problem, gentlemen. I can keep it for my own no longer; it is yours and the country's. The President has been kidnapped."

They stared at her as if she had suddenly begun skipping the rope or standing on her head. She went on: "The news has been withheld, even from you, for five hours. That may have been ill-advised—I don't know—it was done by me and the responsibility is mine."

"I share it." Brownell spoke sharply. "Officially, I take it and welcome it."

There were ejaculations. Three or four were on their feet. Billings, an old friend of the Stanleys, looked like a cretin with his mouth open. Liggett, Secretary of State, exclaimed idiotically, "Kidnapped, how, who?" Vice-President Molleson, hunched forward in his chair, was regarding the President's wife with a shocked and suspicious stare. The quiet composed voice that cut through the confusion belonged to Lewis Wardell, Secretary of the Interior.

"Suppose you tell us about it, Mrs. Stanley."

Brownell asked, "Shall I?"

She shook her head. "Thank you, Harry." Her hands were folded tight in her lap; her voice was strained but steady. "The President had breakfast a little after eight o'clock, alone. We had house guests and I breakfasted with them earlier. About half-past eight he called to me from the hall that he was going outside to look at the morning and would afterwards return to the library—this room—I understood that he did not intend to go to his office, as he was leaving before twelve for the Capitol and had no appointments. That was the last I heard or saw of him."

She swallowed.

"A little before ten Mr. Brownell telephoned to me. He

46

said that there was something of great importance which he wished to tell the President. He had supposed that the President was in his study, or the library, working on his message to Congress; and he had phoned to those extensions, first the study, then the library, and there had been no answer. He had made inquiries and had concluded that the President was with me, and when I said no, Mr. Brownell was concerned and came at once to see me. We went together to the study and the library, and other places. He went outdoors. He thought we should ask as few questions as possible... I continued the search inside, but I did not find my husband... I knew, gentlemen..."

She faltered and stopped. After a moment she looked up and nodded at Brownell, who stood beside her. Brownell spoke:

"I picked up a Secret Service man who was on duty outside. We learned that the President had not been seen to reenter the house, and we found evidence that alarmed us. I consulted Mrs. Stanley. I issued orders that no one was to be permitted to leave or enter the house or grounds on any pretext, without reference to her or to me. I closed the communication with the Executive Offices. Outgoing telephone calls were stopped, and incoming calls were routed to a man I selected. We continued our investigation. The results were meager, but they led definitely to the conclusion Mrs. Stanley has announced to you. The President has been kidnapped."

Brownell stopped. Questions came at him. What emerged was again the quiet voice of Lewis Wardell:

"Ten o'clock was five hours ago, Mr. Brownell. The responsibility you welcome is a heavy one."

The secretary nodded. "Of course. The President was to go to the Capitol at noon. Up till that hour we thought we had reason to suppose that he would appear there. When he did not, for two hours we pursued another line. At half-past two I telephoned you gentlemen."

Oliver, Secretary of War, put in, "You had reason to suppose he would appear at the Capitol? What does that mean?"

"It means..." Brownell started, and stopped. He took a step forward and resumed sharply: "Gentlemen, we're wasting time. To you, this group as a whole, I offer no explanations and no details. I shall answer for my conduct to the proper person at the proper time and place: namely, the

47

President of the United States when he is back where he belongs. Yes, I waited five hours to tell you; and I have not reported to the Chief of the Secret Service or the police or anyone else. Why not? Because I don't trust them. I trust no one! You know Washington and you are acquainted with the present crisis, but I doubt if all of you together know as much as I do of what has gone on here for the past two months: the crescendo of fear and greed, of demands and appeals noble and ignoble, of hatred and avarice, of threats veiled and open. I know, for instance, what happened in the President's study last Friday evening, when one of you gentlemen now present sat not disapproving while three of your brother statesmen in elective offices told him that if he did not come out for war within a week he would be impeached. I trust no one! I suppose the Cabinet has—"

The interruption came from Lewis Wardell. "Mr. Brownell. You might save the oration for later. If the President has been kidnapped, let's find him."

"Yes, sir. I was saying, I suppose the Cabinet has the legal authority. If you will delegate that authority to one of your number who can be depended upon for loyal, prompt and aggressive action, I am ready to tell him all I know and suspect. Otherwise I tell only what I must, and I take whatever action I think necessary on my own responsibility if you don't lock me up. To act as a group would be too cumbersome anyway. Will you name a man?"

Oliver muttered something to his neighbor Liggett. Billings admonished the secretary: "Take it easy, Harry, we don't fancy pushing." Theodore Schick, the fat and shrewd Secretary of Commerce, with his eyes half shut, spoke between a squeak and a growl: "In the absence of the President... I presume... the Vice-President..."

Two or three heads were seen to shake negatively. Molleson almost stuttered: "N-no, Theodore. Not me, boys." He controlled himself to a judicial tone. "It is not a constitutional absence."

A heavy silence. The eyes of the members of the Cabinet looked uneasily around, each at his colleagues, and there was suspicion in all of them. Mrs. Stanley rose from her chair and left the room.

# WEDNESDAY—CONFUSION

# 1

At nine o'clock Wednesday morning the District of Columbia was under martial law. All rights of citizens were suspended; to walk on a sidewalk or drive a motor car or buy an ice-cream soda was no longer a right but a privilege and might or might not be rudely interrupted. Soldiers were seen on the streets of Washington, but not in numbers; they were on post at intervals throughout the city and merely stood, armed, as much onlookers as the passers-by who stared at them. The search for the President of the United States was being carried on by others, city police and detectives and the Secret Service; that is to say, the official search. Unofficially a hundred thousand citizens joined in the hunt, or a million— there was no telling. The Washington *Record,* the newspaper owned and published by Hartley Grinnell, son-in-law of George Milton, which had been savagely criticizing the President for months, appeared that morning with its entire front page a placard:

CITIZENS OF WASHINGTON, VIRGINIA, WEST VIRGINIA, MARYLAND, DELAWARE, PENN-SYLVANIA, NEW JERSEY

FIND THE PRESIDENT!

HE MAY BE IN THE CITY, HE CANNOT BE FAR AWAY. FIND HIM! YOU CAN! IF EACH AND EVERY ONE OF YOU WILL MAKE SURE OF THE BUILDING YOU LIVE IN AND THE ONE YOU WORK IN, AND ADJACENT BUILDINGS, AND ALL POSSIBLE SPOTS OF CONCEALMENT NEAR YOU, HE WILL BE FOUND. TAKE NOTHING FOR GRANTED! IN THIS NATIONAL EMERGENCY, CREATED BY THIS DAS-TARDLY CRIME, NO ONE HAS A RIGHT TO REFUSE YOU COMPLETE SATISFACTION AS TO HIS PREM-ISES. GET IT!

### FIND OUR PRESIDENT!
### and, if necessary,
### RESCUE HIM!

The idea caught on. Papers in other towns and cities copied it in special editions; posters conveying it were printed in a dozen states and displayed on walls, fences, and billboards. Any inhabitant might expect at any moment to find his home or office or factory or warehouse invaded by an individual or a delegation demanding "satisfaction" and the right to search. None might refuse, even in those cases where it was evident that a private grudge was taking advantage of an opportunity to make a nuisance of itself. But though there were such cases, and though there was displayed in the aggregate an incalculable quantity of stupidity, intolerance, and plain nonsense, it was yet an impressive demonstration of the temper and spirit of the American people reacting to an unprecedented outrage. They wanted their President back, and they intended to find him. They made incredible fools of themselves, but that may always be expected to happen, anywhere, when any individual or any group, large or small, loses simultaneously its self-consciousness and its sense of humor. They were crusaders, even the druggists and garage-owners in Delaware villages who put revolvers in their pockets when they left their homes for their places of business, and the plumbers in New Jersey cities who, called to fix a leaky pipe, greeted the housewives with suspicious glances and kept their ears open for strange or unexpected noises.

Destruction and violence, pointless but not unnatural, occurred here and there. In Altoona, Pennsylvania, the local leader of the Gray Shirts was left dangling on a tree and his home was burned to the ground. Similar, though usually less fatal, incidents took place in a hundred communities scattered over the nation. In twelve hours a gray shirt had become the most unfashionable garment in the history of the Republic and it was no longer being publicly worn, nor indeed privately either. Reds were hunted and disciplined too, but with less fury and certainly with less reason. In California Japanese were caught and beaten, arrested, chased through the towns and over the hills; it was reported that more than a dozen were killed.

In the section within a few hundred miles of Washington, motorists found it difficult to get to their destinations. They might be, and were, stopped almost anywhere by almost anyone, questioned, and their cars searched. If at the twentieth such delay they exhibited a little natural resentment, they often regretted it. On the main highway north from Atlantic City a man in a big sedan with another man on the seat beside him—the president of a Philadelphia bank and one of the bank's directors—stopped at a filling station. After he had pumped in the gas and been paid, the attendant observed, "You won't mind if I glance inside," and grasped the handle of the rear door. The banker said that the door was locked and he was in a hurry and a dozen people had already looked inside, and stepped on the starter. The attendant said, "Wait a minute, you'd better unlock it." The car started forward and away. Four or five shots rang out and both rear wheels banged on flats. From a group of men standing there two, one with a rifle and the other with a shotgun, detached themselves and trotted over to where the car had stopped and the banker had got out, choleric at the outrage. One of the men, pointing the rifle from his hip, said, "Open the door." The banker, swearing adequately, did so. The man looked inside, yanked the cushion from the seat, and backed away pulling after him a traveling bag, which he opened, dumping the contents over the running-board and the oily pavement. He kicked the shirts and brushes and slippers around a little before he said, "Okay. You'd better learn some manners, mister." The other man moved to the front of the car and remarked disparagingly, "These tires ain't much good," and pulled the trigger of the shotgun twice. That made four flats. The banker, gone from red to white, demanded to know where the town constable could be found. The man with the rifle said, "That's me." The banker called to his companion to wait here, walked down the street to a drug store, and telephoned the County Attorney in a nearby town. The County Attorney, after listening to the flood of demands, threats, and protestations, said that the best suggestion he could offer was for the banker to take the next train north; there would be one in about an hour.

That, on that Wednesday, was one of the multitude of comic unnoticed episodes of the search for the President.

# 2

Lewis Wardell did not go to bed from seven o'clock Tuesday morning until late afternoon of the following Friday. During that period he took two short naps on a couch in a room adjoining the office of the Chief of the Secret Service, but except for those snatches he was sleepless for over eighty hours.

At five o'clock Tuesday afternoon the members of the Cabinet agreed unanimously upon the following points:

1. The routine affairs of the Executive Offices would be handled by Secretary Brownell, and anything of urgency beyond routine would be referred by him to the full Cabinet.

2. All phases and activities of the search for the President would be under the direction of Lewis Wardell, Secretary of the Interior, and he could be removed from that direction only by a majority of the Cabinet.

3. The Cabinet would meet daily at nine in the morning during the emergency, and all members except Wardell agreed to be present. Secretary Brownell and Mrs. Stanley would have the status of members.

4. The absence of the President was not a vacancy under the Constitution, and would not be considered to be so unless a majority of the Cabinet agreed.

5. The confidential nature of facts learned, positions taken, and actions contemplated in Cabinet meetings was to be doubly inviolable during the emergency.

These points were put in writing and initialed by all members. When it came his turn with the fountain pen Theodore Schick, Secretary of Commerce, hesitated. He had strenuously opposed Point 4, and had really not surrendered on it but had merely been overborne by numbers. Now he read it again, and shook his head.

"How can I initial that?" he demanded.

Lewis Wardell said, "It would seem to be necessary for each of us either to initial it or resign."

Schick smiled at him, then took the pen and added his TS

53

to the row, observing, "I suppose there's nothing very binding about it."

Billings muttered quite audibly, "Only to gentlemen." There was a little stir, and Liggett mumbled to Billings something about the necessity for unanimity, but the latter muttered again audibly, "To hell with him." The absence of the catalytic quality of President Stanley's personality was already making itself evident.

Lewis Wardell was through with that meeting. He was already on the telephone, speaking to the Chief of the Secret Service, telling him to collect his entire available staff immediately and await instructions and authority. He asked the Chief to hold the wire and called to the Attorney General: "Davis, come and tell Skinner I'm his boss. I'm going right over there." He handed the phone to Davis and turned to the President's secretary: "Come along, Brownell. Got that agreement? Good."

On the way through the White House grounds and across to the Department of Justice Wardell fired questions at the secretary. What was the urgent matter that had moved Brownell to seek the President at ten o'clock? Confidential, Brownell said, no possible bearing on this. Wardell darted a glance at him, but did not insist. What was the alarming evidence which he and the Secret Service man had discovered? A chloroformed handkerchief which the Secret Service man had found under a spirea bush, and some trampled grass nearby. Where was the handkerchief now? In Brownell's pocket, in a paper bag to keep the smell in. What other evidence or clues had they found? None. Absolutely nothing, and the Secret Service man, Cramer, was competent and probably to be trusted.

They were on the sidewalk.

What people or vehicles had been seen? A guard patrolling the drive at some distance. A sentry at the rear entrance to the grounds. Neither of them had seen the President. Two gardeners working some eighty yards away from the White House. The President had walked up and spoken to them, apparently soon after he went outdoors, and had walked back the way he had come. They had subsequently heard or seen nothing. Two employees had entered at the gate between eight-thirty and ten o'clock, a cook and the secretary of Mrs. Stanley's secretary; and a messenger from the State Department and the Assistant Secretary of the Navy. A truck, Callahan's, had entered around nine o'clock to deliver groceries and departed as usual; the driver was known to the sentry and had been recognized by him; and about nine-thirty a car had come with plants and shrubs for the gardeners. No one had seen the President after he left the two gardeners.

"Here we are," said Wardell. "I'll want more from you later." They entered the Department of Justice and took the elevator.

Phil Skinner, head of the Secret Service, came to them in the anteroom and took them inside. He was big and heavy but not awkward, imperturbable but alive, with gray doubting eyes and very blond hair. In his own room, when they entered it, a dozen men were standing and sitting around. He said, "Get out, boys. Wait outside. Dick, go and help Birdie with the telephone. Get everybody here—Birdie will tell you."

When the men had gone out and the door had been closed behind them Lewis Wardell said, "Skinner. We can forget the 'Misters,' if you don't mind. President Stanley has been kidnapped."

Skinner looked at him, looked at Brownell, then back again at the Secretary of the Interior. "Sure," he said. "It uses a lot of time standing on ceremony. Sit down." He took the seat at his desk, swinging it to face them as they drew up chairs. He went on: "So the President's been kidnapped."

"Yes. You don't seem particularly disconcerted."

Skinner shook his head. "I quit having hysterics a long time ago. Tell me about it."

Wardell told him succinctly, in less than two minutes, all that he knew. When he had finished the Chief of the Secret Service just looked at him, with raised eyebrows, not only saying nothing, but apparently with no intention of saying anything. Wardell said impatiently, "Well, when you're through staring..."

"Excuse me." Skinner let his eyebrows down. "Maybe I'll have hysterics after all. I don't remember ever hearing a worse cockeyed story, Mr. Secretary."

"Cockeyed?"

"Yeah, cockeyed. The President of the United States disappears, and for five precious hours, goddam precious, his secretary treats it like a family game of hide-and-seek, and for two more hours the Cabinet sits around and plays who's-got-the-button. Maybe that's what you've got to expect from a Cabinet, but if I'm supposed to butt in on this—am I supposed to butt in?"

"Go on."

"I wouldn't bother much about anything else until Mr. Brownell told all about those five hours."

Wardell nodded. "That is in prospect. The bothering will be done by me. You understand that?"

"Yeah. Davis said to follow you, you're in charge."

"Good." Wardell turned to the secretary. "I'll finish with you, Brownell, and you can get back to your office and feed the newspaper wolves. If you'll handle them I'll appreciate it. Let me have that handkerchief." The secretary took a paper bag from his pocket and handed it over; Wardell opened it, sniffed inside, nodded and laid it on the desk. To Skinner: "Chloroform. Smell it." To Brownell: "Why did you suppose, until noon, that the President would appear at the Capitol?"

The Secretary replied promptly, "I didn't say I supposed that. I said we thought we had reason to suppose it."

"And the reason?"

"It will sound fantastic. Last Thursday Tremaine of Allentown Steel told me that he would find a way of having a talk with the President in advance of a public commitment on the war. He said, in spite of hell. He had been trying to see the President for a month."

"Fantastic enough. Do you mean you thought Tremaine had carried the President off just to have a talk with him, and when he was through talking he would drive him around to the Capitol?"

"No. Not like that. There were other things, many of them; Sunday the President told Mrs. Stanley that before taking his stand he would like to hear one able and intelligent presentation of the other side, and that although Tremaine was a hyena he had ability and intelligence. Many things; damn it, the President was gone, and we had to think something!"

"All right." Wardell appeared to accept it. "From twelve-thirty to two-thirty you pursued another line. What?"

"An idea of Mrs. Stanley's. She went to see Sally Voorman, the wife of Voorman the steel lobbyist."

"What for?"

"To play bridge—no, I guess it was checkers. What the hell do you suppose for?"

"I don't know. Not to try to catch her husband in a morning amour, I imagine. I'm asking you."

Brownell got up from the chair. He was controlling himself. He jerked away a step, stopped and turned, shut his lips tight and looked down at Lewis Wardell a moment, and then sat down again. He said, "You're wasting time, Wardell. Of course what you want is to learn why I waited till half-past two to notify someone and start some action. That's easy. Because I didn't know whom to notify. Look here. Suppose someone—a munitions man or a patrioteering maniac like Caleb Reiner—has carried off the President and intends to hold him until Congress has been driven and pushed and bribed into war, or until Molleson has temporarily assumed the office and achieved the same result? Suppose the job of finding the President is placed in the hands of the Attorney-General or the Chief of the Secret Service—it doesn't matter who—anyway, a man whom the munitions crowd owns or the maniac controls? Guess how much chance there would be of his being found until the purpose was achieved! That was the situation that confronted Mrs. Stanley and me this morning. We had no fear that the President had been seriously harmed, or that he would be. We acted as his proxies and lieutenants, in the manner that we thought best calculated to preserve the policy dearest to his heart. Damn it, we love him! We love him and belong to him! She does of course—well, I do too. We acted and shall continue to act *in his interest*. First, we surmised that the people playing this incredibly bold game would have perfected their plans for an immediate coup: they would expect that the absence of the President would become public news by noon, when Congress would meet, and in the excitement, doubtless by a well-arranged sequence, they would get their war. So we fooled them on that; we waited until Congress met and adjourned. Then Mrs. Stanley wanted to try one thing, one stab through a curtain, and I let her; it was without result. We next spent an hour together in the President's study, deciding on a man who must have two qualifications: he must be sufficiently high in authority to stand a chance of being placed in charge, and he must be as completely reliable as possible. Close to the President as we were, we knew only too well that not a single highly-placed man in Washington could be regarded as beyond suspicion. We knew that the Cabinet would never stand for me."

The secretary's eyes were boring at Wardell. "We decided on you. Billings we knew better, but there was too much straw in him. We picked you. I phoned Billings to come early to the meeting, and primed him to put you up. So you've got a job. Find the President. You'll find him. They won't dare to hurt him. Essentially you'll have to do the job alone, because

I swear to God there's not a man you can trust implicitly; not a cop, not even a White House Secret Service man, not a member of the Cabinet. The munitions gang has got its bloody claws in places you'd never suspect; the bankers have sent billions abroad but they know how to use money at home too; the patrioteers that are the most dangerous are the ones who make the least noise; and the Gray Shirts are about as silly and harmless as Hitler's mob was in nineteen-thirty. Find the President, Wardell, find him and bring him back to the White House with his policy still clean and intact in his hands, and then let them tear it away from him if they can. And trust no one except yourself."

Brownell turned, suddenly whirling, and put his eyes on the head of the Secret Service. "What about you, Skinner? What are you like?"

Skinner's gray doubting eyes met the secretary's. He said quietly, "Oh, average. Ornery and suspicious and sometimes honest. But when I'm getting paid for a job I never make a mistake about who I'm working for." He looked at Wardell. "It might be a good plan to get started on this little case before the week's out."

Brownell asked, "Do you want me any more?"

Wardell shook his head. "No. Two orations in one day is enough. Thanks for the hints. I can get you."

Brownell went. After the door had closed behind him Wardell said, "Well, Chief. First, what do you think of Secretary Brownell?"

"Not so bad," Skinner replied. "I rather like some of his ideas, for instance about not trusting anyone. That's why I was thinking it might be a good plan to send three or four men over to account for all the cubic inches in the White House."

Wardell nodded. "We'll do that."

# 3

Lewis Wardell had never done any sleuthing. Previous to his appointment to the Cabinet he had been a practicing attorney in Indiana, active in politics on the liberal side. He had a sharp flexible mind, a skeptical but tolerant philosophy, and a pertinacity notable even among the stubborn Hoosiers. He had, in short, unusual abilities; but he had never done any sleuthing, and that fact was in large part responsible for the mistake he made that Tuesday evening and failed to correct for forty-eight hours: he attempted to carry on the action on all sectors at once and to retain personal command of each sector. The results were that confusion and delay hampered the most valiant efforts of his men, many lines of inquiry were left suspended without either abandonment or conclusion, and he all but collapsed at his desk on Thursday afternoon.

It was not that he disdained help. When the shrewdest inspector in the New York Police Department arrived with twenty picked men from the Detective Bureau at one o'clock Tuesday night, his offer of assistance was eagerly welcomed. Similar offers from other cities were declined only because no use could be made of them. Before dawn Wednesday morning the hunt was well organized and a hundred highways, alleys and tunnels of possibility were being explored. Many scores of the citizens known to the newspapers as "denizens of the underworld" had been rounded up and were being held, and hundreds of Gray Shirts, including their national leader, Lincoln Lee, who had been found sleeping in a room in the apartment of a Representative from Texas. All persons known to have been in or near the White House or its grounds on Tuesday morning had been questioned, and six of them—a servant, two clerks, the two gardeners, and the messenger from the Department of State—had been locked up pending further inquiry. Five men from the Bureau of Investigation of the Department of State were in the offices of the telephone company, checking all long distance calls from Monday morning on. The movements of the car which had brought plants to the gardeners had been verified for every minute of the day. The sentry who had been at the rear entrance was under arrest, likewise the guard who had been in that portion of the grounds and the two men of the White House squad of the Secret Service who had been on duty. The origin of the chloroformed handkerchief—linen, fair quality, not new, hemstitched, no laundry marks—was being investigated by a dozen men, and a dozen more were getting druggists and their clerks out of bed all over the city, inquiring into sales of chloroform for the past several days. Men with electric searchlights from the War Department were examining each inch of the terrain—lawn, pavement, and gravel—of the grounds south of the White House. A small army was combing the city, divided into sections, with orders to question anyone and inspect any premises offering the slightest promise or the slightest suspicion. By three o'clock in the morning Lewis Wardell had reconsidered the tenders from other cities of the assistance of trained and picked men, and was telephoning Baltimore and Philadelphia and Boston to send them on.

Another line was being pursued by a special group of Assistant Attorneys-General, Department of State investigators, and a miscellany selected by Wardell and Billings. These were invading the homes of the great and near-great, official and lay, in many cases rousing them from sleep, and talking things over with them. They were combining suavity with inquisitiveness and making it a point not to offend, chiefly hoping for a careless hint, an unguarded word, that might present a clue.

And by three o'clock a sort of help that was of course inevitable and, however bothersome it might be, could not safely be ignored, was already arriving in volume and threatened to become an avalanche. The telegraph and telephone wires were humming with advice, clues, and suspicions from thousands of alert and sleepless citizens, from counties in every state. When the first such had arrived around seven o'clock Lewis Wardell had issued emphatic instructions that every communication received was to be reported to him! Eight hours later, not yet daylight, six men were doing nothing but receive them—five on telephones and one slitting telegrams—in a room of another bureau of the Department of Justice commandeered for that purpose.

# 4

The men, regular Secret Service, assigned to the trails originating in the White House and grounds scored the first hit.

At four o'clock in the morning Lewis Wardell, in Chief Skinner's room which he had appropriated for his headquarters, was drinking black coffee, reading copy for a telegram to be rushed to all officers of the law in the United States, talking on the telephone to an Assistant Attorney-General, and listening to the man who called himself Lincoln Lee, who, handcuffed, was seated in a chair at the corner of the desk. When he had hung up the receiver he turned to face Lee.

"Now repeat that."

Lee, for one, had not relinquished his gray shirt, though a coat mostly concealed it. Above its open collar the cords of his neck showed hard like tubes of steel; he sat with his backbone strong and straight, poised, if not for action that instant or that night, in any case for action. His wrists on his lap were neither accepting nor resisting the handcuffs; they too were action in suspense.

His voice was contemptuous, assured, and coldly unyielding. "You asked what are my personal ambitions. I said I have none. Do you mean the petty ambition of a bureaucrat like yourself? That is for small men. I am not pursuing ambition, I am following destiny. What I am, I am, I need not become; I need only make myself known to others and I shall be recognized. If the President was kidnapped for political reasons, those who did it are political infants; they are not strong, they are merely desperate. If they kill him, the reaction will defeat and destroy them; if they return him, he will defeat them himself."

"You said you would kill him."

"Of course. If my destiny led me to that. Of course. It is a child's question. But my destiny is not in Washington, not yet; it is in the villages and towns and cities of America. When it leads me here, and I act, there will be no mystery as to the author of the event."

"You would seem to be in Washington now."

"A recruiting tour. Not for action, only a passage of the prelude to action."

"Then why did you sit at a table for two hours Monday night discussing a map of the city of Washington with three of your lieutenants?"

The only perceptible acknowledgment by Lincoln Lee of the impact of that shot on its target was a faint lowering of the twist at the corner of his mouth. He said, "Before I could explain that I would have to remember that it happened."

"I'll do the remembering for you." Wardell's tone tightened. "And is it only a coincidence that Callahan's grocery trucks are kept in the Maryland Avenue Garage?"

"I don't know. I don't drive them."

"Never? Not even Tuesday morning?"

"Not at all. You're talking nonsense, Mr. Secretary."

"To match yours, Lee, about your being in Washington. An employee of the government was present at your meeting in the cork-lined room in the Maryland Avenue Garage Monday night."

"Probably. If he's an American. I am willing to enroll all Americans, and shall."

"Not probably for this one. He was there. Unfortunately he could not hear what was said at the table as you discussed the map. If he had known of its importance he might have managed." Wardell leaned forward in his chair to pin Lincoln Lee with his eyes. "That's what we've been leading up to. That's what you're going to tell me. Why the map?"

Lee did not seem impressed. He shook his head. "No. I prefer not to tell that. It was a private matter, private to my organization. No."

"Oh yes. That, and this; where is the map now? I want it, and the papers that were with it."

Lee shook his head again. "You're wasting your time. I'm telling you, if you want to find your gutless President, you're plowing the wrong field."

"I'll do the plowing. Maybe it will help if I give you the picture: at this moment, in two rooms in the basement of this building, there are two men, one named Grier and another named Fallon. You may remember that they were with you at the table. They are in separate rooms. Some detectives from New York are with them. I don't know exactly what they are doing to them, and I would prefer to remain ignorant, but my understanding is that they are likely to answer any questions that are asked before they become incapable of speech."

Wardell paused, but Lee was unmoved and silent.

"They had in mind offering you the same persuasion, but I paid you the compliment of assuming that with you it wouldn't work. The idea is that they will get your lieutenants' stories and I shall get yours, and we'll compare them and draw conclusions. I know you would rather not, but you must. Make no mistake about it. I figured that with you a different method of compulsion would be required. You can believe that I mean business, and I have no more time to waste. If you refuse to tell me what I think you know, or if your story disagrees with Grier's and Fallon's, I shall at once lock you up in an insane asylum, where you belong—yes, an insane asylum, and you will be kept there—"

Wardell stopped, and involuntarily shrank back in his chair.

Lincoln Lee was up above him, quivering from head to foot, and a gleam sufficiently insane was gathering to points in his eyes. He spoke hoarsely: "You dirty lying bastard!" Wardell straightened up, hardening, forcing his voice: "Sit down! That's where you'll go if you don't talk, an insane asylum—"

Neither of them had noticed the opening of the door to the room; certainly they had no leisure to remark the entrance of the person who had opened it, for Lincoln Lee, his teeth showing and the gleam in his eyes darting the lightning of mania, had leaped forward with his manacled hands upraised, and Wardell, helpless beneath him, unable to get to his feet, was bending his arms in futile defense of his face and trying to throw himself to one side. The newcomer was in on the jump, and he got there in time. He hit Lee just once, with his left because of the angle of his approach, but it was a solid left with all the shoulder in it. Lee went down. Wardell's foot had got against a corner of the desk and he kicked himself back, chair and all, and stood up. The newcomer dangled his left hand around in the air, held it up to look at it, dangled it around again, and said:

"Jesus."

Wardell stepped forward and looked down at Lincoln Lee on the floor, muttering, not very steady, "Confound it, it worked too well."

The other nodded. "He's cold. His head hit the corner of the chair on the way down. Shall I drag him out of the way?"

Wardell looked at him. "Who are you? I think I've seen you. Aren't you from the White House squad?"

"Yeah. Moffat. I phoned you twenty minutes ago; found Kempner, the Callahan manager, and you said to bring him in. He's out in the hall. When I heard your friend here raising his voice I opened the door so I could hear better."

"I'm much obliged." Wardell looked down at Lee, motionless on the floor, his legs stretched out and his manacled hands flung above his head. "How soon will he come out of that?"

"It's hard to say." Chick Moffat grinned. "He was in a good position to tip over and he rubbed that chair pretty hard. Shall I drag him out?"

"No." Wardell had his breath normal again. He was not at all a coward, but the sight of Lincoln Lee above him, iron on his wrists ready to strike and points of fire in his eyes, had been a little unnerving. "Put him over in a corner. Over there. Bring Kempner in. And have somebody bring me a gun to keep on my desk; I don't suppose I could hit anything, but I'll have one anyway. Have you asked Kempner anything?"

Chick Moffat had grasped Lee's relaxed ankles and was hauling him, like a sack of bran, across the linoleum toward a far corner. When he got him there he let the ankles fall and stooped over to feel the pulse. Then he replied, "No, my orders were to deliver him."

"Good. Bring him in."

Moffat went out. In a minute he was back with a man, a short bald blue-eyed man on whose round amiable face astonishment, alarm, and sleepiness were plainly struggling for possession of the field. Moffat put him in the chair Lincoln Lee had recently vacated, and turned and went out again. Wardell, back in his own chair, took in the round face and the blue eyes and thought that if guile was concealed there it had never found a more unlikely hiding-place.

"Your name?"

"Adolph Kempner, K, E, M,—" The bald man's voice was clear and careful, as it had been twenty years previously when he had called back figures looking for a trial balance. Wardell interrupted him:

"Yes. You are manager of Callahan's store?"

"I am. Vice-President of the corporation. May I say—"

"No. Answer my questions briefly and correctly. How long have you been keeping your delivery trucks in the Maryland Avenue Garage?"

"Yes, sir. More than three years. Four years in August."

"How many trucks have you?"

"Well . . . six Reos and the two little Fords."

"Where have you been since eight o'clock tonight?"

"Tonight?"

"Last night."

"At the home of a friend of mine, Mr. L. A. Dippel."

"Doing what?"

"We were playing pinochle."

Wardell looked aside as the door opened. Chick Moffat entered, crossed to the desk and laid on its glass top a dark blue .38 revolver and a box of cartridges. He said, "It's loaded.—What now?"

"Sit down. You've been pretty helpful." Wardell turned back to Adolf Kempner. "Playing pinochle until three o'clock in the morning?"

"Yes, sir. When we get started . . . we're quite fond of it. I got to my rooms—I'm not married—at half-past three, and found this gentleman waiting for me."

Wardell turned to Chick Moffat. "Didn't anyone know where he was?"

No, Chick said; another with him on the assignment had gone off to try to pick up the trail, and at ten o'clock, when news came that the truck had been found, and the other clerks and employees who had been unearthed had sworn to complete ignorance regarding it, a dozen men had joined in the hunt for Kempner. A dozen more were looking for the missing driver. Chick had remained at the rooms, and at three-thirty Kempner had walked up and stuck his key in the lock.

Wardell said to the manager: "A young man named Val Orcutt makes your deliveries to the White House. Why?"

"Why?" Sleepiness had resigned the field on the round face, and alarm was uppermost. "Why . . . because I tell him to."

"Why did you pick on him? Because he's a member of your organization?"

"Of course he's a member of our organization, naturally . . ."

"I don't mean Callahan's. I mean, because he's a Gray Shirt?"

Adolf Kempner blinked and his mouth opened. He shut it again, as the import of the questions seeped through, and his round face took on an unexpected quality of dignity and composed resentment. "That's a lie," he said quietly. "None of our boys are Gray Shirts. I am not. What are you driving at?"

"I'd like to know." Wardell kept his eyes fastened. "Where is Val Orcutt now?"

"I don't know. At home asleep, I suppose he is."

"He isn't. He hasn't been there since he left this morning. When did you see him last?"

"Why, I saw him . . ." The manager was suddenly silent, then suddenly he exclaimed, "My God!" and stared at Wardell with horrified eyes.

Wardell said, "Well?" And with sharper impatience, "Well?"

"Wait a minute." Kempner was pleading. "Just wait a minute." He swallowed. "This is how it was. At twenty

65

minutes to nine Val left for the White House. I always check that order out myself to avoid any chance of error. We always make a special trip for it, we don't want to run any risk of getting other orders mixed with it, but we send a big truck—you understand that, it wouldn't look well, a little Ford delivering provisions to the White House. We appreciate the advantage of people seeing our fine big truck going there every day. At a quarter past nine, I was back in the office then with the mail, Val phoned me. He told me that he had jumped out of the truck onto something and turned his ankle, and would have to lay off for the day."

Wardell nodded. "Your stenographer has told me of that call. So that's what Val Orcutt said?"

"Yes. Yes, sir. My God, he must be at home..."

"He didn't return to the store?"

"No. I offered to send for the truck, but he said he would take it to the garage since it wasn't needed at the store.... I thought in the afternoon I should telephone his home to ask how he was but I didn't get around to it..."

"You didn't telephone the garage to ask about the truck?"

"No, why should I? Val is a trustworthy boy, it never occurred to me, I took it for granted..."

"How did his voice sound on the phone? Was he excited?"

"No." The manager frowned, remembering. "He wasn't excited. His voice sounded funny, I supposed it was his ankle hurting him. It didn't sound like him, too high."

"Why did you think it was him if it didn't sound like him?"

"Oh, it was him." Kempner stared. "Of course it was him, why should I think it wasn't?"

"I don't know. Did you know that the Maryland Avenue Garage is the Washington headquarters of the Gray Shirts?"

"No. I... I can't believe it."

"It is."

Kempner said promptly, "Our trucks will be out of there tomorrow."

"Oh, no." Wardell was grim. "Your trucks will stay there. Your store won't open tomorrow. Your employees are under detention. Yourself also."

The manager went red. He held in for a moment, then sputtered. "The store won't open? Under detention?" His voice rose and his face got redder. "Sir... sir... I am not a man of temper, but this is an outrage... by what right..." He tried to collect himself. "It is the most reputable establishment in the city . . . for the store not to open is impossible . . . it would be a calamity . . ."

"Don't whine," Wardell snapped. "To hell with your store. Val Orcutt, your driver who had one of your trucks in the White House grounds at nine o'clock yesterday morning, has disappeared, and the truck was found at ten o'clock last night in front of an empty house on Fifteenth Street Northeast. It had been parked there all day. And lying on the floor inside of the truck, in a dark front corner back of the seat, was a penknife belonging to President Stanley—one he always carries in his left vest pocket."

Kempner was staring. "My God," he muttered. "In our truck . . . I can't believe it . . . in our truck . . ."

"Just so. Now maybe you'll tell me how many of your men are Gray Shirts, and which ones. Come, speak up."

"How can I?" The manager's hands were clenched tight together and his voice was shaky. "How can I, sir? There are no Gray Shirts at Callahan's, I'm positive. It isn't possible, in *our* truck—it's a calamity. If any of the boys was a Gray Shirt I certainly would know it, I wouldn't stand for it . . ."

"What about Val Orcutt? Where is he?"

"I don't—don't I tell you I don't know? Val Orcutt is an absolutely fine boy, I know that.—And, sir, I want to tell you that it would be criminal not to let the store open. God knows I'm sorry about the President's penknife, but not to let Callahan's open would be—it would be unconstitutional! I can tell you—"

"Be quiet! I'll tear your damned store to pieces if I'm inclined that way." Wardell turned to his desk, poured from the thermos jug another cup of black steaming coffee, and sipped at it. After a minute he put the cup down, reached for the revolver and cartridges lying there, looked them over and put them in the drawer. Then he sipped some more coffee. Finally he spoke again, but not to Kempner.

"Moffat, are you a bright detective? Does this man know anything?"

Chick Moffat shook his head. "Only how to sell groceries. On a bet, no. I'm fairly bright."

Wardell looked again at the round face and blue eyes of the bald-headed manager, then turned to the desk and pushed a button, and sipped some more coffee. In a moment the door opened and a man entered. Wardell glanced at him and indicated Kempner with a thumb.

67

"Lock this man up. Not in the building. I doubt if he's any good."

The man nodded and started for the manager, who had jumped to his feet with a mouthful of protests all trying to emerge at once. Wardell finished his cup of coffee. The man grabbed Kempner by the arm and marched him out of the room, ignoring his outbursts on the subjects of warrants, outrages, and the Constitution of the United States. Wardell spoke to Moffat:

"How's the maniac?"

"He's all right. He's been awake for quite a while."

"I haven't seen him move."

Chick grinned. "No. He's cute. He's just lying there planning how to do his good deed for today."

The door opened again. Another man entered. Wardell looked at him. "Who are you?"

The man had sweat drying on his face and forehead, and he looked discouraged. He spoke from inside the threshold. "I'm from downstairs. Heath of the New York Homicide Squad. Those two babies we're working on have got paralyzed tongues or something. We can't screw a word out of them and they've passed out. We thought you ought to come down and see—"

"No. I don't want to see. No! Goddam it, of all the—" Wardell jerked back in his chair and rubbed his hand hard over his face. "Excuse me. It wouldn't do any good for me to see. Lock them up, and report to Chief Skinner, all of you. Tell Skinner I said it might be a good plan to send you out to Fifteenth Street to try to pick up a trail from that truck. There's a lot of men already on it."

Heath from New York nodded, and went.

Wardell looked toward the far corner of the room and called: "Lee! Get up and come here." There was no movement. Wardell called again. Then he turned to Chick: "He's still unconscious."

Chick, grinning, rose from his chair and walked to the corner, and poked with the toe of his shoe, not rudely, at the posterior of the man lying there. "Come on, Lee, shake a leg." Still no movement, and Chick reached down and grabbed an arm, rudely this time. "Come on, cut out the faking." Then he straightened and took a backward step involuntarily at the incredible and intense ferocity of the voice that came suddenly from the floor:

"Take your hands off. Don't touch me."

Lincoln Lee moved. Without haste, and even somehow with dignity, he lifted himself to a sitting posture, drew a foot back under him and without assistance from his manacled hands came up to his feet. He walked across the room, with Chick Moffat following, and stopped in front of Wardell. There was something in his carriage and behind the composure of his face and eyes which made it not very easy for Wardell to stick to his chair.

"You can't even compare Grier's story with Fallon's, can you?" he said contemptuously. "They are my men. A man is made over when he becomes mine. I'll tell you just one thing: I had nothing to do with the childish kidnapping of President Stanley. As a favor I tell you that. I am not above generosity."

"Thanks." Wardell was looking up at him. "I'll return the favor by putting you where there are a lot of others like you, so you'll feel at home."

"You're a blackguard." Lee was still quiet. "You're a coward and a blackguard, and therefore it is nonsense to suppose that you can interfere with my destiny. Try."

Wardell was still looking up at him, and he did not take his eyes away when he reached his hand out to the desk and moved it around until it came into contact with the block of buttons. He pushed one. The one thing he was sure of about Lincoln Lee was that it was futile to talk to that face. He sat silent, and Lee stood silent. When a man entered in answer to the bell Wardell called him over and said:

"This is Lincoln Lee, head of the Gray Shirts. The men who brought him are across the hall. Turn him over to them and tell them to lock him up."

"Yes, sir. Where, in the building?"

"If there's a safe place. In any case, nearby. I may want him later."

"Right." The detective turned to Lee. "Come on, General, take a walk." They moved off, Lee in front. At the door they stood aside for two men to enter, then went out.

The two newcomers were from the front office. One of them had reports on the chloroform, reports on the search for Val Orcutt, on other searches and gestures and conjectures, a pile of reports that filled a basket; the other had telegrams and telephone messages, those not to be disregarded culled during the past hour from the ocean that was sweeping over them. The telephone on the desk rang, and Wardell took up

69

the receiver. It was Oliver, Secretary of War. He said that a discussion he had just left had convinced him that an approach should be made without delay on George Milton, the financier. He could offer no suggestions as to the kind of approach; Milton was the cagiest man in America and merely to question him would lead to nothing; but some kind of line should be taken, something should be attempted in that quarter. As Wardell hung up the receiver a third man entered the room. A detective had arrived with another person, a woman, who had seen the Callahan truck leaving the White House grounds; also, there was word from the jail, from Chief Skinner, that the sentry who had been on duty at the rear entrance had changed his story and was now saying that he had seen and recognized the driver on Callahan's truck when it entered the grounds, but had not noticed him when the truck left.

Lewis Wardell hunched over in his chair, his elbows resting on his hips, his hands clasped, his head sunk. The others had left the room; only Moffat remained. For a while Wardell stayed like that, then he lifted his head and blinked red eyes at Chick Moffat, who had got out of his chair and started for the door.

"Wait a minute," Wardell said. "You see how it is. How would you like to camp here and help me get it all?"

Chick hesitated. He opened his mouth, hesitated again, and finally shook his head. "I'm not the man for it, I haven't got that kind of a head. You're snowed under; you ought to have the Chief here, and maybe someone else, like Sampson from the Internal Revenue. He's a good man."

"I'll take you."

Chick shook his head again. "Anyway I've got to get some sleep. I'm no good without sleep."

"I've had none. I'm going on to the end."

"Sometimes a general can do that, but an army can't. I'm sorry, sir, I appreciate your offer, but I've got . . . I can't do it."

Wardell grunted, and looked at him without saying anything. He looked a long moment, then grunted again and said abruptly, "All right. After you've had your nap you'll report to Skinner."

"Yes, sir."

When Chick had gone Lewis Wardell sat staring at the piles of reports and telegrams on his desk. As he reached out for the first pile he said to himself half aloud, "Even that man has something on his mind, and it might be anything."

Down on the sidewalk Chick Moffat walked to where he had parked the modest black sedan which he had bought only two months previously in the expectation that Alma Cronin might like to go for a ride now and then. Two or three soldiers were standing around. Dawn had come, but it was not time yet for the sun; life's pulse was at its lowest. The street lights winked and went out as Chick stopped beside his sedan. The mild breeze from the west carried the smell of green growth from Potomac Park and of moisture from the river. Chick looked around with his foot on the running board; there were a dozen or more cars parked here and there, but not much sign of activity. As he climbed in behind the steering-wheel he muttered:

"If that old owl puts someone on my tail may he swell up and bust."

# 5

At eight o'clock that morning, Wednesday, Chief Skinner with six Secret Service men presented himself at the White House. He was received by Mrs. Stanley, downstairs; her eyes were red and tired, her lips were colorless, and she was keeping herself under control. The Chief asked her if she had any special instructions or suggestions.

She shook her head. "I would prefer that you proceed just as you would anywhere. Omit nothing. I suggested that to Mr. Wardell on the telephone, and he agreed. Mr. Brownell and I searched thoroughly, we thought, but of course not professionally, and we were too alarmed and excited to know very well what we were doing. I understand that you are to remove nothing without consulting me, and that Mr. Brownell is to be present when you are in the President's study."

"Yes, madam. Certainly."

After Mrs. Stanley had turned to go she turned back again. "Please let me know when you have finished."

"Certainly, madam."

71

The Chief had already instructed his men; they separated and the search of the White House began.

# 6

Nine o'clock.

The maid weighed not much over a hundred pounds, but she atoned with spunk for the deficiency in size. She was black-haired, with cheek-bones and a pointed chin, and her uniform was not very clean, for she had changed it for work since serving breakfast and had not expected any callers. She held the door firm to its crack of ten inches against the insistent pressure from the outside. She said:

"Mrs. Brownell is out too. I don't know when she'll be back. You'll have to wait downstairs. The elevator man shouldn't have brought you up."

The man in the hall, towering above her as he peered through the crack in the door, said impatiently, "I can't wait. There's something I have to get from Mr. Brownell's room. Let me in and I'll explain."

The maid shook her head and decided to close the door. But it didn't budge; and suddenly she was pushed violently backward as the door felt the force of a shoulder with two hundred pounds behind it. She regained her balance and, disdaining to run, stood and screamed. But the man was evidently as speedy as he was powerful, for the first scream had barely got started when a hand covered her mouth, her arms were pinioned to her sides, and she was lifted into the air. He carried her across the foyer into the living-room, sat down in a chair and stretched her across his lap, on her back, his hand sealing her mouth as tight as the clamped lid of a fruit-jar and his other arm pinning her motionless from the hips up.

He said, "If you'll stop kicking we'll have a conference."

She kicked.

"All right. Listen anyway. I'm a Secret Service man. If you'll give me a chance I'll show you my badge. We're looking for the President, I suppose you've heard of that, and we've got an idea that there are one or two little things in Mr. Brownell's room that might help. I don't want to hurt you—in fact, I'm determined not to. I'm not going to hurt you, and I won't steal the silver or your money or diamonds—I won't even carry off the rugs. If you'll promise to act sensible I'll turn you loose and we can arrive at an understanding. You can watch my every movement and satisfy yourself that I won't even make a mess for you to clean up. Just give me your promise; I can see that you're the kind that will keep it if you make it. Will you behave yourself? If you promise absolutely to behave yourself, raise your right leg."

She had stopped kicking to listen. Now her right leg came up, stretched horizontal, and stayed there. He eyed it—it was small but not without shape—then his arm confining her relaxed a little and his hand left her mouth. She would undoubtedly have got the scream out, and she meant to make it the most shattering scream of her life, if it had not been for the necessity of filling her empty lungs in preparation for it. As it was, though she made the intake a convulsive gasp and at the same time jerked her body to one side, he was quick enough to stifle the scream and keep her from getting loose. He had her again.

"That wasn't nice," he protested. "We'll pretend you don't know your right leg from your left so there won't be any hard feelings. Now excuse me." He went forward from the chair till he was squatting on the balls of his feet, laid her on her back on the floor, straddled her, holding her arms against her sides with his knees, and, with his free hand taking a handkerchief from his pocket and unfolding and shaking it out, stuffed it into her mouth. He did this speedily and not very tenderly, for she was producing quite a racket by kicking her heels against the rug on the floor. He carried her into the kitchen and tied her hands and feet with dish-towels he found in a drawer; with another towel he bound the handkerchief in her mouth; with others he secured her firmly, both arms and both legs, to a kitchen chair. He straightened up and looked down at her.

"Now," he said, "You'll have plenty of time to think up a good way to tell your legs apart." He went back to the living-room, stood looking around, and shook his head. He crossed to the other side, went through a small hall, and found a bedroom. There he began to search for "one or two little things."

73

# 7

Ten o'clock.

In the library in Pittsburgh, Ben Kilbourn stood beside the massive pinkish desk talking into the white telephone. He was saying, "No! Get him then. I tell you we can't—Oh. I'm sorry. Just a minute, Senator Allen, here's Mr. Cullen."

He handed the instrument to the gray-eyed man in the swivel chair, and stepped aside. Cullen spoke.

"Allen? Cullen. What about it?"

Two hundred and fifty miles of wire brought the Senator's careful wary voice, his careful cultured pronunciation. "They haven't found him yet."

"I know that." The steel man was sarcastic, and impatient almost to explosion. "I'm not cut off from civilization. What about Congress? You're meeting today?"

"We're meeting, and adjourning."

"You mean at once? No business?"

"Oh yes, there's business. We pass a joint resolution of concern, trepidation, and sympathy. Then we adjourn."

"Good God." Cullen paused an instant, taking it. "Then you're licked."

"I don't know if we're licked. I would say not. Ten minutes ago Reid remarked to me that the only thing for us to do is to stay under a tree until the shower's over."

"Then you're licked. Reid too, huh? I know you haven't got much guts, you're too clever to have guts, but I thought Reid was a fighter. Listen, Allen.—No, listen to me. I'm through waiting, and the country is through. I've been patient as a coupon on a South American bond for two months, and I'm through. The situation is dangerous. We want action. We'll find the President, or get another one, what's the difference? It's time for action. That's my word to you. You've got yourselves into this mess down there with all your meetings and dickering and coaxing, and the thing for you to do now, today, is what you should have done a month ago. Get it on the floor and fight for it. Put your resolution, a straight war declaration with no belly-aching, and shove it through. They'll scuttle, most of them; the others you can ignore. Get Reid and Wilcox and Corcoran and a few others you can depend on, and as soon as they get through with their concern and trepidation, go ahead."

"Listen, Cullen—"

"There's nothing I need to listen to. Go ahead. Act. Today."

"But you'll have to listen to this." Senator Allen's voice was a little less careful, and was conceding more to the common vulgarities of stress, than it had ever done before. "I'm sorry, Cullen. You know how sorry I am, but you don't know what's going on down here. Wilcox is scared, so scared he stutters. He wouldn't be seen on the street with a war man. Corcoran isn't scared, but he not only would not help in the move you suggest, he would violently oppose it on the floor. I told you what Reid said; he isn't scared either, but that's what he thinks. A war resolution today would get one vote. Mine. The next incident of my career would be my burial."

Cullen said, "Huh. You're scared too. Where did all the cold feet come from? You're a fine bunch of statesmen. We need a new crowd down there. Why are they all running?"

Allen said, "Because a war man kidnapped the President."

"Do they know that? Who?"

"No. They surmise it. They don't even surmise it, they feel it. They suspect everybody. They suspect you. I wouldn't be surprised if this line has been tapped and we're being listened to."

"Jackasses."

"You know of course that Wardell has been placed in charge by the Cabinet. That makes it worse for us, in fact impossible. Brownell is responsible. You don't realize what the atmosphere is, not only in Washington. A mob threw stones at Albert Courtney in Philadelphia this morning and would have dragged him out of his car if the police hadn't saved him. Voorman here in Washington is sticking to his house on good advice. I have it pretty straight that at this moment the Cabinet is in session, making a list of men to be summoned and questioned and perhaps detained. The first on the list is George Milton; another one is yourself."

Cullen said, "Huh? The damn fools are crazy."

"That's what I'm telling you. If you are summoned to Washington, I would advise you to come only by train, don't try to drive, and don't use your private car, it's too conspicuous."

"Why should I go to Washington? To hell with them."

"Of course, you will do as you please."

"I'll try to."

The steel man replaced the receiver. He sat with his hands on the desk in front of him, two tight fists, tricky, powerful and dangerous, but with nothing to hit.

He said, "And by God, those are the men we pay to run our country. One of them lets himself get kidnapped and the rest have got nothing but milk in their livers."

Suddenly he yelled at Ben Kilbourn, "What the hell are you grinning at? With your damn pink cheeks! Are you taking a tonic?"

Kilbourn said, "Yes, sir, it's a tonic."

# 8

At twenty minutes past eleven Lewis Wardell and Chief Skinner sat in the office at the Secret Service Bureau and looked at each other. Wardell looked tired, tense, and determined; the Chief looked skeptical and acutely concerned. The latter was saying:

"I know all that, but I'd go to the Cabinet. I've seen a lot of circumstantial evidence since I put on long pants. If it proved to be a washout it would be mighty handy to have them on record back of you."

Wardell said, "I have the authority of the Cabinet. Why start an argument and waste a lot of time? I think you'd better go and get him."

"If you say so. You might as well put it in writing."

Wardell sat a moment with folded arms and tight lips, then with sudden decision turned to the desk and took pen and paper and wrote.

Since Chick Moffat had left that office at dawn, a few things had happened. The District of Columbia had been placed under martial law, with Major General Francis Cunningham in direct charge but reporting hourly to the Secretary of War, who in turn reported to the Cabinet. The unofficial search of premises by aroused citizens, throughout an area of over a million square miles, was under way—inefficient, unorganized, and anything but thorough, but for the most part well-meaning and indisputably in deadly earnest. Another attempt by Wardell to get something out of Lincoln Lee had been totally without result, and Lee had been sent to the

District jail. Liggett and Billings, Secretaries of State and Agriculture, had brought Wardell a communication from the Cabinet suggesting that a bold and strong line be taken immediately with certain of the nation's financial and industrial leaders, naming names; Wardell thanked them and suspended action, for by that time, past ten o'clock, he had received two reports both of which pointed in an amazing and most unlikely direction. Chief Skinner had returned from his search of the White House; nothing had been found which by any stretch of fancy would be considered a clue, and the search, thanks to Mrs. Stanley's coöperation, had covered every inch within the building. But the enterprise had not been entirely fruitless, for outside, in a covered passageway at the rear, one of the men had discovered an interesting object buried halfway down in a filled garbage pail: a bottle of chloroform two-thirds full. The garbage pail had been there twenty-four hours; the man who had filled it thought he remembered that it had been partly filled on Tuesday morning and the remainder dumped in this morning, Wednesday. He did not remember seeing the bottle, and could not tell whether it had come from one of the house receptacles or not.

The Chief took the bottle from his pocket and handed it to Wardell. "We had to wash it off. It was good and messy. No chance for any fingerprints."

Wardell took the bottle and got up from his chair. "Wait here," he said. "I'll be back in a minute. There's someone across the hall I want to show this to." He went out; and it was when, after a short absence, he returned, that he began the tale and the discussion which resulted half an hour later in Chief Skinner's advice—ignored—that he go to the Cabinet before taking action.

# 9

At eleven-thirty Harry Brownell sat at his desk in his private room in the Executive Offices. He had left the Cabinet meeting—the others remaining in session—an hour previously in order to meet the newspaper men, and that uncomfortable business had just been finished. The representatives of the press had been next door to savage. When Brownell offered them one or two thin morsels and said that was the lot, they snorted with rage. One of them, dignified and impressive in a morning coat, protested in a voice which excitement betrayed into a squeak, "Do you realize, Mr. Brownell, that is our function and duty to let a hundred and twenty million American citizens know what is being done to find their President?" A chorus supported him; one shouted indignantly that he had hung around the Secret Service Bureau for eight hours, with the reward that at sunrise he had been escorted to the sidewalk and told to stay there. Brownell threatened, warned and cajoled, gave them another little morsel, and finally got rid of them.

They had been gone only a few minutes, and Brownell had barely begun to get his thoughts in order for some proposals intended for the Cabinet in the afternoon, when his secretary entered to say that Chief Skinner was there to see him. At Brownell's nod the secretary went out.

Chief Skinner entered with his hat in his hand, walked across the room, stopped smack against Brownell's desk, and stood there looking at him with his head cocked a little on one side.

Brownell said, "Good morning, Skinner." He returned the look at the other's silence. At length he put his eyebrows up and said it with another inflection, "Good morning?"

Skinner sighed, and said, "Mr. Wardell says he would like to see you over at his office. The one that used to be my office."

Brownell's eyebrows came down and moved towards the center. "He must be getting delusions of grandeur, using you for a messenger boy. What's wrong with the telephone?"

The Chief shook his head. "Beyond me. He has an idea he would like to see you right away and you should come back with me. Can that be managed?"

"Why..." Brownell stopped. Skinner looked at him; saw him wet his lips and saw the working of his temples; and reflected that a man who couldn't control his temples would never make a good poker player. Brownell resumed, "I can go, of course, if it's important. Has he got hold of something?"

"Maybe. He'll tell you about it."

Brownell got up and went to the closet for his hat. In the outer room he paused to tell his secretary where he was going and give some instructions; then the two left together, out through the side and across the grounds.

When they arrived at the Secret Service Bureau they

found that the stage had been set. At any rate, the Chief found it so, and threw Wardell a glance of approval; Brownell merely saw that a dozen or more men were in the room, standing around apparently with nothing to do; Wardell was seated at his desk bent over an open drawer. At Brownell's approach he closed the drawer and straightened up.

Brownell nodded a greeting. "Skinner says you want to see me."

"Yes." Wardell stared at him, into his eyes. "I need a talk with you. I won't stand on ceremony. First I must ask you a favor. Will you stand there with that group of men, among them?"

The men had collected at one end of the desk. Brownell looked at them, and back at Wardell. "Certainly. If there is any reason why I should."

"Only the obvious one that you are to be identified."

Brownell opened his mouth, then closed it again and without speaking moved to the group. It made an opening and he mingled with it. Wardell left the room. In a moment he returned, ushering before him a woman—a woman of substance as to flesh but not fat, middle-aged, not excited but not entirely composed. Wardell stopped her three paces from the group.

"Mrs. Delling. Is the man you were speaking of among these?"

The woman looked at the men, a face at a time. She saw tall ones and shorter ones, big ones and medium-sized, and was not at all disconcerted by the dozen pairs of eyes returning her regard. She took her time and finished the group. At length she nodded, and pointed an unwavering finger.

"That one. The well-dressed one in black, with a blue tie and a big nose."

Wardell spoke. "Will you step forward, Brownell?" The group fell back; Brownell moved directly in front of the woman. "You mean this gentleman, Mrs. Delling?"

Her tone was positive. "That is he, yes, sir."

"How sure are you?"

"I never make a statement unless I am sure. We owe it to truth, I think, never to abuse it."

"Very good. Thank you. Now if you will go back where you were, and wait there. Under no circumstances are you to leave.—That's all, men. Wait in front for assignments."

The woman left. The men filed out after her. Chief Skinner started along at the rear, but Wardell called to him to remain, and he closed the door and came back. Brownell did not move from the position he had taken in front of the woman. When the door had been closed he turned only his head to say to Wardell:

"Of course this is some kind of nonsense, but it's fairly irritating. The explanation?"

"Sit down." Wardell took his own chair and jerked his thumb at another. "Come on, sit down, I'll explain.—Sit there, Skinner." The President's Secretary moved to the chair with deliberation, flipped apart the tails of his morning coat, and sat.

Wardell said, "I'll explain if necessary, but it would be quicker and better if you did it yourself. Suppose you tell me all you know about the disappearance of the President."

The Chief of the Secret Service, on a chair at one side, was thinking to himself, *He's made a mistake. He shouldn't have let him see that woman. Brownell was absolutely worried, now he's relieved.*

Brownell said, "I've told you all I know. You are the first person I told, and the only one."

"You told me a tale. Now I want the truth."

"You have it. All there is of it, from me."

"No good, Brownell. I know things. I want the truth. No matter what it is, it's your best bet now."

Brownell sat and looked a moment, then leaned forward in his chair to get his eyes into Wardell's. He said slowly and bitterly, "So someone's got to you, have they? Even you. And you think if you can shut me off you can go ahead. What's the game? How have you framed it?"

For long seconds the two pairs of eyes met, hostile, suspicious, and pointed with purpose. Wardell finally abandoned it. He snapped, "All right," turned in his chair, and reached down and opened a drawer of the desk. From it he took first a stack of handkerchiefs, then the bottle of chloroform, and placed them on the desk.

He said, again getting Brownell's eyes, "Here are three facts for you. First, Monday night at nine o'clock you bought from Mrs. Delling at her husband's drug store on Acker Street, a bottle of chloroform. Second, here are nine handkerchiefs, taken this morning from the bedroom of your apartment, identical with the one found on the White House lawn smelling of chloroform. Third, this bottle, still two-thirds full, found by Skinner this morning at the White House, is the one you bought from Mrs. Delling. It is the

80

brand they sell." Wardell paused, and made his voice a whip: "Now I've explained, let's hear you."

Brownell said quietly, "It's a fairly good frame-up. I'm handicapped by not knowing for certain whether you're in on it. If you are, it would be a waste of time talking to you. I'll go to the Cabinet."

"You'll go nowhere. Frame-up hell. Come, Brownell, for God's sake give it up. You can't go through with it, it's hopeless. Tell me about it, let's wind it up. Where is he? Let me put him back in the White House and you can settle with him."

Brownell was still quiet. "I didn't know you were so clever, Wardell. I don't believe you are. Perhaps you're straight after all. Maybe I've been put up on you."

"You've put yourself up. What did you do with the chloroform you bought on Acker Street Monday night?"

"I bought no chloroform."

"What! You saw her pick you out."

"I bought no chloroform." Brownell leaned back in his chair, crossed his legs, and slowly rubbed the palms of his hands together; and though his face certainly was heavy with concern, Chief Skinner was thinking to himself, *He's just too damn pleased about something.* Brownell said, "Look here, Wardell, let's say you're straight. God knows I am. I didn't buy any chloroform, and I've never been in Acker Street; I don't even know where it is. I don't know anything about that woman picking me out, but it could be done from pictures; whoever arranged it with her could handle the details. Haven't they got any other witnesses who saw me? They should have. As for the bottle which you say Skinner found in the White House, wouldn't it be fairly stupid of me to leave it there? Similarly, it was stupid of them to plant it there, but that's their business."

"It wasn't in the White House. It was in a garbage pail outside, and it is the kind and size you bought from Mrs. Delling."

"The kind I didn't buy. No. If it was outside perhaps it wasn't planted; it may be the one that was actually used. As for the handkerchief, that may also have been arranged, or it may be only a coincidence. The Secret Service man, Corliss, found it; I carried it in my pocket for some hours before turning it over to you; I didn't realize that it resembled any of my own. Whoever burglarized my apartment for you, if that was straight, must have reported that he found several different kinds among my supply, mostly quite common varieties; I am informed by my wife that I am not as particular about handkerchiefs as I should be. So. If others have arranged this show and you've been taken in by it, there's my explanation. If you're a member of the cast, forget I've bothered to explain. In any event, it won't work, and you're wasting a lot of precious time. Don't think this isn't going to the Cabinet, because it is."

Lewis Wardell sat and looked at him, and finally said, "It will go to the Cabinet. I'll take it myself. You're a damn fool not to give it up. If you let go now you might come out alive."

"The Cabinet is sitting now. We'll go together."

"Oh no, we won't." Wardell pushed a button on the desk. "I'll go alone, and I'll make sure right now that it won't be hushed up. A little publicity might help.—One last chance, Brownell. Will you talk?"

"You're wasting time, and you're making an ass of yourself."

A man entered the room. Wardell turned to him. "Send two men in here." A telephone on the desk rang, and Wardell, asking the clerk to wait, turned to answer it. There was a little trouble getting the conversation started, but after some impatience Wardell said, "Yes, I get it now, Erasmus Hospital. What is it?" Then he did little but listen, with an ejaculation or two and a few questions; and when he finally replaced the receiver he turned again to the clerk:

"Make it four men, and move."

The clerk moved. Wardell said, "This may mean life or death for you, Brownell, do you realize that? Will you talk?"

The President's Secretary only looked at him. The Chief of the Secret Service cleared his throat and shifted his feet around, his grey eyes looking more doubtful than ever. Four men entered; and inside, stood in a line.

Wardell said, "I don't know your names." He looked at one. "You, come here." The man stepped forward. "This is Mr. Harry Brownell, Secretary to President Stanley. Take him to the District jail and lock him up, have him well guarded, and let him see no one without permission from me. Be sure those instructions are followed."

The man took a step; Brownell moved to meet him, without a word, and they went. Chief Skinner sighed. Wardell called another man forward:

"Across the hall, Room Nine, is a woman, Viola Delling. A

detective, a New York man, is with her. Lock her up downstairs, if there's any room left. If not, take her to jail. Then you and the New York man find out everything you can about her, particularly whom she has seen and where she has been the past week. He knows where she came from; he got her. Also get a line on her husband. She'll raise hell, but I don't want to see her. Take her away. Remember we're under martial law and civil rights are suspended."

The man turned and left. Wardell spoke to the two remaining: "Do you know Washington? Do you know where Erasmus Hospital is?"

They nodded.

"At that hospital, in the accident ward, is a young man named Val Orcutt. Bring him here as quick as you can; take a car if you've got one, or a taxi. He's had a crack on the skull, so handle him carefully; if he gets amnesia again he won't be much good to us. Do you know what amnesia is?"

One of the men said, "You forget things."

"Just so. Be careful with him."

The men went.

Wardell got out of his chair, bent and flexed his arms and drew his shoulders back with his chest out, breathing. "Damn it," he said, "I'm groggy."

The Chief nodded. "There's a quart of bourbon in the drawer there."

"No, thanks. How about some cheese sandwiches and coffee?"

"I could manage some."

After the clerk had been summoned and the order for sandwiches and coffee given, Wardell said to Skinner:

"I suppose there's some newspaper men out front. Would you go out and tell them Harry Brownell has been arrested? The news might start something somewhere."

"It will," the Chief agreed as he got up for the errand.


# 10

At a few minutes before noon Chick Moffat was going down the sidewalk, neither briskly nor leisurely, merely going, nearing the entrance to the Department of Justice. He had been assigned that morning—one in a hundred—to the task of finding Val Orcutt, the driver of the grocery truck, and on phoning in from Isherwood for instructions on a lead, had been told that the quarry had been flushed and he should report at headquarters. Almost at his destination, though, chance intervened to delay him, for as he was about to turn in at the entrance he heard his name called, in a voice that swung him around in the middle of a step.

It was Alma Cronin, on the sidewalk. "Chick! Thank goodness."

"Me too." He grinned. "I'll thank anybody you say. Who are you running from?"

"I'm running to, not from. Don't you ever go home any more? I tried to get you on the phone a dozen times last night, and again this morning."

"You would pick last night for wanting me. I'm finding the President. I went to bed at dawn and slept a hundred and forty minutes."

They had moved to the edge of the sidewalk not to get bumped. Chick looked down at her, and she looked up at him, and there was more color in their faces and life in their eyes than there had been two minutes before.

She said, "I wasn't wanting you. I mean, I wanted to ask you something."

"I get the difference. Much obliged. Did you try Information at the Union Depot?"

"No. It's something very . . . I'm on my way now to see Mr. Wardell. I tried first to see Mr. Brownell, and couldn't find him. I could ask you now, I suppose, but here on the sidewalk . . ."

"Let's go to lunch."

Alma said she was supposed to be back at the White House at one o'clock, and Chick said that would be double his usual allowance of thirty minutes for eating. Her hesitation was brief. Chick said he knew a place nearby where they cooked lamb chops with chives and floated them in a swell brown sauce, and marched her off. Two blocks away and a little down a side street they entered a revolving door. It was one of those places—there are not many—where the kitchen is so close that all the smells fill the air, and the cooking so good that your appetite thanks your nose.

After they had ordered Chick said, "Do you want to ask me something now or save it for coffee?"

Alma looked around. It was early, and there were not many in the restaurant; the adjoining tables were not occupied. She said, "I didn't want to ask you on the phone. I wanted to see you. I'm half afraid to talk about it, even to you. I had no idea people could be the way they are."

"What's wrong with people?"

"Everything. They're such awful cowards. Me too, I suppose I can't blame them. Did you know that a lot of the White House staff are under arrest? That Secret Service men searched it this morning from top to bottom? Everyone talks in a whisper when they talk at all. This morning when I went to work someone was following me, I'm sure of it."

"That was only me, being handy in case you wanted to ask me something."

"Don't joke, Chick. It's no joke. It's terrible."

"Well . . . I've followed so many people, and nearly always nowhere.—Here's the lamb chops. I tried to do them this way at home once, but they burnt on me. Of course it's terrible, and it's apt to be worse before it's better, but you have nothing to do with it. Thank God. Push your plate."

He transferred the chops, spooned sauce over them, fixed his own, and ordered beer. They ate, and discussed the chops.

Alma looked around again. She leaned forward. "What I wanted to ask you, Chick. I want to know what to do." Her voice was low; she lowered it more. "Last night around eleven o'clock, about half an hour after I got back from being questioned by your colleagues, a man came to my place and offered me five thousand dollars to steal Mrs. Stanley's diary and give it to him by noon today. He said the last two weeks of it was all he wanted. When I said no he offered ten thousand."

Chick chewed and swallowed. "H-m-m," he said. "So the First Lady keeps a diary."

"Of course. Everyone knows that. There have been pieces about it in the papers."

"Well . . . congratulations. That's a pretty good haul. It's enough to get married on if you happen to be inclined that way."

"Don't be silly. After I said no to his first offer I had a few seconds to think in. I pretended to hesitate. He urged me. I said that even if I decided to do it there would be no opportunity before noon, but there might be later. He said it

85

would have to be today. I told him he could come to my place at eight o'clock this evening, and maybe I would have it and maybe I wouldn't. He said he would come."

Chick asked, "Why was it silly for me to mention your being inclined to get married?"

"Because this is something serious."

"Getting married is serious."

"Is it? I know nothing about it. Chick. What shall I do? Shall I tell Mrs. Stanley? Shall I go to Mr. Wardell without telling her?"

"Look here." Chick laid down his knife and fork. "I've been waiting for an opening to get your ideas on marriage for over three months, and now that we've got the subject started we might as well dispose of it. There's nothing inherently silly about marriage, is there?"

Alma, meeting his gaze, looked exasperated; but she felt the exasperation going, and, in an effort to save it, she let her eyes fall. She stuck her fork into a chop and sliced at it. "Inherently? No."

"It really isn't a damn bit silly, is it?"

"I suppose not. How do I know? I see no reason to think it silly. Do you?"

"Good. Me? Good Lord, no. I think it's simply swell, I think..." She looked up; and since his gaze was still upon her he got the shock of her eyes all at once, like the sudden flood of sunlight after the darkness of a cave. He gasped. The words that he had been expecting to come next, naturally in the sequence, got lost somewhere below his throat and it seemed unlikely that they would be available. He said, "Well...I'm glad that's settled. It's nice to have that settled. What kind of a looking man was it that offered you ten thousand dollars?"

Alma smiled. The smile was saying, though only to herself, *He is absolutely a darling and I love him and I want him, but if I catch myself descending to guile at this juncture may I fry in hell*. She said, "He was big and strong with blond hair and dirty finger nails, and he wore a brown necktie."

She thought triumphantly, *Show me any female guile in that!*

Chick asked, "What are you going to do?"

"That's what I'm asking you. Whatever you tell me to."

With the last word of that Alma clamped her teeth on her

lower lip, sharply, and Chick wondered why. He signaled to the waiter and ordered coffee; and then said:

"You haven't told Mrs. Stanley?"

"I've told no one."

"Good girl. This thing's an ungodly mess and there's no use your getting mixed up in it without reason. It's even possible there's no connection—"

"Shouldn't I tell Mr. Wardell?"

"What for? So someone can hide in your closet and jump him when he comes?"

"If jumping is necessary, yes."

Chick nodded. "Of course that's the card to draw to. But you might be letting yourself in for it. For what, I don't know; but everyone's gone crazy. It might be better just to warn Mrs. Stanley to lock the diary up and when your friend calls this evening tell him nothing doing."

The restaurant was filling up. A newsboy had entered and was passing among the tables, offering an extra with black headlines four inches high. Chick bought one and unfolded it, holding it so that Alma could see with him:

## PRESIDENT'S SECRETARY ARRESTED

## BROWNELL BOUGHT CHLOROFORM

Alma said, "Good heavens. No!"

Chick said, "I told you everyone's crazy. You keep out of it."

"I don't want to. I mean, I want to be in it." Alma had started stirring her coffee, and forgot to stop. "You see, Chick, this thing is maturing me. Like young plants when they open up the windows to prepare them for going outdoors; I'm being hardened off. After all I'm only twenty-four, and I didn't know much about people. I had studied ideas and systems a lot, like Communism and Social Credit and Capitalism and the housing problem and international finance and war, and apparently I thought that people were just another idea. This kidnapping the President, and the martial law, and the fear and suspicion in everybody's faces, and the jealousy and hate coming out—I've only been on the edge of it, looking on, but it's showing me that people aren't just another idea, they're far more—or far less, I don't know which. They're animals with blood in them, and they don't only talk and write books and play bridge, they really do things. Hateful and terrible things, and maybe sometimes grand things. It's exciting and it scares me to realize that I'm one of the animals and I have to live with them. I thought I hated war, but I see now that I merely disliked the idea of war. Now I do hate war, anyway I think I do, and I know I hate the obscene pigs who have kidnapped the President for fear he would keep us out of war. That's why I say I want to be in it. I have no idea what Mrs. Stanley's diary has got to do with it, but it must have something. So I want to help catch this man, and if they beat him up to make him tell who sent him I wouldn't like to see it but I wouldn't have an ounce of regret and I'd do it again."

She stopped. Chick said, "You through? That was quite a talk."

"I'm through. Don't be smart."

"I'm not smart. I said it was quite a talk because I meant it. You see, I don't know about ideas. I was brought up among people, the kind you mention. The next-door neighbor on one side beat his kids, and the one on the other side paid fifteen dollars for a dog to get one big enough to lick ours. I'm the same with ideas as I am with booze, I know when to let them alone. I'm not anti-war and I'm not pro-war; if there's a fight I suspect I'll be in it. I'm just an animal."

He said it not apologetically, but not proudly either. Alma exclaimed, "Chick! Why, Chick.—All right, you're just an animal. There are lots of kinds."

"Sure." Chick grinned. "Now about purloining this diary. I'm glad you've decided to turn down the ten thousand, because if you ever decided to marry an animal and it happened to be me, it wouldn't work. I couldn't ever marry for money. But you say you want to catch this millionaire, and I say you want to keep out of it. How would it be if I came and hid in your closet at a quarter to eight, and then walk out and sit on him, if you object to jumping, while you beat him up."

"Chick. I don't object to the words you use."

"I thought probably you thought it was vulgar when I said *jump him*. I gathered that."

"You're too sensitive. Even if I thought it was vulgar, would you stop it?"

"Hell, no. I might."

"You wouldn't. You'd better not."

"I will. But it's one o'clock, and you'll have to walk because

88

I had to park practically in the river. Have I got a date to hide in your closet at a quarter to eight?"

"Of course. You know darned well that's what I wanted to suggest at the beginning. I must run."

Chick beckoned to the waiter for his check.

# 11

At about the moment that Chick Moffat was ordering coffee for Alma Cronin and himself, the two detectives who had been sent to Erasmus Hospital arrived at the Secret Service Bureau with Val Orcutt and his mother. Lewis Wardell and Chief Skinner had finished the cheese sandwiches and coffee. Oliver, Secretary of War, had come over from the Cabinet meeting to propose drastic action with regard to the war editorial which had appeared in the late edition of the Washington *Record*—the paper, owned and published by Hartley Grinnell, son-in-law of George Milton, which had at the same time, on the front page, printed the appeal to citizens to find the President. That had been settled with dispatch. Oliver had other suggestions. Wardell listened with a frown. In the middle of the discussion that followed a clerk entered to say that the men had arrived with Val Orcutt.

Wardell said, "I'm sorry, Jim, we'll have to put this off. It's the man who drove the grocery truck; we've found him. Come back later."

Oliver got up, looking not too amiable. "Wouldn't it be just as well, Lewis, if you left details of that nature to Chief Skinner and gave us a little more time on larger questions of procedure and policy? When we gave you authority we didn't have a dictatorship in mind."

"Take back the authority when you want it."

"We don't want it. Level up a little, Lewis. I think we're being reasonable."

"I'm not. I haven't time to be. I got no sleep last night and I don't expect any tonight. As long as it's my job I'll do it my way. I've arrested Brownell and sent him to jail, and tell them they don't need to try to see him."

Oliver stared. "Good God. When? Why?"

"At noon. Here in this office. The papers have got it. I

haven't time for explanations now, Jim. Come back later." Wardell turned to the clerk: "Send them in."

Oliver stared, shook his head, turned and left.

The Chief of the Secret Service spoke: "Do you mind if I shove this chair over a little? I'd just as soon catch a glimpse of this young man's face while he tells us things."

Wardell nodded wearily. "Of course."

When the detectives entered it appeared that they had caught two fish on one hook. They had Val Orcutt, taller than either of them, his red face redder by contrast with the clean white bandage which completely swathed his head, and they also had a plump little woman with graying hair who was stubbornly and aggressively beside him. She kept it a compact group. One of the detectives said to Wardell, defensively:

"It's his mother. There's no use talking to her."

Wardell said, "Take her out." To the other detective, "Put him in that chair."

Val Orcutt moved, got to the chair, and sat down. His mother moved with him and stood by the chair with her hand on its arm. Wardell repeated: "Take her out." The first detective took a look at the woman's face, shrugged, and observed, "We'll have to carry her."

"All right, carry her." But Wardell's eye caught the grimace on Chief Skinner's face. "What's the matter, Skinner?"

"Nothing. Excuse me for showing my feelings."

"What kind of feelings have you?"

"Just ordinary. Let her stay. He'll feel more at home."

Wardell looked at Val Orcutt, at the Chief again, and grunted. "Push a chair up for her." When the chair came forward Mrs. Orcutt turned and looked at it, sat down and wiggled back, folded her hands on her lap, and twisted her head to smile unobtrusively at the detective. Wardell told the detectives to wait outside and they left. He said to the woman, "You can stay there as long as you keep your mouth shut."

She spoke, for the first time. "My boy's head is busted open."

Val Orcutt glanced at her and said, "You keep quiet, mawm."

Wardell asked, "How is your head?"

Val put his right hand up and moved it, pressing, on the bandage. "This side's all right." The right hand went down

90

and the left one up. "There's a bruise here. I'm kind of woozy, but I'm all right."

"Your name is Val Orcutt."

"Yes, sir."

The woman said, "Valentine Orcutt."

Wardell glared at her. "What did I tell you?" Her son said, "If you don't keep quiet, mawm, they'll put you out." She nodded, acquiescent but unimpressed.

"You drive a truck for Callahan's."

"Yes, sir."

"You made a delivery to the White House yesterday morning."

"Yes, sir."

"What time did you get there?"

"I don't know. I mean I don't know exactly." Val was sitting straight in the chair, not using its back, his hands on its arms, his eyes steady at his questioner. "I left the store around eight-forty. I must have been at the White House by ten minutes to nine."

"How long have you been a member of the Gray Shirts?"

Val blinked twice, but his eyes kept steady and his tone did not change. "I am not a member."

"How many of the men at Callahan's are Gray Shirts?"

"None that I know of. I'm pretty sure, none."

"Now look here." Wardell leaned forward. "The very worst thing you can do is tell me lies. Some of these questions I am asking you, I know the answers already. The others will come out in the end. The only chance you have of the slightest consideration is to tell me the truth, not part of the truth, all of it."

"Yes, sir."

"How long have you been a Gray Shirt?"

"I told you. Never."

"How long have you known Harry Brownell, Secretary to the President?"

"I don't know him. I've never seen him."

"Nonsense. He has been arrested. He's in jail, and we have his story. You deny that you know him?"

"I've never seen him. Not that I know of. Not to know who he was."

Wardell leaned back. "All right. Suppose you tell us what happened at the White House yesterday morning."

"Yes, sir." Val blinked. "I got there about ten minutes to nine. I delivered three baskets of groceries and vegetables

91

and a basket of meat. That was all I had in the truck. There were some empty baskets to go back, and I threw them in at the rear end. Both the doors were open; the truck has double doors at the rear. I was shoving at the empty baskets when I heard a noise and I started to turn around and something hit me. That's all I know."

Wardell stared. "For God's sake! That's all you know?"

"Yes, sir."

"You expect me to believe that?"

"Yes, sir." Slowly, Val Orcutt put up his left hand and passed it gingerly across the bandage, and then rubbed at his forehead. "It's all I remember. I didn't remember that much until a little while ago, when Mawm came. I think he must have hit me with a wooden club. It cut the skin open but it didn't break my skull. The doctor at the hospital thinks it wasn't iron, either."

"Who hit you? Did you see him?"

"No, sir."

"Saw nothing of him?"

Val started to shake his head, and stopped with a grimace. "No, sir. I didn't see him at all. I had my back turned. I just heard a noise."

"Who took you to the hospital?"

"I don't know. I mean, I don't remember. They told me that a cop sent me in an ambulance. That's all I know."

"Where did the cop find you?"

Val frowned, and rubbed his forehead again. Mrs. Orcutt looked at his face, and said to Wardell, "If you want to know ask me. They told me at the hospital. He was walking on the grass in Potomac Park with blood all over him, and when the cop went up to him he didn't know his name or anything else—"

"What time was that?"

"About eleven o'clock yesterday morning. The cop called an ambulance, and at the hospital they thought he had been hurt in one of the street fights, and at first they thought he just didn't want to tell his name because he was a Communist or something, and they didn't pay much attention anyway because the ward was full of men that had got hurt. It wasn't till this morning a doctor found out he really didn't have his memory. When he didn't come home last night I worried and then about nine o'clock men began coming to ask about him, and later some more men came and asked my husband and me millions of questions, the same ones over and over again, and two men stayed in front of the house and two out back all night. I guess they're still there. As soon as it was daylight I started out to hunt for him and made my husband stay at home in case he came back. The men out front wouldn't let me go at first, then one of them decided to go with me. I went to the police station where the lieutenant's wife is a friend of mine, but he said more than a hundred men were looking for Val already and he couldn't help me any. I tried to find Mr. Kempner, that's the manager of the store where Val works, but he wasn't at home and I couldn't find him. I went to two hospitals and then I went to the morgue and looked at four dead men. Then I went to Erasmus Hospital and Val was there in the accident ward. He just stared at me and didn't know me. I asked him things and he pretended he didn't know what I meant. So I made him blow his nose."

She paused for breath. "Oh," Wardell said. "You made him blow his nose."

"Yes, sir. He had good color and they told me he ate a big breakfast, so I knew there was nothing serious wrong only he needed to clear out his head. I held a handkerchief against him and told him to blow hard like I used to do when he was little. The nurse yelled at me not to do it, but I made him blow, and he yelled because it hurt his head, and then he looked at me and said *Mawm* and I began to cry. The nurse called the doctor and he said it was remarkable."

"Yes." Wardell nodded. "Remarkable, yes. Is your son good at pretending things?"

"No. Val don't pretend. You asking him if he was a Gray Shirt, you ought to be ashamed of yourself. The President smiles at him and speaks to him. You ought to hear his opinion of the President, how he admires him—"

Wardell cut her off. "You said he pretended he didn't know what you meant."

"Well, I guess you know what I meant. I meant his head wasn't clear."

"You mean he was pretending. You said so."

Mrs. Orcutt unfolded her hands, lifted them palms out, pushed air at Lewis Wardell, and folded them in her lap again. She said with some contempt, not unamiably, "If you can't talk sense there's no sense talking at all."

Wardell looked at her. He pushed a button on the desk. A clerk came, and was instructed to send in three men. In less

93

than ten seconds they entered. Wardell told one of them to go to the hospital and bring the doctor and nurse who had attended Val Orcutt, another to go to the Orcutt home and bring Val's father, and the third to find the policeman who had picked up Val in Potomac Park. They went.

Chief Skinner had slid down in his chair, his hands in his pockets, his chin on his chest, his brows upraised to let his eyes, inquiring and not satisfied, rest on Val's boyish red face. Wardell looked at him. "Well, Skinner?"

"Go ahead." The Chief kept his eyes on Val. "You can't be too curious. I was just thinking, what if I pressed good and hard on the spot where he was hit, might it have the effect of making him remember more about what happened? For instance, what if he got hit by that heavy cane the President carries? It's missing, you remember. But just for fun you might pretend you think he's telling the truth."

Wardell looked at Val Orcutt and said, "Pressing that spot on your head would be a new kind of third degree, wouldn't it?"

"Yes, sir."

"We'll consider it. So the President has smiled and spoken to you. When, yesterday?"

"No, sir. A few times, last summer mostly."

"Did you see him yesterday?"

"Yes, sir."

"Ah! Where?"

"He was standing on the grass by some bushes as I drove by. Looking at flowers on them. Rhododendrons."

"Did he speak to you?"

"No, he was looking at the flowers."

"Who else did you see?"

"I saw the sentry at the gate, that was all."

"No gardeners?"

"No, sir."

"They were there."

"They must have been to one side, I didn't see them."

"No guards?"

"None except the sentry. They're not often close to the drive."

"Did you notice the sentry on the way out?"

"No, sir. How could I notice anything on the way out?"

"True. You had been hit by a wooden club, like a heavy cane. But your head was all right on the way in?"

"Yes, sir."

94

"Then you'll know this. Do not make any mistake when you answer this. Who was in the truck besides you when you entered the White House grounds?"

"No one."

"Is that the truth?"

"That is absolutely the truth."

"How do you know?"

"Why . . . I would know. The truck has a closed body, with doors at the rear. From the seat of course I can see in. When I got to the White House I opened the doors to take the baskets out, and how could there be anyone in there without me seeing him?"

"But someone was there. Someone hit you. How did he get into the grounds if not in your truck?"

"I don't know. I suppose there are ways to get in. The guards can't be everywhere."

"Of course. You would know." Wardell hunched forward. "That's one of the facts about you. You deliver to the White House every day, and you know where the guards would be around that hour. You know the President's habits of going outdoors around that hour. You're lying." Wardell's tone went up. "You're lying, when your only chance for life is the truth. Do you realize what the end of this is for everyone concerned? Death. Do you realize that, Val Orcutt? You're going to die. You don't stand a chance. Unless you tell me the truth now, then maybe you do stand a chance. It's your only one. How could anyone else—"

Val's mother was yelling. She had started her interruption in a lower key, stating that her boy did not lie and there was no sense in threatening him like that, but when she found herself ignored and Wardell kept on she slid forward in her chair and began to yell. Chief Skinner got up and started for her. His grasp on her arm, not tender, forced her attention. He said, "Out you go." One glance at his gray eyes was enough for her. She said, "Please, I'll shut up. Please don't." The Chief let go.

Wardell went on, "No one but you could have known of the opportunity. No one else could have known your truck would be there at that hour. Even if they could have got into the grounds—what for, without the truck? Anyway, this settles it: The sentry saw you driving out. That's enough. You're done for."

When he stopped Val Orcutt waited a moment and then said, "Yes, sir."

"What do you mean, *Yes, sir?* Good God, don't you see the only thing for you is the truth?"

Val said, "I mean I see I'm done for. I've told the truth, but I see you're not going to believe it. Only one thing: I don't know how they got into the grounds and I don't know how they would know the truck would be there, but I suppose lots of people would know that. I go every morning about the same time. But one thing: the sentry didn't see me drive out. He couldn't have, because I didn't drive out. I suppose they put me in the back of the truck after they hit me and I was in there, I don't know. How could the sentry see me? But listen here, of course I see what you mean talking about my being hit by the President's cane. I wasn't, but I see what you mean. But even if I was, how could the sentry see me driving out? Whatever hit me, it didn't leave me in any shape to drive a truck."

Mrs. Orcutt distributed a grin, first to her son, then to the others. Chief Skinner did not acknowledge it; Wardell glared at her. He then transferred the glare to her son, and kept it there to cover the effort he would make to recover the attack. Apparently the only thing for it was a bullying explosion, but it was halted before it became vocal by the ringing of the telephone. Skinner got up, but Wardell turned and reached for it. He said, "Hello."

It was one of the clerks out front. The clerk said that Mr. Billings, Secretary of Agriculture, insisted on speaking to Mr. Wardell and refused to leave a message. Mr. Billings would not take no. Wardell said, "I'll take it."

In a moment Billings' voice, urgent almost to trembling, was in the receiver: "Lewis? I'm talking from the White House study, Mrs. Stanley is with me. The Cabinet, all of them but Molleson, are in the library. You've got to come over here right now."

Wardell snapped, "I can't come."

"You'd better. You've got to. Mrs. Stanley and I are holding off a vote, but the best we can do is that they'll wait ten minutes for you. Three minutes are already gone. It will go against you, no question about it, and that will be hell. Come at once."

"What is it, Brownell? I told Oliver—"

"It's not only Oliver. Brownell partly, yes. It's complicated. Don't talk, come. If they once vote you out—"

"Let them."

There were a couple of clicks and a scraping in the receiver, then Mrs. Stanley's voice was in his ear: "For God's sake, Mr. Wardell, come at once!"

Wardell opened his mouth, shut it, opened it again and said, "All right. Hold them. I'll be there in five minutes."

He replaced the receiver and turned to Chief Skinner. His eyes were bloodshot, his hair a tangled mess, his collar dirty and crumpled from sweat. He got up and started for a corner to get his hat, saying:

"Skinner. I'm going to the White House. You go on with this. Until you hear to the contrary from me or the Cabinet, you have full authority. Don't hesitate to use it."

He went out on the run, not stopping to shut the door behind him. The Chief of the Secret Service got up and went over and closed it, then he returned to his chair. He looked at Val Orcutt with his gray doubting eyes and said:

"Well, my lad. Let's begin over again at the beginning and see if we made any mistakes. For instance, before the doctor comes, who did you think you were when you had the amnesia?"

## 12

At four o'clock Wednesday afternoon there were a dozen men in the library of the Grinnell home. Hartley Grinnell, newspaper publisher, whose home it was, was there; old white George Milton, whose money had bought the home and whose daughter's cultured taste had furnished it; and Martin Drew, New York financier, who had stayed the Monday night after all and after Tuesday's startling developments had explosively remained. Robert A. Molleson, "Bob," Vice-President of the United States, too much blood in his face, dark puffs under his eyes, and a long cigar stiff between his teeth, sat on a leather sofa with its back to the long table; the man standing before him, tall and thin, with scraggly dark hair, yellow-green eyes and a large sensitive mouth but certainly not tender, was D. L. Voorman, the steel legislative agent, the highest-paid lobbyist in the world. The others, either of the circle around the sofa or hovering at its edge, only less famous than Martin Drew and less astute than George Milton, were mostly from New York; one lived in Washington and one was from Chicago. Highball glasses, full, half-gone or empty, were scattered around, and even with the windows open the smoke was so thick that George Milton had long since given up waving his hand in front of his face and was perforce contenting himself with pinching his nostrils now and then to take the smart away.

It was a gathering full of possibilities for commentators. A philosopher would have found occasion for melancholy strictures on the adequacy of the vessels the human race selects as the grand reservoirs for its accumulation of vast and terrible power; an editor of the New York *Herald Tribune* would have gone lyric with amazement that so tremendous an aggregation of sapience, glory, and righteousness should be confined within one room; a Communist would have frothed with fury that the monsters dared to disguise themselves in human shape; an undertaker, referring to the tables of mortality, would have rubbed his hands at the prospect of an early pick-up in business; a statistician would have calculated with dry accuracy that the dozen individuals (specimens) before him represented the control of over five billion dollars of American wealth. Of course their observations would all have been correct, and totally ineffectual to sway the business in hand by the breadth of a hair.

D. L. Voorman was speaking to Vice-President Molleson.

"Tomorrow and tomorrow, that's it. I think they're right about that, but believe me, Mr. Vice-President, there is no question of coercion." Voorman had been in and out of Washington for ten years. He had gone fishing with Molleson half a dozen times but never called him anything but Mr. Vice-President; with Senator Allen and two amiable young ladies he had once spent a genial week-end in a Virginia cabin, but never called him anything but Senator. He was the highest-paid lobbyist in America. "They have no thought of coercing you. They appeal. They're nervous, that's all. So are you, so am I, so is everyone. We have to try to keep our heads. We don't ask you to do anything rash, God knows we don't want anything rash. An emergency requires a man, and you're the man for this one."

Molleson shook his head. His teeth were so tight on the

cigar that it barely wiggled. He took the cigar out. "No, Voorman. I've made my position clear. The step you gentlemen suggest may become necessary—"

A shattering voice broke in, a voice meant to shatter and accustomed to it. It came from a tall heavy man, big-jawed, with gray hair, in a miraculously fitting brown suit. "I coerce. Appeal if you want to, Voorman. I coerce. Get that, Molleson, if that's what you want to call it. You're just squealing like a rabbit, and in times like this you'll find out what happens to rabbits."

Voorman's large sensitive mouth twisted a little. He waited until the shattering voice was done, then turned and wedged his way out between two chairs. The man in the brown suit stood there. Voorman waited until other voices had started up in the circle facing Molleson, then under their cover muttered, "I'd like a word with you, Mr. Denham." He started towards the other end of the room and the man in the brown suit followed.

There, near the windows, the shattering voice made only the concession of a little lowering. "You're an ass to coax him, Voorman. If that's your technique no wonder it's been a mess down here for the past month."

Voorman said, "You ride horses."

"What if I do?"

"Were you ever on a scared horse? Not a mean one or a contrary one, a scared one. Did you try to bully it? If you did, what happened?"

"Beside the point. You can't handle things like this by thinking up fables."

"Maybe not. I'm just illustrating. You called Molleson a rabbit. You couldn't have said a worse thing because of course that's what he is. I tell you, Mr. Denham, it is an absolutely desperate situation and we can't afford to make any mistakes at all. I'm sorry Mr. Drew got you and the others down here; it makes it harder instead of easier. You're so used to obedience that you think it meets all demands. We've got to have more than obedience from the Vice-President, we have to have courage from him. It isn't a question of his not wanting to; of course he wants to. He's scared. I can't think of a poorer way to talk courage into a man than to tell him he's a rabbit."

Denham stared briefly. Being a dominant and masterful man, he could not very well continue on that line except by firing Voorman from his job, and that at the moment was impractical. So he switched: "We've got to have war this week."

"I know that. We may get it."

"We must get it. The Russians have been pushed across the Tunguska River. Another month will finish them. There will be soviets in Berlin and Rome in two weeks and the fronts will crumble. Federal Steel sold today at twenty-eight. The day our warships leave the coast the market will triple its prices in three hours."

"Yes. Oh yes." Voorman's tone carried soft smooth impatience. "That is the necessity; the point is how to satisfy it. My advice regarding the Vice-President has been ignored; he has been badly handled. There's no use trying to force him to commit himself because he never does. What was needed with him was to get the idea in his head, get him gently accustomed to it, and give him the feeling that he will have a preponderance of support behind him. That's as far as he can be got until the Attorney-General is ready to act."

"And where's the Attorney-General? Sitting over there with that crew of half-baked—"

"Of course. Mr. Davis would be where he belongs; with the Cabinet. He's not like Molleson; he has plenty of courage, he likes action; and he is totally impervious to any pressure we might try to use on him. He has imagination; he is patriotic, and he fiercely resents the restrictions by force which the belligerent governments have placed upon our commerce and the movements of our citizens. The men—"

"That's double-edged. They're all doing that."

"But it isn't feasible, even for Mr. Davis, to enter both sides of a war. He must choose, and of course the choice is made. The men in the best position to swing him will be with him tonight, at Corcoran's. They have been carefully selected, and they will be there. If they put it to him right he'll like it, and if he likes it he'll waste no time doing it. He'll go to Molleson tomorrow morning and tell him that the Attorney-General is prepared to issue an opinion that the office of President is vacant under the Constitution, and that Molleson is therefore President of the United States. He knows Molleson as well as I do, and he will know how to handle him; he will not mention war; he will simply tell him he is President of the United States. With the bait offered like that, Molleson will be unable to resist it. Davis will render the opinion,

Molleson will assume the office, and then will be the time for our avalanche which he will be even less able to resist. We can get the declaration of war before sundown tomorrow."

"Wardell will fight, and Liggett. And Sterling and Jackman—they'll have Molleson enjoined."

"By whom? The Supreme Court will not act. Where is the judge who will dare to assume jurisdiction? Anyway, there will be no time. Before a move can be agreed upon and made, war will have been declared. Then who can stop it? Not even Stanley himself... should he return an hour after the declaration."

Denham considered. His eyes were half-closed, his loose self-indulgent lips pushed together, his head down onto his shoulders. With the slow vagueness of undirected movement, his right hand felt for the coat pocket of the miraculous brown suit, found it, and came forth again. He realized there was something in his hand and brought it up to open the tooled leather cigar case. It was empty.

"You got a cigar, Voorman?"

"I smoke cigarettes. There are some in the humidor."

"Panatelas. I'd just as soon suck a straw.—Voorman. We're paying you sixty thousand a year?"

"For a while, you have been."

"You earn it. Where have you put the President?"

The lobbyist's sensitive mouth twisted, and the yellow-green eyes laughed. The sudden laugh in them was startling. "No, Mr. Denham. Sixty thousand a year wouldn't pay for that."

"I know it wouldn't. You may expect to get paid. Where is he?"

"I haven't a ghost of an idea. Like everyone else, I have a guess, but I wouldn't draw to it to save an ante."

"Correct." Denham nodded. "You won't trust even me. Quite correct. I understand they've searched your house."

"They've searched half the houses in Washington. No, sir, on that I wouldn't trust even you, if the question presented itself. But it hasn't. It doesn't."

"That's straight?"

"As straight as a projectile from one of your guns."

"What's your guess?"

"George Milton." Voorman shrugged his shoulders. "Not by evidence, not even by intuition, just for the sake of a guess. It hangs on two pegs: his money feeds the Gray Shirts, no doubt of that; and he is too positive of his own theory regarding the President's disappearance."

"He's always positive."

"Yes. But never about anything so improbable as his idea that the President is in ambush in the White House, awaiting his opportunity to crush us. It's nonsense. The White House has been searched; and anyway a thing like that couldn't be done, there would have to be too many in on it. I don't believe it. George Milton says we underrate Stanley. He pretends to no interest in the enterprise with Molleson and Davis; he says it can come to nothing because Stanley is ready and waiting for us. Preposterous. That's why I guess George Milton. Look at him, sitting there. He's letting us do it, and we'll do it."

"If you're correct, his part is done.—All right, Voorman. About Molleson. If you know him that well. All right."

Denham turned and moved off, towards the group around the sofa across the room. Voorman, in no haste, followed him; there was no laugh in the yellow-green eyes now, and no calculation or concern; there was only a dream, beyond guessing if there had been other eyes to see it.

The door, the massive paneled door in the center of the wall opposite the windows, was opened by a footman to admit a newcomer. Voorman stopped, observing; the dream left his eyes, receding back of them to its retreat, leaving nothing there but fox. He moved again, towards the door.

"Mr. Secretary! We hardly knew whether to expect you."

Voices came from the group around the sofa, that of Martin Drew above them: "Ah, Schick! Abandon ship!" The newcomer, much too short and fat for a fox, having shaken hands with Voorman, waddled across. Seven or eight pairs of eyes appraised him, coldly hostile and hopeful at once like veteran bidders at an auction. Vice-President Molleson, his face suddenly even redder than before and his eyes too uneasy to manage a straight regard, removed his cigar from its vise to say: "Did you give it up, Theodore? I hope you fellows got more things settled than we have." Voorman spoke: "Gentlemen, Mr. Theodore Schick, the Secretary of Commerce." He pronounced some names; there were perfunctory nods. Martin Drew said, "Are they still biting their nails over there, Schick?"

Theodore Schick's shrewd eyes looked more amused than impressed. He nodded but once, at old white George Milton at the end of the table ten feet removed from the group, who was not even looking at him. Schick addressed Hartley Grinnell: "Could I have a drink? Bourbon or Irish. I haven't been drinking the damned sherry, but I couldn't help smelling it." He turned to Molleson: "Well, Bob. I thought you were going to a ball game. It didn't matter; it would have been Wardell's show anyhow. They would have loved to unhorse him, but they were all afraid to try his job. He rode them down and made them like it. It wasn't bad; Lewis has character."

Molleson inquired, "Is Brownell still under arrest?"

Schick nodded, and then nodded thanks to Grinnell as he accepted his drink. "Incommunicado. And likely to remain so." He sipped. "Wardell is now going to look under all the stones there are. There will be a lot of discomfort." Schick smiled at Molleson. "He is curious about your leaving the meeting, Bob. He asked leading questions about you."

The Vice-President grunted without removing the cigar from his mouth. "He can go to hell. Did they adjourn?"

"No. They're considering... certain proposals. Various steps have been decided upon, various others are being pondered. I opposed nothing and supported nothing. As soon as Wardell had gone, victorious, I left. I came here at the request of my friend Martin Drew." He smiled at Drew, and then around at the others. "I suppose you eminent gentlemen came to Washington to call on the President. Unfortunate, isn't it? He's out." Schick sipped at his drink. "Is this highball what I came for, Drew?"

Martin Drew said, "We've got to have a President. If the office is vacant, Molleson is it. We're telling him that. I thought it probable you would agree."

"I would have, yesterday." Schick's shrewd eyes half closed. "Today, I'm afraid not. I'm opposing nothing and supporting nothing. In the past twenty-four hours the country has turned into a keg of dynamite. I will not help light the fuse; it's too dangerous for my taste. It suits my temperament to find shelter and watch through a hole. I knew your game, of course; those who do not know it can guess at it. I have today heard it discussed, by the Attorney-General, among others. I tell you, Lewis Wardell has character; he dominates Oliver and will not hesitate to use the army in any emergency that presents itself. You gentlemen will need a strong hand. Additional troops are on the way from Fort Myers. Voorman, you have no equal at intrigue; can you shoot? I can't. I have no inclination that way at all."

Voorman said, "You went to a good deal of trouble to come here, Mr. Secretary."

Schick smiled at him admiringly. "To the point as usual, Voorman. And so nicely. But for the handicaps imposed by the clumsiness of democracy, you would be a Cardinal Prince manipulating a kingdom. I came here neither to bless your project nor to spike it, but on a personal errand. I am all for shelter." Schick moved; the chairs were close in the circle and he sidled between two of them to get out. He went beyond the end of the table and stopped directly in front of George Milton; and said, without any effort to make it tête-à-tête by lowering his tone:

"You know me."

The old white head nodded. "Sufficiently, Mr. Schick."

Schick smiled. "Still no concessions, sir? Quite right. My personal errand is with you. You helped me once. I am aware that it was incidental to your own interests, but that made it no less vital to me. I came here to tell you that within an hour the Cabinet will decide upon your arrest. You are not very young, and I thought you might wish to avoid it."

George Milton nodded again. "Thank you. It is impossible to avoid the consequences of the activities of fools."

"That may be. As you please, sir. The idea, I believe, is to extract from you the facts as to your dealings with Brownell, and as to the kidnapping of the President by the Gray Shirts and his present whereabouts."

"Good. Not a bad idea, for donkeys."

"Yes, sir. I would advise..."

Schick went on with his advice, but an interruption caused it to receive even less heed than it might otherwise have got. A footman had entered the room, walked around the group at the sofa, approached George Milton and stood at the proper distance waiting for Schick to finish. Schick stopped. George Milton asked, "Well?"

"There's a man to see you, sir."

"Who is it?"

"He said, Kramer. The man who was here yesterday."

George Milton put his hands on the arms of the chair to lift himself up and, ignoring Schick's proffer of assistance, got to his feet and straightened himself. He said, "Schick. More donkeys." He directed a long white finger at the group around the sofa and wiggled it back and forth to include them all. "You are right to despise them. You appear to have discernment. Have you, or are you merely a coward?"

"Both." Schick smiled. "I believe I may say, both."

"What would you say if I were to furnish evidence tonight or tomorrow that the President's disappearance was arranged by himself and his wife? Would that interest you?"

"If it went beyond conjecture. If it went into evidence, yes, indeed. I would find it very entertaining."

"Good. Am I correct in assuming that such evidence would turn the country and Congress overwhelmingly against him?"

"If the evidence were good he would not have a vote or a follower. But . . . evidence."

George Milton nodded, and turned to the footman. "Go slowly. I am not a racehorse."

Schick watched them as they crossed to the door, the footman holding back his steps, the octogenarian banker-capitalist-entrepreneur clinging to his lifelong contempt for his enemies—here, the advancing years—by keeping the efforts of his old muscles below the level of their remaining powers.

In the hall the footman turned to the left. George Milton followed. They passed around the head of the wide stairs and to the other side of the house. The footman opened a door and George Milton went through; the door was closed softly behind him. It was a room much smaller than the library, with a desk, a few chairs, and books and newspapers. Standing by the desk was a man, large and muscular, with blond hair, wearing a greenish-gray suit and a brown necktie. George Milton said to him:

"You're late."

"Yes, sir. There's more soldiers on the streets, and they're stopping—"

"It doesn't matter. What about it?"

"Well . . . I've come for the money."

"Will you get anything for it?"

"I don't know. She had no package when she left the White House a little before noon, and she met a Secret Service man in front of the Department of Justice and ate lunch with him. She hasn't seen Wardell; of course she may have phoned him. Brownell is in jail. I've got a man on watch, but she probably wouldn't carry a package anyway; she would fasten it under her clothes."

"You will see her at eight o'clock."

"Yes, sir."

George Milton went to the desk and unlocked and opened a drawer. From it he took a small package, neatly wrapped in brown paper and held by rubber bands. "Ten thousand dollars in hundreds. If she delivers it, look at it before you pay her. Bring it here at once. If you don't get it, come anyway. I don't like to leave money out all night."

"Yes, sir." The man put the package in his inside pocket and buttoned his coat.

"And Kramer." George Milton's lower jaw was working. He was aware of the fact, and hated it, but it would not be controlled; it was too late to attempt to subdue the inner convulsions of excitement which for half a century had dotted the days of his adventures into power, possession, and greed; and latterly it had become no longer possible to keep the convulsions entirely within. They tore cruelly through the defenses weakened by age, and he could not keep his jaw still. But his voice told him, and others, that he was still George Milton. "And Kramer. I have known you to show energy and initiative. If that girl doesn't get it? If obtained tonight, I will pay you twenty thousand dollars for that diary; and if it contains what I hope for, fifty thousand."

The man shook his head. "No, sir. There would be no possible way."

"If it contains what I want, a hundred thousand."

"It couldn't be done, sir, not for a million. I'd take the risk, I don't need to tell you that. Around every foot of the boundaries of the White House grounds soldiers are touching elbows."

"Bribe them. Create a diversion. Are you a man or an errand boy? What are a few soldiers?"

Kramer shook his head. "I wouldn't try to touch it. I'm working for you, and I'll tackle most anything short of suicide. No, sir."

"What are you afraid of?" The old white man's voice was thin with contempt and derision. "You could bleed nothing but water. Are there no men left? The only one to be found with iron in his juice is the lunatic who calls himself Lincoln Lee. Miserable trepid little worms." The lower jaw would not stop working. "Worms!"

# Introducing the first and only complete hardcover collection of Agatha Christie's mysteries

Now you can enjoy the greatest mysteries ever written in a magnificent Home Library Edition.

# Discover Agatha Christie's world of mystery, adventure and intrigue

Agatha Christie's timeless tales of mystery and suspense offer something for every reader—mystery fan or not—young and old alike. And now, you can build a complete hardcover library of her world-famous mysteries by subscribing to The Agatha Christie Mystery Collection.

This exciting Collection is your passport to a world where mystery reigns supreme. Volume after volume, you and your family will enjoy mystery reading at its very best.

You'll meet Agatha Christie's world-famous detectives like Hercule Poirot, Jane Marple, and the likeable Tommy and Tuppence Beresford.

In your readings, you'll visit Egypt, Paris, England and other exciting destinations where murder is always on the itinerary. And wherever you travel, you'll become deeply involved in some of the most ingenious and diabolical plots ever invented ... "cliff-hangers" that only Dame Agatha could create!

It all adds up to mystery reading that's so good ... it's almost criminal. And it's yours every month with The Agatha Christie Mystery Collection.

**Solve the greatest mysteries of all time.** The Collection contains all of Agatha Christie's classic works including *Murder on the Orient Express, Death on the Nile, And Then There Were None, The ABC Murders* and her ever-popular whodunit, *The Murder of Roger Ackroyd.*

Each handsome hardcover volume is Smythe sewn and printed on high quality acid-free paper so it can withstand even the most murderous treatment. Bound in Sussex-blue simulated leather with gold titling, The Agatha Christie Mystery Collection will make a tasteful addition to your living room, or den.

**Ride the Orient Express for 10 days without obligation.**
To introduce you to the Collection, we're inviting you to examine the classic mystery, *Murder on the Orient Express*, without risk or obligation. If you're not completely satisfied, just return it within 10 days and owe nothing.

However, if you're like the millions of other readers who love Agatha Christie's thrilling tales of mystery and suspense, keep *Murder on the Orient Express* and pay just $7.95 plus postage and handling.

You will then automatically receive future volumes once a month as they are published on a fully returnable, 10-day free-examination basis. No minimum purchase is required, and you may cancel your subscription at any time.

This unique collection is not sold in stores. It's available only through this special offer. So don't miss out, begin your subscription now. Just mail this card today.

☐ Yes! Please send me *Murder on the Orient Express* for a 10-day free-examination and enter my subscription to The Agatha Christie Mystery Collection. If I keep *Murder on the Orient Express*, I will pay just $7.95 plus postage and handling and receive one additional volume each month on a fully returnable 10-day free-examination basis. There is no minimum number of volumes to buy, and I may cancel my subscription at any time.                                                07013

☐ I prefer the deluxe edition bound in genuine leather for $24.95 per volume plus shipping and handling, with the same 10-day free-examination.                                                                     07054

Name_____

Address_____

City_____ State_____ Zip_____

**X 1 2**
**Send No Money...**
**But Act Today!**

# BUSINESS REPLY CARD

FIRST CLASS    PERMIT NO. 2154    HICKSVILLE, N.Y.

Postage will be paid by addressee:

The Agatha Christie
Mystery Collection
Bantam Books
P.O. Box 956
Hicksville, N.Y. 11802

"Maybe. Lee's in jail. Even if he wasn't, I don't see him climbing the fence at the White House tonight. The girl may get it. Or she may set a trap."

"Well? That means?"

"Nothing. I'll take care of that."

"Indeed. Praiseworthy, Kramer. Bah! Worms! Errand boys. Go on. Go!"

"Yes, sir." The man picked up his hat from the desk, felt at his breast pocket to make sure of the money, opened the door, and went. He descended the broad stairs, nodded at the footman who stood in the lower hall, and left the house. Outside, on the terrace, he met a man approaching to enter—a stocky young man moving briskly with springs in his calves. Kramer slowed up to appraise him in passing, and the other did likewise. Kramer took in the other's face, but his own face did not appear to be the focus of the other's eyes; their point of interest seemed to be below his chin, say, his brown necktie. Kramer passed, and proceeded down the path through the lawn, muttering, "Well I'll be damned, I know where *that* guy ate lunch." The other had gone to the entrance and pushed the button, and at the release of the latch from within had instantly made use of his shoulder to ensure an opening, against the caution of the footman, wide enough for an entrance. In that manner he got inside without delay, which was no reflection on the footman as a footman, since he had been selected by Mrs. Hartley Grinnell, daughter of George Milton, not to repel invasion by force, but adequately to fulfill his function as an appurtenance to gentility.

Upstairs, George Milton had returned to the library. He had found the group around the sofa still intact except for Voorman and Theodore Schick, who were over by a window talking, the latter with a fresh highball in his hand. Apparently Denham, prompted by Voorman, had maneuvered them into a new position in the attack on Molleson, for the Vice-President had lit his cigar and was sitting back, thoughtful and judicial, nodding in agreement as Martin Drew expounded the crisis anew. George Milton crossed over and stood at the edge of the circle, surveying contemptuously its members and the object of their enterprise, but he was not in fact either hearing them or seeing them. He was reflecting bitterly that he was too old to permit himself to be apprehended and conveyed to an unfamiliar terrain for an encounter with a Lewis Wardell. And more bitterly, that this unparalleled clash

107

of all the weapons of a nation, this grandest engagement of his career, should have come perhaps too late, when the temper of his own sword could no longer be trusted to withstand any strain he or the enemy might put upon it. Twenty years ago... even ten... ah...

Behind him he heard the door of the room open, and footsteps across the strip of wood to the rug. He did not bother to turn; he knew the footman's steps. The servant passed him and approached the master of the house, who sat at the other edge of the circle.

Hartley Grinnell looked up. "Yes, Thomas."

"A man to see you, sir. He says he is from the Secret Service. He has a badge."

There was a murmur. A pause of silence. George Milton, who seldom waited for his son-in-law to speak, snapped at the footman, "Fool! Mr. Grinnell is not at home."

Voorman, coming over from the window, spoke. "Don't let him in."

The footman was red. "He is already in. I'm sorry, sir—"

They all turned. The door had opened again, and a man had entered. He came towards them, briskly, not at all menacingly, just a man with business in hand. They stared at him. Grinnell rose to his feet and said, "Get out of my house."

"Yes, sir." The man stood up to them, and took a pad of paper from his coat pocket and a pencil from his vest. "Mr. Hartley Grinnell? In a few moments. You will pardon me, gentlemen; I am instructed to report the names of all I find here. I think I know all of you." He began writing.

Grinnell stepped towards him. "Get out. Thomas! Put him out. Get Allers. This is unlawful invasion—"

"Nothing's unlawful, sir. That's what martial law means." The man went on writing.

Molleson said, "Hello, Moffat."

"How do you do, Mr. Vice-President."

He finished scribbling and returned the pad to his pocket. George Milton moved back a few paces. He could hear the breath coming and going in his nostrils, and he would not have others hear it. The man said:

"Mr. Grinnell. I am instructed to take you to the Department of Justice, and to tell you, if you inquire, that you are to account for the war editorial in your newspaper this morning." He turned. "Mr. Voorman. You also."

Voorman's mouth twisted. He asked softly, "And to my inquiry, why?"

"I am instructed to tell you that the Attorney-General will be there to question you. Come, gentlemen. Go ahead of me."

Hartley Grinnell was white. He would have blustered: "Do you mean I am under arrest?"

"I'm to take you. Come, let's go."

There was a movement in the group. Chick Moffat stepped back for room. Denham emerged and moved towards him. Chick put his right hand in his coat pocket and said sharply, "Talk from there."

Denham stopped. "Look here, sonny. Mr. Grinnell and Mr. Voorman are not here. You will understand that. Martial law is for the preservation of order, not for outrages on prominent citizens. They are not here. Get out."

Chick said, "I'm ignorant on those points, Mr. Denham. Come along and explain them to the Chief.—You two, come on. Step."

But Denham was born to shatter resistance. He moved forward, calling, "Drew! Come on, let's throw him out." Martin Drew responded, not reluctant. Chick went back another pace or two, drew his pistol from his pocket and displayed it, saying crisply, "This is as far as I go. Don't come closer." Denham and Drew paused; Drew said contemptuously, "He won't shoot, come on," and started. There was a shattering explosion, simultaneous with cries of warning, and Drew crumpled to the floor. For an instant there was no sound and no movement, then Denham and others started for Drew. Chick commanded: "Back!" They stopped. Drew was pulling himself up, holding to a chair. Chick said:

"Take it easy, Mr. Drew. I took you in the leg because if I'd tried for your arm I might have killed someone behind you. The rest of you keep back till I'm out of here. A little further —Thanks. Mr. Voorman, Mr. Grinnell. We'll go now. To the door, please, and make it snappy."

The publisher and the lobbyist moved to the door. "Open it, and don't try any tricks." He sidled after them, and followed them out. The footman went over and closed the door. Denham went to Drew, and said for someone to phone for a doctor. George Milton pinched his nostrils to take the smart of the powder smoke away.

## 13

At half-past seven Wednesday evening Alma Cronin was in her room eating crackers and mushroom soup which she had taken from a can and heated on the electric plate she kept in her bathroom. She had not been able to get away from the White House until six-thirty. The flood of personal telegrams and letters which had been arriving since dawn for Mrs. Stanley were for the most part going disregarded, but it had been Alma's task to sort out from them the few that might require acknowledgment or prove pertinent to the crisis. Mrs. Robbins had asked her to return for the evening, and she had promised to do so later.

At six-thirty she had left. She was worried. The man who was to call on her at eight o'clock surely wasn't such a fool that the possibility of a trap had not occurred to him. Would he not be watching in front of her house to observe those who entered? He might even know Chick Moffat, a member of the White House squad, by sight. The house she lived in was not large, three stories, built of stone up to the sidewalk, one of the better classes of those hundreds of buildings in clusters here and there in various parts of Washington, consisting of room-and-bath apartments designed for the profit of the owners and the convenience of privates and lesser officers in the army, male and female, which carries on the work of the government. It had a small garden-court in the rear. Alma's room was one flight up, in front, with windows on the street.

She bought crackers and a can of soup and hurried home, to telephone Chick a warning. She could not get him. She tried his apartment several times; there was no answer; and even called the Secret Service Bureau; he was not there. She gave it up, and ate the crackers and soup, and worried. She was restless and uncomfortable and on edge. Various elements were contributing to her inquietude, but they were all merely differing aspects of the central fact that she was twenty-four years old and that life, which had hitherto presented itself to her as an arena for interesting and lively discussion, had suddenly begun to display to her the realities of its passions and conflicts. Harry Brownell, with whom she had several times spoken, who had been to her eye a discreet and polished person impressively intimate with power, had become a man in jail, suspected of an execrable treachery. Mrs. Stanley, who had been an affable, amusing and ubiquitous First Lady, a central figure in the national tableau, had become a woman whose husband was missing and who, far from appearing stricken with grief or anxiety, seemed rather to be filled with a pleased excitement at her opportunity to contribute to the noise of affairs and alarms. Arthur, the nice little man with spectacles in the receiving-room downstairs, to whom one went for lead pencils or fertilizing tablets for the flower-pots, was, like Harry Brownell, in jail, and all day and all night a detective sat on the stool in the room downstairs. Chick Moffat—though this was not a part of the public cacophonous tone-poem of hatred, jealousy, suspicion, and fear, but a private tune in another key—Chick Moffat was the most disturbing phenomenon of all. It was he who chiefly had jerked life out of all the formulas she had got ready for it. It was as if she had been watching an exciting play on a stage, absorbed but properly detached, and one of the actors had suddenly descended from the platform, walked up to her and begun addressing his lines to her and . . . well . . . for instance, bent down and kissed her. Of course, Chick Moffat had not actually kissed her, but what the devil, there must come a time when even a man as backward as he was . . .

There was a knock on the door. She went over and opened it, dashing cracker crumbs from her lips with the tips of her fingers.

"Chick! Hello. Come in. I've been trying to phone you."

Chick Moffat stepped inside, shut the door, and grinned at her. He kept his hat in his hand. Alma said, "I hope you've dined. As you see, nothing very fattening here."

Chick looked at the cracker package and the empty soup bowl. "I haven't had a bite since our lamb chops, but I'll tend to that later. No time; I was afraid I wouldn't be able to get here at all; we're arresting everybody in the phone book, starting with the A's and going right through. What were you calling me for? Is the deal off?"

"Sit down."

"I hadn't better, unless your friend's not coming. In that case, I'll go out and bring in a couple of hindquarters and we'll have a feast."

Alma said, "You're so businesslike."

"Am I?" Chick looked surprised. He stood, considering the idea, looking at her. Their eyes met, and they both stood. Alma was making desperate clutches, within, at the only straw in reach, the good old stand-by of her sense of humor and unfailing appreciation of the ridiculous. She thought: I know what was in the cup Tristan and Isolde drank out of, it was mushroom soup. But since it could not have been that thought which encouraged Chick, there must have been something else in her eyes; for all at once he let his hat drop to the floor, put his arms around her, and kissed her. For an instant she held her breath, and then helped him. His embrace was close and tight, and tighter; his kiss was not expert, but unquestionably earnest and thorough. She began to feel dizzy, and pushed at him; then she was free; he had released her and stepped back. She realized that she was holding onto the sleeve of his coat, and dropped her hand.

Chick said, "Is that what you mean, businesslike?"

Alma nodded. She laughed, and stopped. "Chick. Oh, Chick, kiss me again.—No, don't. No! There isn't time."

"Is the deal off?"

"No. Not that I know of. How long have you been wanting to kiss me? I was trying to phone you to come in the back way, because I thought that man might know you and if he saw you come in he wouldn't come."

"For a long time, about seventy years I think."

"Would he be watching?"

"I expect so. I parked in Brush Street and came in through the court. You see, I'm studying to be a detective."

"I might have known you'd have that much sense. It's ten minutes to eight."

Chick nodded and stopped to pick up his hat. "I've got to get under cover. If you don't mind, I'll use the bathroom instead of the closet, it's in a better position. No talking now, no nothing. When he comes, stall. Pretend you've got it and you want to see the money. Anything. I won't wait long." He started for the bathroom.

"But Chick! What are you going to do? Isn't it dangerous—"

"I'll do something. Take the money away from him and cut his throat. I'll think up something." He opened the bathroom door.

"But, Chick—"

"Now's the time to shut up." He was in the bathroom, but

112

stuck his head out. "Just one little thing. Will you marry me?"

"Certainly."

"Okay." The door closed.

Alma took three steps toward the bathroom door; then stood and smiled at it. There was danger, no doubt of it; the man was much bigger than Chick and looked strong as an elephant; but why shouldn't there be danger? Chick would know what to do; certainly he was armed. But suddenly she went white: what if the man was armed too and Chick got shot? She started for the bathroom door; she would stop this business. She was afraid of guns and detested them; she could see a gun in that man's hand pointing at Chick... but she stopped. There was no chance of Chick's getting hurt now; he and she would never hurt each other, and nothing would ever hurt them. Never.

She crossed and got the cracker package and the empty soup bowl and put them out of sight in a drawer, brushed crumbs from the chair and the rug, and glanced around the room. Then she sat down in the chair and picked up a book, but did not open it; it rested on her lap as she sat and smiled at the bathroom door. She became so lost in the feeling of the smile that she was not at all startled when a knock sounded on the entrance door; she was halfway across the room toward it before she remembered what the knock meant. Then her heart, already fast-beating, changed to a new rhythm and she went on and opened the door.

The man was there. She looked up at him; he was even bigger than she had remembered. He nodded. She said, "Come in." He entered, and she closed the door.

She said, "You're on time."

He nodded. "Right on the dot, Miss Cronin."

She was resisting an impulse to glance at the bathroom door. She moved away, towards the middle of the room; the man hesitated, and followed. When she turned he tapped at the breast pocket of his coat. "I've got the money. Ten thousand dollars. If you've got the diary we can do our business in one minute. I'll just take a look at it."

She said, "I suppose I may take a look at the money?"

"Certainly, Miss Cronin. But I'll look first, if you don't mind. Where is it?"

"I haven't got it." Alma put her hand to her mouth, horrified; she had not had the slightest intention of saying

113

that. But she was saved the trouble of attempting a recovery; she saw that her part was over as she observed the change that had suddenly come over the face of the man. Her back was partly turned toward the bathroom door; the man was partly facing it. Alma heard Chick's voice behind her, sharp: "Put 'em up. Alma, jump away, quick!"

She was too slow. Being not at all familiar with the play of guns, it took her half a second to get the import of it, and that was too late. The man with the brown necktie was as fast as he was big; in one swift rush he had Alma in his arms clasped against him, and was halfway across the bathroom; she was no more to his strength than a feather pillow. Chick saw he could not shoot, leaped forward and tried for a blow with the metal of the gun; the man ducked, jumped back, crouched, and tossed Alma, hurled her through the air straight at Chick. With it he jumped forward again, swung at Chick's jaw and staggered him, and before Chick could recover enough balance to get his gun up the man had his own revolver out and was swinging it. It landed, glancing a little, on the side of Chick's head, and this time he went clear down.

Alma was on her knees, scrambling up. The man pushed her back, muttered with plenty of breath, "I'd sock you too for a dime," turned, and went, closing the door behind him.

Alma didn't get up; she went on her knees to Chick. He lay still, his arms flung out, his legs bent double. There was a little blood on his head, creeping from the edge of the hair. She shook him; he flopped back. She felt his pulse; it was there, and did not even seem weak. She called his name, looked around, shook him again, called his name. She scrambled to her feet, started for the door, turned and came back again. Coming back, something on the floor not far from Chick glistened at her eye; she picked it up and looked at it, and the sight of it stunned her; momentarily Chick was out of her mind, everything was out of her mind except the paralyzing and incredible fact that she held in her hand President Stanley's wrist watch, with the engraving on the back—the watch she had once before held in her hand, the day she had carried it down a corridor of the White House and met a Secret Service man coming for it. Then—it had dropped from that man's pocket! He had had it! The President's watch, which he always wore!

She ran to the telephone. She waited five seconds that

seemed a thousand for the operator; then another wait for an answer from the number of the Department of Justice. There was a sound from the floor; Chick was stirring; she called his name, but stayed at the telephone. There was a voice on the wire, and she demanded to speak to Lewis Wardell at once. The clerk demurred; she must give him the message. Chick was on his elbows; on his knees, on his feet. He was speaking to her; she was telling the clerk she must have Wardell.

Chick was beside her. "Alma, I'm all right, don't, I'll be all right in a minute..." She opened her hand and showed him the wrist watch: "It was on the floor, he had it, they must catch him." Chick's face was above her so she could not see it, but she felt his hand on the receiver pulling at it, and he was saying in a voice suddenly alert and sharp, "Cut it. Ring off." But she was saying to the transmitter: "Tell him it's Alma Cronin, a man that was just here had the President's wrist—"

Chick's hand had pushed down the hook and cut the connection. She grabbed at it. "Chick! Are you crazy?"

"No. Turn loose, Alma. I'll explain."

"You can explain later—they must catch him—are you crazy?"

"Here—listen—"

"No. Chick! They must catch him!"

"They don't need to catch him. That watch didn't fall out of his pocket, it fell out of mine. I tell you, drop it! I'll explain."

Alma stared at him, at the grimness of his jaws and the hardness of his eyes. She did not see the trickle of blood on his temple, trickling to his cheek. Her own face went white. She stared, and finally said: "Out of your pocket, Chick."

"Yes. And I was wrong, Alma. I can't explain. You'll have to trust me."

She would not have dreamed his eyes could be so hard. She made her own voice hard: "Mr. Wardell will have to trust you." She had the receiver again; the hook was up; she gave the number of the Department of Justice. Chick said, "Alma, for God's sake. Alma, please."

"Whatever happens, Chick, I am going to tell Lewis Wardell that I found that watch on my floor. Secret Service Bureau? This is Alma Cronin, my message for Mr. Wardell..."

She could not see Chick, who had stepped behind her. She could not see the desperate resolve on his face, nor his double fist drawn back. Certainly after the fist had been driven against her jaw she could see nothing, for it had been

115

scientifically directed and propelled for a "sleeper." As she crumpled up Chick caught her in his arms before she could go to the floor.

He hardly looked at her, unconscious in his arms. He was losing no fraction of a second. He laid her on the bed, left the room and ran down the flight of stairs. In the lower hall he departed by the rear, crossed the garden-court, and went through a passage between two houses into the other street. There, parked under a tree, was his sedan. He got in and started it, drove to the corner and turned, down a block and again a right turn. Two hundred feet brought him in front of the entrance of Alma's house; he stopped, and left the engine running. Out on the sidewalk, he looked around, twice in every direction; the street was quiet, there was no light for some distance, and no army patrol in sight. He entered the house and ran upstairs and into Alma's room, meeting no one. She was still quiet, dead quiet, on the bed. He took a dark coat from the closet and wrapped it around her, got her in his arms, crossed and opened the door a crack, and listened. There was no sound save a faint hum of voices from the floor above; the way seemed clear. He entered the hall, not bothering to turn off the light, and closed the door behind him. With his burden he could not run down the stairs, but he made good time. In the hall below he turned the light off and then opened the street door. A couple were passing on the sidewalk; he waited; a woman came along; he waited. It seemed clear, and he ventured to the stoop. No one was in sight within a hundred yards. He dashed for it.

He shut the door of the sedan. She was inside, on the floor in the back, with the coat for a pillow. He opened the front door and got behind the steering-wheel, shoved the gear, started. If only the moving and jolting didn't rouse her! It could not be done in less than twelve minutes. If only she would sleep that long! Alma... my beloved Alma... for God's sake sleep!

# THURSDAY—STALEMATE

# 1

Ordinarily a hundred men rule the United States. The statement is subject to numerous and complicated qualifications. The hundred rulers have their advisers, lieutenants, and influential followers; they act with varying degrees of awareness and responsibility in their rôles; they are organized loosely and informally and often defeat their own ends by their contradictions and jealousies. But in the large, they rule; against a majority of them no major policy can be pursued; against their united opposition any program or design is without hope. They have developed a complex and fascinating technique for the assertion of their will; unlike the kings of divine right, who had merely to command openly the obedience which was due to them by common consent, these modern princes conceal their scepters under all the disguises which necessity may suggest and ingenuity can invent. But though the scepter has relinquished its gilt and its ceremonial function as a royal toy, it has abandoned none of its power.

By noon of Thursday seventy or more of those hundred men were in the city of Washington. They came from Atlanta, St. Louis, Chicago, Philadelphia, Detroit, Cleveland, Kansas City, Boston, New Orleans, Pittsburgh, Baltimore, New York. They arrived by automobile, train, and airplane. It was not especially noteworthy that they were for the most part in a state of astonishment, indignation, alarm, and bewilderment, for such a condition is habitual with rulers and masters of men; it is apparently an occupational peculiarity induced by the constant impingement of large and grave affairs. *Uneasy lies the head* would cover that. What was remarkable about their condition was their impotence. It was unprecedented and outrageous. They had arranged for war, and when rulers arrange for war that is traditionally what they get. Not that they had expected war as one expects interest coupons on a bond; simply it had happened that way. Many of them regretted the necessity; but when their loans to belligerents were endangered, their shiploads of munitions stopped or destroyed, their foreign investments wiped out, their profits annihilated and their market holdings reduced to pitiful fractions, war was inevitable. Too bad, but inevitable. They had forthwith communicated with the persons who exist for that purpose: editors, legislators, radio executives, clergymen, professors, patriots. Good; that was arranged. But there had been exasperating delays, one after another. They were not confronted with any open and organized resistance, except from inconsequential groups of fanatics here and there, but there appeared to be an amazing quantity of reluctance that came from nowhere and everywhere. They had one point of disaffection spotted: President Stanley. He did not openly oppose them, but they knew what was going on. He was soft; he was beset with sentimental squeamishness in the face of the sterner realities of the national need and the national honor. They accepted his weapons, and refrained from open attack; they undermined him. On the Monday afternoon before the Tuesday of the joint session D. L. Voorman had prepared a list of 304 Representatives and 59 Senators safe for war. Thank God; it was arranged at last, and barely in time. They all knew it was arranged, and were confidently and feverishly preparing for the sequel, the cyclone of steel and blood they had ordered. They had their breasts against the tape. Then the wires and the wireless brought the news of the adjournment—another delay, when destiny had begun to count not only hours but minutes; and then, incredibly, the word that President Stanley had been kidnapped. It was intolerable, a ridiculous and fatal disaster; no other President had ever been kidnapped; trust that sentimental ass to let it happen to him at this terrible juncture vital to the welfare and honor of the country!

They rushed to Washington.

They found there a situation without precedent and beyond calculation.

## 2

Reviewing from this vantage-point the activities of the rulers on that Thursday, them and their lieutenants, advisers, followers, and opponents, the chief impression one gets is that of a chaotic and helpless lunacy; but that view is far too uncharitable. It was not the case, as it might superficially appear, that confronted by a unique crisis they were all suddenly reduced to imbecility; on the whole their composure, their fertility of resource, their audacity, their bellicosity, their tactical talents did not desert them. But they were unequal to the situation because they did not know what it was. The most important element in it was a question mark. Had they known President Stanley was dead, it would have been simple. Had they known where he had been taken and by whom, it would have been equally simple. Had they even known but one thing, that it was certain the President would not be returned for forty-eight hours, the situation would have been handled with dispatch and when the President was returned it would have been as the Commander-in-Chief of an Army and Navy at war. But of the President they knew nothing and could learn nothing, and by that uncertainty many of them were paralyzed and the remainder frustrated. On account of that uncertainty, because at any moment of the day or night the word might come that the President was found, rescued, on his way back to the White House, no one would commit himself to a course or compromise himself by an action; Molleson would not move, Attorney-General Davis would not decide, Senators and Representatives would not speak. In a hundred offices, libraries, and hotel rooms the rulers threatened, exhorted, cajoled, and cursed; to no avail.

It could not be said that the legislators and high officials were in revolt against the rulers. It could not even be said that they were standing firm on principle or in loyalty to an absent leader. They were merely reflecting the temper of the country as evidenced by telegrams, air-mail letters and telephone messages from their constituents, reports from their observers at home, newspaper dispatches, all the sensitive threads of feeling, opinion, and prejudice which form the enormous nation-wide web having Washington for a center. The people had loved their President. Latterly doubts and strictures had begun to find expression—no matter how they came; the fabric of his popularity had worn thin; but they had loved him. Now they wanted him back; they wanted him back and until they got him they wanted nothing else; to hell with corn-planting, trial balances, monthly bills, leaky faucets and war, until the President was found. Especially, for the moment, to hell with war; they were sick of hearing about it anyway. The feeling was overwhelming, from ocean to ocean and lakes to gulf, and they let Washington know it. It was enhanced by the one of the thousand contradictory rumors which had gained most credence and had in many communities supplanted all others: that the President had been kidnapped by an international banker and was being held in the basement vault of a Wall Street building until he would agree to war. Negotiations were supposed to be going on behind the scenes.

Representative Binns of Georgia was funny. That is, he was a wit. Thursday morning he said to a group of his colleagues:

"It looks to me perfectly obvious. Who has profited by it? The pacifists. Tuesday afternoon Congress would have voted war no matter what the President said; if the question got to the floor today not one would dare to vote at all, they'd duck and run to a man. Of course, if and when he comes back it might be different again, but as long as he's gone there's not a chance. It certainly looks obvious. Gentlemen, I'll tell you where he is: the Women's League for Peace has got him. They've got him at their headquarters, sitting on him. And I don't blame Wardell for not storming the place and rescuing him; personally, I would prefer to paddle a canoe across the Pacific and attack a Japanese battleship."

They laughed, a little. Not much, and not long.


3


Binns's logic was used, seriously and more to the point, an hour later by Senator Corcoran. He was talking to Lewis Wardell. After repeated requests, by phone and messenger, Wardell had given him fifteen minutes. Since his victory at the Cabinet meeting the afternoon before, Wardell had grown more irritable, more frantic, and more humble. He had delegated various important lines of inquiry to Assistant Attorney-General and men from the State and Treasury Departments, with instructions to report to him nothing but results. He had listened to Chief Skinner and taken his advice. He had sent Grinnell and Voorman and a score of others equally prominent to jail, and had so far refused to see them, but they were soon to be released as part of a new strategy devised by Skinner. A hundred men were to be placed in the central offices of the telephone company; all calls from and to a long list of numbers were to be listened to. More experienced detectives were on their way from the nearest cities; all persons, including Brownell and Lincoln Lee, who had been apprehended, were to be set free and kept constantly under surveillance. Skinner's point was that nothing could be learned from a man under detention who would not talk; free but observed, betrayal sooner or later was certain. He would, he said, try a little talk with Lee himself before he let him go.

Wardell was not disheartened, he was only frantic. He would not have believed it possible. The most intensive search, for two days and two nights, by the largest and most expert body of investigators ever assembled, aided by the unanimous ardor and determination of the citizens, had failed to discover the trail. The mass of details they had collected sifted into nothing so far as the main objective was concerned. Brownell had, or had not, bought chloroform; it had or had not been his own handkerchief. Wardell had seen him again, Wednesday midnight, with the Secretaries of State and War present, and Brownell had stuck to his assertion of innocence and ignorance and demanded to be released. Liggett and Oliver had agreed that there was sufficient evidence to warrant holding him. Hundreds of people had been found who had seen the truck at various points on the streets of the city, but in no case was there any positive proof that it had not been another of the Callahan trucks, and there had been so many conflicting descriptions of the driver that all of them were useless. All persons who had seen the truck, or thought they had, had been given a look at Val Orcutt; the dozen or so who claimed to identify him had not been sufficiently convincing to invalidate Val's own story. The sentry at the entrance, who had at first claimed to have seen the driver leaving as well as arriving, and who had later admitted he could not definitely remember the leaving, had Wednesday night confessed that he had not seen the truck leave at all; he had merely heard it; he had been watching a flock of pigeons. The man in the receiving room of the White House basement had seen or heard nothing unusual. He had not gone outdoors at all that morning after arriving at work; he had taken the delivery from Val and given him the empty baskets, and had gone on, whistling, arranging things on his shelves.

In two hours' questioning after the departure of Lewis

Wardell on Wednesday afternoon, Chief Skinner had extracted from Val Orcutt nothing whatever. He had finally given up and sent him back to the hospital under guard, but he had not been satisfied. He had reported to Wardell, "The boy is honest, but there's something wrong with him. He's honest, and he hasn't got anything to scrape off his conscience, but there's a filter in his throat he has to push his words through. The cop found him in the park just as he said, and the doctor thinks he had amnesia, but his being so careful when he talks makes me itch. I asked him some cute questions, and his frown *may* have been only because his head hurt. I didn't chastise him with scorpions; shall I do that?"

"Would it do any good?"

"No. He's tough. If he's buried something he won't be digging it up. After all he did get cracked on the head. Of all the things we're curious about, the one we really would like to find out is where the President is, and I doubt if the boy knows that."

Mrs. Orcutt and her husband had been investigated; nothing. Viola Delling and her husband the druggist, likewise; nothing. She, confronted with Brownell's denial that he had bought chloroform in her store, had been indignant, positive, and scornful. The articulation of her scorn had got her into hot water, when she protested that it was preposterous to question her good faith since she had patriotically furnished all the assistance in her power to prosecute the search for a President of whose policies she did not and could not wholeheartedly approve. Ha, they said, ha, you admit it then, you disapprove his policies! That gave her a difficult and unpleasant hour, but in the end they conceded the probability that she had not kidnapped the President.

A thousand other sales of chloroform were investigated, as well as doctors and hospitals in that connection; the bruise on Val Orcutt's head was examined by a dozen doctors for a possible hint of the weapon used; an effort was made to check up on every conveyance seen on Tuesday morning within five blocks of the empty house on Fifteenth Street Northeast, where the truck had been found abandoned; a thousand false scents were started, pursued, and reluctantly given up; the telephone call to Kempner, manager of Callahan's, which Val Orcutt said had not been made by him, had been traced to a booth in a cigar store and a score of men were working on that. All possibilities were being clutched at, not with the desperate indiscrimination of the proverbial drowning man and his straw, but with all the acumen and determination of an army of the most highly trained and competent investigators in America.

So far as they or Wardell or Chief Skinner could tell, they were on Thursday noon as far from the solution of the mystery as they had been when they began. Three main lines were being followed:

1. Pursuit of clues at hand: the chloroform, the handkerchief, the truck, the persons involved.

2. Search for new clues: the White House grounds, the streets and premises of the city, the highways, railroads, airports near and far.

3. The other end, motive: leaders of the munitions industry and allied interests, Gray Shirts, patriots (jingoes), international bankers, representatives of foreign governments (belligerents). These were all under suspicion, a few had been "detained," some had been or were being questioned, and many were under surveillance.

The suggestion which Senator Corcoran had to offer, when finally Lewis Wardell granted him fifteen minutes, was with regard to the third line of inquiry, motive. Corcoran wanted, he said, to do two things: lodge a protest and make a suggestion. He did not criticize the imposition of martial law on the District; no doubt that had been necessary and indeed essential; but he did vehemently object to the arrogance and violence with which the honor and reputation of prominent citizens were being attacked. It was unreasonable, unjust, and futile. The emergency created by the crime against the person of the President should not be taken advantage of for the establishment of a dictatorship attempting to justify itself by brutality, abuse, and calumny. So far as he knew, there was no reason to suppose—

Wardell stopped him. "Nonsense. How would you like to have my job? You've had dealings with me, Senator, you know it isn't my habit when I'm criticized to yell shut up. But that's all you'll get out of me now: shut up and let me alone."

Corcoran insisted; he was speaking not only in the interest of the citizens involved, but of the country as a whole; even—especially—with regard to the welfare of this administration—

"Shut up!" A thousand fruitless endeavors, sixty sleepless hours and a dozen quarts of black coffee had ruined Wardell's nerves as well as his appearance. "I'm telling you, shut up and get out!"

With his protest thus tabled, Corcoran had eight minutes left for his suggestion. He proceeded with it, beginning with the exposition with which Representative Binns had prepared the way for his sally of wit. If the target of suspicion was to be determined by reference to motive, it seemed to him clear that a grave error had been made and much valuable time lost. Who could have reasonably expected to gain by the kidnapping of the President? Those who desired war? Obviously not. They had their goal in sight. The President would have addressed the Congress on Tuesday noon and, no matter what he said, before adjournment that day Congress would have declared war. Of the correctness of that statement Corcoran was convinced, but even admitting that it was doubtful his argument held good. With the President left undisturbed in the exercise of his office, the worst that could be said of the position of the war supporters was that they stood better than an even chance of victory; whereas now they stood no chance at all, unless and until the President was returned. It was true that was chiefly because the citizens of the nation were foolishly but overwhelmingly convinced that war supporters were responsible for the kidnapping; but would not whoever committed the crime foresee that? Apparently they were clever enough. This logic was so unassailable, said Corcoran, that it was even being suggested in one or two quarters that the whole thing was an Administration plot, executed with the connivance of the Cabinet; the President was in the White House; the arrest of Brownell and similar activities were red herrings—

Wardell snorted. "Rot. What are you doing, suggesting—"

Not at all, the Senator hastened to say with obvious sincerity. Even granting the wish and the intention, which he did not, such a plot, with so many persons involved, would have collapsed within six hours. But the suggestion, ridiculous as it was, showed, as a weather vane shows the wind, the direction where logic pointed. The kidnappers of the President were not the supporters of war, they were its enemies.

"Neat," said Wardell. "Thanks. It is neat, too, your saying *supporters* of war; you can't very well support a war till you have it; personally I prefer *instigators* of war. Say I accept your logic, what do I do next, start after the Carnegie Foundation for Peace?"

Corcoran ignored the sarcasm. He observed that his fifteen minutes was up, and rose from his chair. He would take, he said, but a few seconds to add that there were two elements in the community, both sufficiently capable of violent and audacious action, whose interests were being served by the present situation: the representatives of four European governments and one Asiatic, and the Communists. The governments did not want us in the war on the side we should certainly take; the Communists didn't want us in at all.

Wardell said, "Neat. Your time's up."

Senator Corcoran went.

That interview turned the third line of inquiry into a farce. Wardell was not persuaded by Corcoran's analysis to dismiss from consideration any of the previous suspects, but the possibility of its correctness could not be ignored. He called in the Chief of the Secret Service and various other lieutenants, and fresh dispositions were made. An investigation was set on foot of the activities of the representatives of the five foreign governments; that was unquestionably farcical, both sides under suspicion at once, but logic and farce have slept together on various occasions. It appeared now that any person in the country might have had reason, or thought he had, to kidnap the President; as to motive, all were in the same boat; detection must look for opportunity, competence, and the requisite boldness and pugnacity.

They went after the Communists. Where yesterday Gray Shirts had been herded into the basement rooms of the Department of Justice, the jails, and their own kitchens and living-rooms, and questioned, threatened, and entreated, today the Communists got it. With the same lack of result, and at least an equal display of contempt, defiance, and derision on the part of the new suspects. Trails were started, minor "subversive" activities were uncovered, stool pigeons were betrayed, headquarters were found and raided—and that was the sum of it. If the Communists had the President, it became clear that they had adequately arranged to guard the mystery as perfectly as their political forbears had guarded the execution of the Russian Czar.

But not even in Washington and New York were the Communists run to cover as the Gray Shirts had been the day before. This pursuit remained official, orderly, and organized.

You can usually pretty well tell, if you have time and resources enough and are good at research, where a hundred million people got an idea; so many newspaper and magazine articles, so many scenes in the movies, so many radio talks, so many inspired preachers and lecturers; but it would be impossible to say how the American people became invincibly persuaded in a few short hours that a "war gang" had kidnapped their President. Spontaneous combustion does start fires, and it probably started that one. At all events, they knew it; and when Senator Corcoran's suggestion propelled Lewis Wardell willy-nilly into the middle of a farce, and Wardell conscripted a thousand investigators and a million suspects for its cast of characters, it got little attention from the citizens of the United States either as participators or as spectators. They were busily engaged with the drama as it had at first unfolded itself to them; they had their villain spotted and they were after him. Any day would be a good one for chasing Communists; at the moment they had more pressing business on hand.

4

At one o'clock Thursday afternoon a handful of Senators and Representatives were gathered in the office of Senator Reid. They had repaired there, singly and inconspicuously, a few minutes past noon; for both houses, following the example of the day before, had convened at twelve and immediately adjourned. They were in Reid's office, with the door closed; outside, in the hall, with the back of his chair squarely against the closed door, sat Reid's confidential secretary, instructed that no person whatsoever was to be permitted to enter. All who had been made privy to the meeting had arrived.

The portent and gravity of the matter under consideration can be best conveyed by mentioning that the vigilant solicitude on the face of Senator Wilcox made him look like a statesman. To look like a statesman was no trick at all for a Tilney, a Jackman or a Corcoran, for nature had fashioned them properly to begin with, they had had a great deal of practice, and they actually had some statesman in them. But though Wilcox might have been thought, on this occasion or that, to have displayed the appearance of a panther, a wolf, a hyena, or a fox, it had never occurred to anyone that he resembled a statesman; and the present shocked concern exhibited on that face was an eloquent tribute to the consequence of the crisis he and his colleagues had gathered to discuss.

Sumner Horner, Speaker of the House, with hunched shoulders and chin on his broad chest, his left hand deep in his trousers pocket and his right forefinger wagging its well-known emphasis, was speaking to the group in general and Senator Corcoran in particular: "I'll go along if that's what you decide. I'm not sure I'm right and I don't see how the hell anyone can be sure he's right. I'll go along, on one condition: that we pledge ourselves to maintain this group for the period of the emergency, to act as a unit on majority decisions, to have as our sole purpose the preservation of parliamentary government, and to keep our proceedings inviolably confidential. Each must take his oath on that, or we achieve nothing but futility."

Senator Allen snorted. "Confidential? The reason we're here is because Reid was at a confidential meeting this morning, and he told Corcoran all about it within an hour. In a time like this the only thing you can trust a man not to tell is what he doesn't know."

"That's convenient for you," Senator Sterling observed drily. "You, at least, need suffer no dislocation of habits."

"Bill!" Bronson Tilney was in a chair, his arms folded, his legs stretched out, his exhausted brown eyes moving only to necessity. They moved to reproach Sterling. "If you want to call Allen a lowdown Catiline, find a better time. Didn't he make a point that deserves an answer? I agree with Horner. A pledge won't hurt us, it may even furnish a little cohesion."

Reid, too, was in a chair; he never stood for long when it could be avoided, probably because when sitting it was not so apparent that he had been able to achieve only one inch over five feet. He said to Allen, "I gave no pledge to Drew or Cullen or anyone. Not that I wouldn't betray a confidence on occasion. I have my virtues, but they are my servants and know their place." To Tilney: "Does that mean that you consent to an adjournment *sine die*? Is that the way to do it?"

"I don't know." Tilney slowly shook his head. "I don't know, Tom." He looked around. "Gentlemen, I'm not an intriguer, you know that, I haven't the capacity for it.—Tom, I don't know. I have reached the age where the startling becomes the incredible. I cannot believe that men like Martin Drew and Daniel Cullen are plotting with United States army officers to expell Congress from its halls and seize the government. Oh, I know they are; you have told me so; but I can't believe it."

Wilcox muttered to Representative Morton, "He's too old for this; why did they drag him in?"

Tilney smiled at him. "I hear you, Wilcox. I hear you, sonny. They dragged me in because they know that devotion sometimes triumphs where vigor fails. You may be ready to fight for your future and the arena you have chosen for your combats; I am ready to die for the traditions I love and the institutions I hold sacred. There are a lot of people here and there who know that. How about it, Jim? Is that us?"

Corcoran, big and shaggy, looked down at him. "It's me, Bronnie. I've taken a lot of orders in my time, but I can't see myself taking them from army officers. Maybe our time has come. You're a student of history. I'm not, but I know that in the past ten years many men just as good as us, in Italy and Germany and Austria, have faced as an accomplished fact one day what they had ridiculed as preposterous the day before. Maybe our time has come."

Tilney nodded, slowly. "It may be, Jim."

"And you are partly responsible for it. I warned you; we have got to get into the war. Of course certain people demand it for the sake of their selfish interests; others think we are morally obligated; others believe we are in danger if we don't; still others merely hold that it is inevitable and therefore the sooner the better. I am one of the last. I warned you. Drew and Cullen are not merely in favor of war, they must have it; and of course an army always wants war, that is, its leaders do. With the President gone, Congress will not vote it; well, it's a damned good time and a damned good excuse to send Congress where half a dozen other parliaments have been sent, to the dump heap. I made a mistake this morning. I told Wardell that the persons whose interests were being served by the President's disappearance were those who opposed war, not those who favored it, and right now he has a squad of detectives rounding up Communists and tailing Japanese embassy men. I think I was wrong. I think I have been a jackass for three months, let charity put that limit on it. I think this business comes from a deeper plot and a more sinister purpose than any of us suspected, and if it is what it now seems to be, there is only one man in America astute enough to conceive it and bold enough to carry it out. Old George Milton. Older than you are, Bronnie, and a hell of a lot shrewder. He knew, before anyone else dreamed it, that the time was at hand for us to take the road other nations were traveling; a year ago he began to finance the Gray Shirts. Now, in the hornet's nest busted open by the kidnapping of the President, he thinks he sees a chance to go straight to the Army for his strong-arm, and Drew and Cullen and the others are doing it for him. Then who do you think kidnapped the President? What does it look like?"

Jim Corcoran doubled his fists and clamped his elbows against his sides—a gesture familiar to the Senate floor for twenty years—and looked around the group. "Gentlemen, I'm through. We may or we may not get into their damned war, I don't know, but I'm through with anyone who thinks he can play tiddlywinks with the elected representatives of the people of the United States, and any game that's theirs is not mine. We must make common cause with Wardell and the Cabinet, no matter what their views are on war. We must prevent at all costs a spectacular coup on the Congress, and if the best way to do that is to adjourn *sine die* until the President's return, that is what we must do. We must cement this group on the principles suggested by Horner; and in that connection I request Senator Allen to leave us, and if he does not leave I demand that he be expelled forthwith. Also that Senator Reid be asked for the fullest and most circumstantial assurances that his aims are in agreement with ours."

There was a stir. Reid smiled. Sterling said, "Good for you, Corcoran. That's better than sniping at him." Jackman was nodding with grim satisfaction.

Allen was silent, with a red face. Reid said, "That's not nice of you, Jim. Who brought you the story? After all, you're in my office. I only double-cross people when it is to my own advantage."

Corcoran looked at Allen. "We don't want you, Senator." He looked around. "Do we?"

There were No's and shaking heads from all but Reid. Allen rose to his feet, still big and slick and wary, but visibly disconcerted. His sneer, by force of habit, was successful. "Thank you, gentlemen." He stopped in front of Bronson Tilney's chair and looked down at him, opened his mouth and shut it again. At the door he turned. "In my opinion, gentlemen, it's about time for the army." As the door was opened Reid called to his secretary, on guard:

"Allen's leaving, Johnson. As you were."

Tilney's exhausted brown eyes were appraising Reid, and were met with a smile. Reid transferred the smile to the group: "I am ready to furnish whatever assurances you may require, gentlemen. I wish to be one of you, from different motives from those which activate my friend Jim Corcoran. I have an intellectual fondness for parliamentary government, and for its sake would betray my oldest friends. If I am to be questioned in detail, may I suggest that Senator Jackman be selected for the purpose? I believe that he is the only one of you who really dislikes me, and it will be an excellent exercise in urbanity."

# 5

Of the long and heterogeneous list of persons who had been placed under arrest by order of Lewis Wardell, the last to be released was Lincoln Lee. This was because the others had been set free on a general order, with instructions that each be followed and reported upon periodically, whereas Lee was forced to wait until Chief Skinner of the Secret Service could make opportunity for an interview. The truth was that the Chief had not been entirely candid with Wardell when he had told him that he would have a try at getting something out of Lee before letting him go; he really had little hope of it; his main reason for the attempt was his desire to have a look at the leader of the Gray Shirts, the man who by repute was displaying in ever-widening circles the organizing genius of a great executive, the fire and eloquence and audacity of a born leader of men, the egomania of a Napoleon, the reckless frenzy of a Hitler. Skinner had taken plenty of salt with this, but he did want to give the fellow the once-over.

At two o'clock Wardell had left for the White House to confer with the Cabinet, and Skinner was in command. He was not the Skinner whom his subordinates had known and respected and obeyed for more than six years; whereas he had always been distinguished by his composure in any emergency, his quick grasp of complexities, and his uncanny ability to pick the main thread of a knot, he was now irascible, confused, and explosive. At last a job had got on Phil Skinner's nerves. He knew that no Chief of the Secret Service, no investigating officer anywhere in the world, had ever had so rare and sensational an opportunity to distinguish himself; he knew that none had ever had at his command so large a body of trained experts; and he, Phil Skinner, with this opportunity and this equipment, was getting nowhere. It wasn't so much that in forty-eight hours he had failed to find the President, he knew how to be patient for victory when that was a requirement for it; what exasperated him and got him off balance was the fact that every trail they had started had petered out into nothing. None of them appeared to have either a point of departure or a destination. The moment it had been learned that Mrs. Delling had sold chloroform on Monday night to Harry Brownell, Secretary to the President, a rapid and rigorous investigation had been begun of Brownell's past and connections, especially his activities for the past month. Result, negative. No traffic with warmongers, no discoverable mutuality of interest with Administration enemies, no flirting with intriguers or itchings of personal ambitions—an impeccable secretary; and, of course, his own denial. Then there must be something wrong with Viola Delling; but that reconnaissance, too, had failed to yield a grain of gold from the dust of her commonplace days and years. The truck, abandoned on the street with the President's penknife lying on the floor; God knows that was a clue; it was hardly possible to believe that a chloroformed President had been removed from it and transferred to another vehicle without a single observer of any portion of the operation; but no observer could be found. There was the truck, and that was that: a dead end. Brownell bought chloroform, or didn't; another dead end. Still another was Val Orcutt. He had been actually present at the scene of the kidnapping, actually there when it happened, and he had no more information regarding it—as to the number or identity of the criminals, what they looked like, where they came from, whether they were men or women or chimpanzees or Japs—than if he had been a thousand miles away.

Chief Skinner thought to himself for the twentieth time that there was something phony about it. Phony, or crazy. He did not suspect Val Orcutt of complicity; that made no sense either. He did not really suspect Brownell; probably the chloroform purchase was a case of mistake in identity and the handkerchief a coincidence. But he had a feeling that there was something wrong with their stories. There was something wrong in the core of the thing, some central fact which perhaps even they did not know or had overlooked, but which would have to be dug up or all the detectives in the world would end by getting to the destination they had already reached—nowhere. Skinner even reverted to one of the ideas that had popped into his head on Tuesday afternoon, the idea which had resulted in the exploration of the White House; but he had conducted that search himself with five of his best men, with a method and thoroughness that made the resuscitation of the idea preposterous.

The Chief thought to himself, "I'm cuckoo, and I might find a better way of spending my time than sitting here on the back of my lap hunting an alibi. I might go fishing, for instance, or go out and climb trees. Some bright boys have put over a fast one, and so far they've just been too fast for me. I'm getting old and blind and deaf. I'm going to resign and go and live in the country, but before I can do that I'll have to find President Stanley, because the Attorney-General will want to consult with him in his despair of finding a worthy successor for this office."

He opened a drawer of the desk and took out a bottle of bourbon, poured an ordinary drinking glass a third full, gulped it down, and cleared his throat with an explosive rasp. Then he took up the telephone and said to the clerk who answered: "Who's out there?... Who?... Go on... Where's Anderson?... All right, send in Moffat and Kilpatrick and Sam Carr." He scowled at the bottle, took another drink, and returned the bottle to the drawer.

The three men entered. The Chief pulled at his ear and looked them over. He ended with his eyes on the one in the center. "Moffat, do you know Lincoln Lee?"

Chick Moffat nodded. "I know him by sight. I saw him in here yesterday."

"Yeah. I remember now. Wardell told me. I had forgot it was you. Since you've been at the State Department and the White House I haven't seen much of you. You look to me as if you're getting fat. Are you as good as you used to be?"

"Better." Chick grinned. "There's more of me. I'm not getting fat. I'm a pretty good detective. As a matter of fact, Chief, I've had it in mind to ask you to put me back in the

133

barn with the work horses. It's not so good over at the White House, it's too soft, and it costs too much to buy clothes."

"The hell you say. If it's so damn soft at the White House, where's the man you were sent there to protect? It was a break for you that you weren't on duty Tuesday morning. —All right. I guess you'll do. Get this. You others too. Across the hall in Room Nine a man has got Lincoln Lee. He just brought him from jail. Go and tell him to bring him in here.—Wait. Then go to the street. Lee will be leaving here in about ten or fifteen minutes, maybe a little longer. You, Moffat, will be responsible for keeping him on the touch night and day. Carr and Kilpatrick will be under you. Make routine reports to the office. If there's anything urgent see that it gets either to Kiefer or to me without delay."

"Yes, sir. That all?"

Skinner nodded. The men went.

The policeman who brought Lincoln Lee in was taking no chances; he had a chain to the handcuffs and was glued to it. He came in with him and the pair stood. Lee was disheveled and unshaven, and his open coat showed his gray shirt none too clean. He had no hat. His shoulders were pulled forward by the twist the handcuffs gave his arms; but his chin was up, and his eyes were level, concentrated—always concentrated—on Chief Skinner.

Skinner said, "All right, unlock him." The policeman looked doubtful, hesitated, then without a word removed the handcuffs and stood back dangling them from his fingers. The Chief nodded, "That's all, you can go."

The policeman said, "He's been awful nice down at the coop, but I wouldn't trust him."

Skinner thanked him for the advice, and he went.

Lincoln Lee was bending his wrists around, first one then the other, working them back and forth. Skinner sat and watched him. So that was the personage: compact, well balanced on his legs, nervous little hands, a hard-looking head on a strong short neck. Skinner watched him, and finally said:

"What's your right name?"

Lincoln Lee for a moment kept on looking at his wrists, rubbing them. At length he looked up and said, "You don't need to bother about it. I don't."

"I was just curious."

134

"I am making my name. A man makes his name. A great man makes a great name."

"Yeah." Skinner kept casual. "By kidnapping a President, for instance."

"Nonsense. That was a job for a fool. You have a name, I suppose? I don't know it."

"Oh, excuse me. I'm Phil Skinner, Chief of the Bureau of Secret Service."

"I see." Lee's mouth twisted. "Little men have little problems, and you solve them. Do you think that is service to your country? Or that it makes you a name? You have a good pair of eyes; you can see. If you wish to serve, why not serve greatness? If you love your country, our America, why do you degrade yourself in obedience to the knaves that are betraying her?"

"Well, I'll be damned." Skinner laughed; he needed to laugh in order to hear it, for he saw and felt the force in the man before him; it was electric, a vibration that was at your nerves like the air at your skin. He laughed. "I *will* be damned. How would you like to use my office for a recruiting station? Apparently you like it all right. Some other day, Lee. Get this. I've got a surprise for you. You may remember you had a talk here yesterday with Secretary Wardell. You may remember he promised to send you to an insane asylum—you know, a bughouse. I've talked him out of it. I have no doubt that that's where you'll end, but that doesn't concern me. We're going to turn you loose. I *think* we are."

Lee said quietly, "Do as you please. Yesterday with Secretary Wardell I lost control of myself. It enrages me to deal with fools."

Skinner nodded. "He baited you a bit, didn't he? Well, we're going to release you. But before you go I'd like to make you a proposition. Were you concerned in the kidnapping of President Stanley? Wait a minute, wait till I'm through. Do you know anything at all about it, who planned it, who did it, where he is, what's happened to him? Don't think you're dealing with another fool because I ask you this. I want an answer; I'll know what to do with it. Well?"

Skinner's gray eyes, which Lee had justly called good, bored into Lee's. Lee was not interested in the boring, he merely maintained his gaze. He said, "No. I know nothing about it. I have my own concerns, and my country's. I have no interest in the games of children and criminals. Nor should you have. You have the quality—"

"Hold it, Lee. We'll discuss my quality some other time, I'd be glad to. I believe you. I don't think you're mixed up in this, I think you're too smart. That's why I'm making you a proposition, because I think you're smart. You know who I am. I'm at the head of the Secret Service of the United States. I doubt if I'll ever have the job of chasing you; if you ever get far enough along to be chased they'll probably have to set the army on you. In the meantime it wouldn't hurt you a bit to have me feeling friendly to you. You know, just not hostile. That's the way I'd feel if you happened on a chance to help me out on the job I'm on now. I'm setting you free. You know a lot of people and you get around a lot and you hear a lot of things outside of church. If you get a hint, no matter what, about the President, will you let me know? If it's any of your friends of course you won't, but it may not be. You might happen to hear almost anything. Will you let me know? It wouldn't hurt you any; you don't give a damn about the President one way or the other anyhow, you've got your mind on bigger things. Will you help me out?"

Lincoln Lee's mouth was twisted, contemptuous beyond all considerations of ordinary amusement or scorn. His tone did not descend to resentment: "You know I won't."

"You won't?" The Chief's brows went up. "The hell you won't. Would you like to think it over?"

"I don't think things over."

"No?"

"No."

"Why don't you try it once? I'm not expecting you to betray your friends; all I ask is a little coöperation."

"You're asking me to stool for you. I forgive you the insult, Chief Skinner. But don't repeat it."

Skinner looked at him not quite with credence, like a botanist at a familiar plant off on a sport. At length he shook his head, turned to the phone and told the clerk to send in a man. He turned back again: "You're a specimen all right, Lee. You're quite a little guy. I hope to God I haven't offended you. I'd hate to think there was anything between us except some good strong bars."

A man entered. Skinner said, "Take this nut out of here and turn him loose at the door. And don't let him sell you a gray shirt on the way down the hall."

# 6

At four o'clock Thursday afternoon Ben Kilbourn sat in the library of the Daniel Cullen home in Pittsburgh, reading a book with red and yellow primulas stamped in color on the cover, beneath the title, *How to Build a Rock Garden*. It was chilly, and he sat before a fire in the fireplace, with his legs stretched out on a stool and his shoulders halfway down the back of a large leather chair. He was reading, some. Now and then he stuck his finger into his place in the book and got up and walked to a window and looked out, and after a little returned to the fire. He was listening for two things: for a possible telephone call from Washington, from Cullen who had gone there the night before, and for noises from the street.

At half-past two he had been rung up by Arkmore, one of the vice-presidents of the Federal Steel Corporation. It seemed that certain of the citizens of the steel capital and its environs, unemployed Reds and similar scum, had determined upon a more lively expression of their prejudices than holding meetings and sending delegations to the Mayor's office. A gang of them had attacked the main office of the corporation in the city itself, broken windows, smashed in a couple of doors, and got themselves beaten up by the police. Other gangs had besieged the homes of two steel officials in McKeesport and one in Donora, captured the car of a couple of state troopers in Monessen and manhandled them, and made various other sorties here and there throughout the domain. Arkmore had called Kilbourn to tell him that one mob, obviously headed for the exclusive residential section on the hill, had already been intercepted and turned back, and that a squad of police was being sent to the Cullen home as a measure of precaution. The police were there now, scattered along the sidewalk and among the shrubbery at the rear, and that was why Kilbourn was listening for noises from the street.

After reading a paragraph or two on the desirability of incorporating plenty of grit and stone-chips with the soil between the rocks, Kilbourn would pause to reflect that if he were the Mayor of Pittsburgh he would wire the Governor at Harrisburg without delay for a detachment of the National Guard. For the two hours following noon he had had the radio turned on, and he had gone through an early edition of an afternoon paper. It appeared to him that each little item of the day's news shared with all the others a more ominous tone than could be occasioned by the routine bubbling of the chronic scum. The New York Stock Exchange was closed. Martial law had been extended to Maryland and Delaware and parts of New Jersey, Pennsylvania, and the Virginias. The outbursts of violence had nowhere assumed formidable proportions, but they were occurring hourly, all over, and many of the reports came from unheard-of places and were informed with strange and grotesque characteristics. In Cumberland, Maryland, the citizens had thrown stones at the soldiers! There was certainly nothing to be made out of that, you couldn't possibly find any sense in it, but it didn't have the appearance of a bubbling scum. Conjecturally, ordinary people, those who commonly pay their taxes and eat chocolate candy and vote for Republicans or Democrats, had really got mad about something.

Ben Kilbourn thought, if it's really like that, if they've really got enough spirit in them to keep a rage going overnight, they'll turn this country upside down and anything can happen. He read another page, and stopped to decide that his guess was Fascism.

He got up, stood listening, and went to a window to open it and lean out. It was a gray afternoon, raw for late April, with a gusty ill-tempered wind. Across the wide lawn, he could see over the shrubs and between the trees that a car had drawn up at the curb and two policemen were getting out of it. Those on the sidewalk gathered around. One of the newcomers did not stop, but came trotting up the path toward the house.

Kilbourn went back and sat down. In a few minutes there was a knock at the library door, and the butler entered. He came over to the fireplace and told Kilbourn:

"An officer, sir. He says that people appear to be coming here, but it is not expected they will arrive. He says that it was thought we should be informed. Would you care to speak to him, sir?"

Kilbourn smiled up at him. "Are you scared, Ferris?"

"No, sir. I see no occasion for it."

"I suppose not. I suppose you really aren't. You were in the World War."

"Yes, sir. I was at Ypres. And of course other places on the Continent during three years."

"Yes. On the Continent. Quite. Well, we won't get scared; I doubt if our guests are equipped with pineapples. Mrs. Cullen has not returned?"

"No sir. Around seven o'clock, she said."

"Good. If we are besieged you can telephone her to stay away. I'm glad Miss Cullen is not here; she would be for arming us with thirty-sixes and potting them from the windows. Thank you, Ferris. I think I needn't see the officer."

The butler bowed and went. Kilbourn resumed his book.

Twenty minutes later he put it down. Unquestionably, this time, there were noises. He went to the window. At first he could see no one, no policemen at all, but leaning out and stretching his neck he caught sight through the screen of leaves of a small knot of them on the sidewalk at the far corner of the grounds; he could not see what they were doing, but they were moving. Noises now were quite distinct, and were coming from various directions; the loudest seemed to be from around the house, from the rear; it was a confused hum, the low preamble to a roar, the mob murmur of anger not to be mistaken for any other collective human sound. Suddenly, also from the direction of the rear, there was a volley of shot, the swift rattle of explosions nearly simultaneous. The roar swelled, and shouts and yells could be distinguished with it.

Kilbourn stood back from the window. Certainly he was not scared, but he was trembling and his lips were working. He said aloud, "By God, they still do. Hear that? They still do." He started to the window, but a knock on the door turned him. It was Ferris back again.

The butler said, "Another officer, sir. A captain of police. He says the—er—persons will not be permitted to enter the grounds. The police have been instructed to shoot. He says we need feel no alarm."

Kilbourn laughed, so sharply and suddenly that the butler could not stop his surprise before it got to his face. He erased it, promptly and successfully. Kilbourn said:

"That's damned nice of him, Ferris. Don't you think so? I'd go down and thank him, only I must wait here for a telephone call from Mr. Cullen. Mr. Cullen is in Washington, giving

139

them hell for not delivering the war he ordered. Thank the police captain for me, Ferris. Tell him how nice I think he is."

"Yes, sir." The butler hesitated, swallowed; and then, obviously, plunged. "Don't let yourself get excited, Mr. Kilbourn. It doesn't pay to get excited. We—we should do these things calmly, sir. Like me, sir, if I may say so. I have been contemplating a step for some time; it is as good as decided; I have in mind becoming a Communist, sir."

Kilbourn stared. He stared for all of thirty seconds, and then exploded. "Oh for Christ's sake! No! Oh for Christ's sake!" He roared with laughter, into the gently perturbed face of the British butler.

# 7

The modern large American hotel is an ideal meetingplace for clandestine affairs. If you are properly dressed, not in need of a shave, and have the trick of looking decently aloof, you can enter an elevator and be carried to any floor, and the bustle of the lobby crowd leaves you satisfactorily unnoticed; and in a case requiring extraordinary precaution it is a simple matter to get off at the sixth floor and walk two flights up to the eighth, or off at the tenth and walk two down. House detectives and elevator starters are alert and vigilant observers, but even they see only what they are looking for, and those at the Pilgrim Hotel in Washington, late Thursday afternoon, had no suspicion of the singular gathering assembled in Suite D on the eighth floor. The name after which that suite was entered on the register of the hotel was A. R. Thomas of Chicago; the man occupying it, expecting to sleep in one of its beds that night if he slept at all, was Daniel Cullen, arrived early in the morning from Pittsburgh.

Vice-President Molleson was there, licked. He had too many vulnerable spots; the structure of his personal fortunes leaned shakily on too many borrowed timbers to withstand any serious pressure; and Cullen and Caleb Reiner, the oil king, had put the screw on him. The joining of the Cullen and Reiner interests was alone enough to stamp the gathering as unique. Denham was there, and Arthur Porter King; Voorman, Senator Allen, and the Pierce Brothers of the Wall Street house. But what gave the group its central and sinister significance was the presence there of four men of a totally different type, men who were presumed to work for a living and receive their pay from the government of the United States: three Major Generals, Hedges, Jones, and Kittering, and Brigadier General Ridley.

If D. L. Voorman had been kept in jail incommunicado, Cullen and Reiner would have managed a collection of generals anyhow, but it would not have been precisely that quartet. Voorman had been released shortly after noon on the general order. He was of course completely ignorant of the nature of the developments of the past twenty hours; he had no notion why, after having been suddenly arrested, he had as suddenly been released. He walked down the sidewalk away from the jail, stopped at a newsstand and bought a paper, walked farther, entered a bookstore and came out again, and was a little annoyed at his discovery that he was being followed. People on the sidewalk had preoccupied faces and seemed all to be bound for somewhere; there were, in this section of the city, three or four soldiers to a block, their guns on their shoulders and their cartridge belts filled. Voorman stopped a taxi and gave the driver the address of his home.

His wife, slim blond Sally, was at home with a welcome for him. Voorman had to have a bath and change. While he soaped and brushed Sally sat on the corktop stool and told him things. She had much gossip, a little information, and two items of instruction: he was not to use the telephone for anything of importance, and he was to call as soon as possible at the office of Coulter, President of the Potomac Trust Company. Voorman got a bite of lunch, took a taxi to Coulter's office, and was told by that discreet and dignified gentleman, "Go to Suite Eight D at the Pilgrim. Get off at the ninth or tenth and walk down." Voorman said, "If you have a car you can spare for half an hour, would you tell your man to drive it up the alley to the back entrance of Howard's hat shop and wait there for me?" Mr. Coulter would be glad to do that. In a few minutes Voorman left the bank, walked three blocks to Howard's shop, nodded and beckoned Walter Howard to the rear, and was let out at the back door. Coulter's car got him to the Pilgrim Hotel in less than fifteen minutes.

That was why the generals were so well selected. Voorman got there in time to prevent overtures to several, particularly Cunningham, who he knew were either dangerous or incompetent. He knew which of them were itching for the big job, the top command, when war came; which were close to Oliver and which were outside of the clique; which were likely to prove most susceptible to the sophistry all prepared for them, and to offer least resistance to the dazzling temptation likewise all prepared.

A snap judgment might have called the four military men either gulls or rascals, or both, for embracing the plot contrived that afternoon in Suite Eight D, but were they such fools after all? As it was presented to them there appeared to be no question of turpitude involved, certainly no mutiny or treason; it was merely a difference of opinion on the interpretation of the law of the nation, and if the august and erudite Supreme Court could split five to four on that, as so often happened, might not the army be granted the benefit of a choice? Especially in this unprecedented crisis, with no time, not a minute, to waste, with the enemy overseas ready momentarily to gorge his present prey and poise himself for a leap at the criminally unprotected throat of Uncle Sam.

Was the office of President vacant? The Cabinet autocratically said no, and stopped the wheels of government. Congress, inept and cowardly, declined to function; it was even rumored—Senator Allen was authority for that—that tomorrow they would adjourn *sine die*. Secretary Wardell, with the Cabinet behind him, was violating the rights and restraining the liberties of innocent and prominent citizens, disrupting the morale of the people with lies and misrepresentations, endangering the very existence of the government by his usurpation of the functions of law and his blindness to the vital and urgent necessity for national defense.

But there was another answer to the question, was the office of President vacant? The answer was yes, and there were plenty to uphold it, representing the most responsible, influential, and "patriotic" elements of the country. One was Vice-President Molleson; it was his duty under the oath, and his desire through his devotion to the Constitution, to assume at once the burdens of the office which was lawfully his. He was under the Constitution the President of the United States, and he intended forthwith to act in that capacity. A program had been prepared and had received his sanction:

1. Molleson would announce to the Cabinet that evening his assumption of the office of President. If a majority of the Cabinet acquiesced, well and good; if

142

not, Molleson would formally demand occupancy of the Executive Offices. It was to be expected that that demand would be refused.

2. Tomorrow (Friday) morning Molleson would function from his office in the Senate Building. A guard of soldiers would protect him. Any executive orders issued by him would be transmitted to the proper officials; those who refused to comply would be placed under arrest, and the orders handed to the army for execution.

3. Molleson's first act would be to demand of the Congress leaders that they meet at noon Friday, receive a message from him, and pass a declaration of war. In case of their refusal, the Congress halls would be locked and guarded, and Molleson would declare war by presidential decree. No Representative or Senator was to be arrested under any circumstances.

4. The dispositions of army units, at the White House, the Capitol, and all strategic points, were to be arranged by the four generals, who would act as a Military Council and select one of their number as Commandant of the area. They and he would be directly subordinate to President Molleson on all matters of policy.

5. The operation was not considered in any respect in violation of the Constitution, but on the contrary was undertaken primarily to uphold the Constitution, which was being defied by those who were refusing to carry out its provisions. Such extralegal acts as the declaration of war by Presidential decree would be legalized when the emergency had passed.

6. Any army officers of whatever rank refusing to assist with the program would be placed under arrest. Attempts at resistance would be instantly and vigorously suppressed.

It was only after many objections, waverings, and arguments that the generals finally committed themselves. The bluntest of them, as well as the ablest and most intelligent, Major General Hedges, very nearly ended the affair in an impasse, time and time again, by his insistent demand for a guarantee that President Stanley would not be returned to the White House for one week. The repeated and impassioned declarations of Cullen, Reiner, Denham, Voorman, and the rest that they had no knowledge of what had happened

143

to Stanley or of his present whereabouts, remained without effect on the general's open incredulity. He finally refused to continue the discussion unless they would sign a document stating their complete innocence of complicity or knowledge in the matter of the kidnapping of President Stanley. It was drawn up, signed, and Hedges sat and read it with a scowl of dissatisfaction.

Voorman said, "See here, General. If we signed a thousand papers like that it wouldn't clear up the point that bothers you, and all of us, most. What really bothers you, and us too, is not who kidnapped Stanley and what has happened to him, but what if he is found alive and well tomorrow afternoon? Well, if he is, he is. I can't answer that for you, none of us can. I don't know whether he's dead or alive, in the bottom of the Potomac River or up in an airplane or locked in the basement of the Japanese embassy. We have to take our chance on that and go ahead. What is the alternative? Wait to see if Wardell can find a President when we have one right here, under the Constitution? While the whole country goes crazy and God knows what will happen, and our friends abroad are beaten into impotence, annihilated? We've waited two days and two nights, two of the most crucial days in the history of modern civilization. What is the alternative? Just go on waiting? Certainly there is a risk; where there is no risk there can be no daring; and I think this country needs a little daring for a change."

Hedges still scowled. He nodded, and read the paper again, and folded it up and put it in his pocket. "All right," he said. "But you understand the extra risk we assume, my brother officers and myself. We are officers of the United States Army, but we are also men. We are devoted to the interests of our country, but we are also devoted to our own interests. That's natural. If Stanley does return tomorrow, and we are in the war, he will be Commander-in-Chief of the Army. Granted that we will not be punished, that he will show respect for our good faith in choosing the authority to be recognized in his absence, what chance do you think there would be of my name being mentioned when he is discussing the high command?"

"None whatever, General. None whatever."

"Then why won't you guarantee us a week? In a week the situation may be so well developed that a name will be inevitable."

144

Voorman threw up his hands. "Then you don't believe that paper?"

"I don't believe a damned word of it."

"Very well, then you don't. The risk, the peculiar risk, that you describe exists. Of course. But there is the reverse of it too. What if President Stanley doesn't return at all? What if he is dead? If the Gray Shirts got him, he probably is. In that case, Robert A. Molleson, seated before you, is the President of the United States—not for a day or a week, but for three years. That's the reverse of your risk."

Hedges stared at him. He said, at length, and meaningly, "By the favor of assassins."

"I'm not interested in the assassins. I know nothing about it. But that would be the fact."

In the end Hedges surrendered on that point. He had others. His brother officers likewise. They wanted assurances from Molleson that he would stand firm and not shift his position on any detail, and got them. They demanded guarantees from Cullen and King of the coöperation of railroad officials, and of ample and immediate funds until the usual Treasury channels were unobstructed. They began to talk in terms of a campaign; they brought up details of strategy; they sat forward in their chairs and their eyes gleamed; Kittering demanded a map of Washington and one had to be sent for.

It was after seven o'clock when Voorman pushed his chair back, crooking a finger at Molleson. He rose and started across the room, toward the little inside hall which led to a bedroom of the suite, and Molleson got up and followed him. When they were inside the bedroom Voorman closed the door and confronted the other with a tired and sympathetic smile.

He said, "It's time for you to go, Mr. President."

Molleson could not stand still. His hand wouldn't stay in his pocket, his head would not rest at this angle or that, his feet could not find solidity. He had no smile of acknowledgment for the "Mr. President." He said, "It's only a quarter past seven."

"I know, but you should be at the White House not later than half-past eight, and you must have something to eat. Go to Willy's and devour a steak and a couple of highballs. A man's no good on an empty stomach—remember when we couldn't find our lunch on the Rapidan? Give it to them straight over there; I wouldn't waste much time arguing if I

145

were you. There's always a chance that they'll go with you. Don't take it for granted that they won't. If they do, so much the better."

Molleson shook his head with certitude. "They won't." His head wouldn't stop shaking.

"All right. In any event, come back here as soon as you leave. No matter when. I imagine we'll be here all night. Have a good meal now, you'll need it."

"I'm not a damn bit hungry."

"You will be after a cocktail or two." Voorman took his hand, firm, reassuring. "Good luck, Mr. President."

# 8

When the general order was issued Thursday noon for the release of persons under detention, a few exceptions were made. More for punishment than precaution, the guards who had been on duty in the White House grounds and the sentry who had been at the rear entrance were kept locked up; and Val Orcutt had been returned to Erasmus Hospital, to a private room, and a guard maintained. Chief Skinner did not fancy taking a chance of losing the one person who had been present at the scene of the kidnapping; besides, Val's head had been pretty well bruised and hospital care wouldn't hurt him any. No one was permitted to see him but his mother, and she was limited to one visit a day.

At nine o'clock Thursday evening Mike Nolan of the New York detective force sat on a chair tilted back against the wall of a corridor on the third floor of Erasmus Hospital, pressing the tips of his thumbs together to keep awake and wishing absentmindedly that the nurse with a patient in Room Fourteen would walk past again. The door of Room Six was on his left, a couple of feet from his chair.

Footsteps smacked on the linoleum, from the right, and Nolan idly turned his head for a glance. It was a man new to him, a large man on a stride, with blond hair, wearing a greenish-gray suit, carrying a felt hat in his hand. He was taking in the numbers on the door. Catching sight of Nolan, he came straight up.

"I'm looking for Val Orcutt."

Nolan shook his head. "No can do, mister. He's not receiving."

The man pulled some papers from his pocket, found a slip among them, unfolded it and handed it over. Nolan looked at it. It was on a sheet torn from a memorandum pad, with *Department of Justice—Bureau of Secret Service* printed at the top. Written in ink was the date, and *Permit bearer to talk with Val Orcutt. Lewis Wardell.*

The man said, "We've got a new line on him. We think maybe we can jog his memory a bit."

"Maybe you can." Nolan had stood up and was looking him over. "My orders are pretty tight. I'll have to telephone."

"Sure, go ahead. Nobody can okay it but Wardell; he's at the White House. Say Extension Nine. He's with the Cabinet."

Nolan glanced around; there was no orderly in sight. The nearest telephone was at the desk around the corner, by the elevator; it would not do to leave the door unguarded, and he didn't care to leave the stranger there alone. He shrugged his shoulders, put his hand on the knob of the door of Room Six, and said, "All right, come on."

The man shook his head. "Sorry, but I have to see him alone. That's orders. You'd better telephone."

"Yeah? What's so deep and confidential about it?"

The man smiled. "There's plenty of things confidential about this case, Sergeant. Everybody knows something that no one else must know. If you're going to phone, hurry up, this isn't supposed to wait."

"When did you get this paper?"

"Fifteen minutes ago. At the White House."

"It says Bureau of Secret Service."

"Yes. Wardell had a pad in his pocket. What do you want me to do, show you his fingerprint on it?"

"Now don't froth at the mouth." Nolan stuck the paper in his pocket. "You're not counting on abusing him any?"

"Of course not."

Nolan nodded, turned, opened the door of Room Six, and went in. Val Orcutt was in an armchair with his back to the floor lamp, reading a newspaper; there was a pile of them on another chair beside him. He was dressed; his head was still enclosed in a bandage, but his face certainly exhibited no pallor. Nolan said, "Here's a visitor for you, Orcutt. Official. I told him you don't need any massage."

The man had entered. He nodded at Val, and stood. Nolan looked at his face, thoroughly in the better light, shrugged his shoulders again, and went out and closed the door. The man said, "If you don't mind," picked up the newspapers from the chair and put them on the bed, and sat down. Val watched him and said nothing.

"Your name's Valentine Orcutt."

Val agreed. "That's it."

The man smiled at him. "You're not a bad-looking lad."

"Much obliged."

"Sure. You're just a nice young fellow. I've got a kid, but he's only eight years old. You live with your father and mother out on Acker Street? I've seen the house. It's all right. Does your father own it?"

"No." Val folded his arms.

The man was smiling at him. "You're not going to wear your tongue out, are you, sonny? Correct." He had kept his voice down, and now made it still lower. "You don't need to be afraid of me. I'm not official."

"I'm not afraid. I answered your question, though I don't know why you asked it."

"No reason. Just a friendly question. I'm not official, I've come to see you on private business. Did you ever hear of George Milton?"

"Certainly I've heard of him. If you mean the banker."

The man nodded. "That's the one I mean. Only he's not exactly a banker—that is, he's a good deal more than a banker. He's the richest and most powerful man in America."

"Good for him."

The man hitched his chair up a little. "That's what he is, Val. And he wants to make a deal with you. The difficulty is that he can't very well see you just now, and the deal must be made quick. I may get kicked out of here any second, if that detective decides to use a telephone. You'll have to take my word on this. You'll have to believe that I'm a man that never goes back on his word, and neither does George Milton. He sent me to see you. Look me in the eye."

Val Orcutt was doing that; he met the other's gray-blue eyes without effort or challenge, without inquiry. The gray-blue eyes were earnest, steady, intent.

The man said, "George Milton will give you five hundred thousand dollars. Half a million dollars, in cash, if you will tell what you know about President Stanley. If you will tell me, now. You'll have to take my word for it. My word and his word, and they're good, Val. Five hundred thousand dollars in cash."

The expression on Val's face did not change. He said, "That's a lot of money."

"It is that. You see, George Milton's not cheap. He doesn't offer you a measly ten or twenty grand. He makes it worth your while. He'll pay it to you in cash, as soon as you get out of here and it's safe. This is straight, Val: half a million dollars. Think of what you can do with that, the home you can buy for your father and mother, the trips you can take, all the things you ever thought of. Just tell me. You can trust me."

Val was silent. He remained so. The man said, "Tell me. My God, Val, five hundred thousand dollars!"

Val shook his head.

"You don't trust me, Val. You can. You must. Absolutely."

Val spoke. "Sure I trust you. The trouble is I couldn't tell anything that would be worth a five-spot. I've already told everything I know."

"Now come, Val. You see, I know better. I know a little, but not enough. It's bound to come out in the end, and what's the difference if it's tomorrow or a week from now? The difference to you is half a million dollars. If you don't tell me now it will become known anyway, and you'll go on driving a grocery truck. You wouldn't be such a fool. I know it's hard for you to trust me, but George Milton would rather lose his eyesight than break his word, and so would I. Don't be a fool, Val. Don't pass up the only chance you'll ever have to meet real money."

"I'm sorry, mister." Val pulled his shoulders up and let them fall. "I could use the money all right, but I haven't got anything to tell."

"Listen here." The man hitched his chair up again. But before he could go on there was an interruption. Seated with his side to the door, he heard the turning of the knob, and swung his head that way. The door moved, came in fast, wide. The man started fast too, but he stopped. There was no girl around to use for a shield, and the steadiness of the automatic in Mike Nolan's hand and the readiness of the look on his face made a bad combination.

Nolan snapped, "Right straight up! You lousy pup. Keep 'em good and high.—Orcutt, you'd better fix your necktie, you'll be having more visitors pretty soon, and this time they'll be official. They're curious why someone wants to see you so bad he steals memo pads and forges signatures.

—Come on, you. Walk out slow. There'll be a limousine here for you in a few minutes. So you thought it would be a good idea for me to phone, did you? You're cute. You thought I really ought to phone. You . . ."

He had intended to say, "You ornery bastard," but he became aware, without glancing aside, that a nurse was watching with open mouth from down the hall, and that it was she from Room Fourteen. So he said instead:

"You cute little cameo." It sounded so silly that he blushed as he heard it coming out, and he wondered where the hell he had ever picked up an expression like that.


# 9


A woman and ten men ate fried chicken and hot biscuits at the White House at half-past seven Thursday evening. Many matters had been considered by the Cabinet during the afternoon, but others which they had expected to decide had been perforce postponed on account of the time consumed in a heated and prolonged discussion of the status of Harry Brownell. That had finally been brought to a conclusion by Mrs. Stanley, by her announcement that she would withdraw unless Brownell was readmitted to membership in the Council without prejudice. There had been further telephonic communication with Oliver at the War Office and Davis at the Department of Justice, and Brownell had kept his seat. Not by unanimous consent: Theodore Schick, Secretary of Commerce, who had been present in the morning, had gone off no one knew where; Vice-President Molleson could not be found; and Lewis Wardell refused to budge, even after the appeal and ultimatum of the wife of the President. But he acknowledged grudgingly the right of the majority to decide, and Brownell stayed.

An additional reason for the failure of the Cabinet properly and promptly to fulfill its functions during the afternoon had been the occurrence of the famous affair of the *Cranmer*, with its four hours of feverish excitement and its subsequent bitter and faintly ludicrous disappointment. The *Richard Cranmer* was a British freight-boat which had been at a Brooklyn dock for some days, taking on cargo. At noon Thursday she had steamed out of the harbor, bound across the Atlantic for Liverpool. At one o'clock two United States warships, cruisers, hurriedly got up steam and started out after her; and though no public announcement was made either of the fact or the reason for it, it was soon whispered, and then screamed from the headlines of the papers in extra editions, that three dockworkers had definitely and unmistakably seen the President of the United States on board the *Richard Cranmer*, being carried on a stretcher along one of the lower decks toward an officer's cabin.

Of all the ten thousand rumors that the President had been found, during those three days, this one aroused the most hope, furnished the bitterest disappointment, and made the most trouble. A wireless to the freighter requesting her to turn around and head back for the port got from her the reply that she was sorry, but her cargo was urgently needed in England, she had properly and legally cleared the port, and she would continue on. A second wireless peremptorily ordering her back got a similar reply, more regretfully but equally firm. By that time the cruisers had a head of steam on, and they weighed anchor and took after her.

At noon that day the American people had been unquestionably and overwhelmingly anti-war. No argument against war, good or bad, had persuaded them; the wave had rolled in under the crest of a typical collective syllogism: a war-gang had kidnapped the President; those who had kidnapped the President ought to be shot; therefore, they would shoot no one except those who wanted them to begin shooting somebody else. But four hours later it was quite different. Ten million radios were turned on, none lacking an audience, while fields waited for the plow and the remains of luncheon ham and eggs dried on the dishes. The dirty treacherous English had their President out on the ocean, carrying him around on a stretcher; he was sick, he was hurt, he was badly wounded, he was dead. But the cruisers would get him, blow the English boat to the bottom of the sea, and bring him back; and then . . . If a diminutive fraction of the threats uttered that day against the English had been fulfilled, the skeleton in Napoleon Bonaparte's tomb would have grinned in ghoulish glee.

A little after four o'clock word was flashed throughout the nation that the *Richard Cranmer* had been overtaken, stopped, boarded, and searched. The stretcher had been found on which, according to the captain of the freighter, a mate with a busted knee-cap had been carried to his bunk; but no President. The American people found themselves in the silly and uncomfortable position of aiming a cannon loaded to the muzzle with vindictive rage, and the target suddenly removed. Some shrugged their shoulders and ate their dinner; some got drunk; most stuck by the cannon and began looking around for the war-gang.

The members of the Cabinet had credited the tale of the three dockworkers barely sufficiently to instruct the Secretary of the Navy to send out the cruisers; they had not really believed that the President would be found on the freighter, but the chance of it and the waiting for it disrupted their proceedings, already hindered by the Brownell wrangle. They had to consider the reply to the Japanese representations regarding an alleged Russian base in the Philippines; the reported decision of the Congress leaders to adjourn *sine die;* the continuance of the contraband list for American ships leaving home ports; various similarly vexing questions; and the total failure of the efforts to find the President or even a clue of any promise. It was none of these, however, not even the last, that caused their most anxious concern. Vice-President Molleson had not appeared at the White House since Wednesday morning. Wednesday night two detectives, assigned to the task by Wardell, had picked up his trail as he was leaving the home of Hartley Grinnell, but it had been lost again towards noon of Thursday, when Molleson had entered the Senate Office Building and not come out again. What with the tunnel to the Capitol, and the various entrances to the two buildings, it was simple for him to escape surveillance there if he was aware of it and had reason to circumvent it.

The Cabinet knew nothing of the gathering in Suite Eight D at the Pilgrim, but they were aware of the desperate determination and the resourcefulness of the opposition; and they knew that Voorman was lost, Daniel Cullen and Caleb Reiner were lost, and the Pierces had come down from New York and gone from the Union Depot no one knew where. A little after six o'clock fresh and doubly disquieting information came over the telephone from the Secretary of War. Oliver reported that he had had occasion to get in touch with Major General Kittering and had been unable to locate him. On account of Kittering's notorious devotion to duty, that had seemed strange; so strange that upon reflection Oliver had entertained an incredible and disturbing suspicion. He had instituted a systematic effort to reach every officer of high rank in the vicinity of Washington. They had all been found, more or less where they should have been, except four; Major Generals Kittering, Hedges, and Jones, and Brigadier General Ridley. The fact that it was this particular four, Oliver said, from various considerations which he need not detail, made the suspicion somewhat less incredible and vastly more disturbing.

Billings, who had been on the phone, gave the information to the Cabinet. After a brief discussion they called up Oliver and asked him to leave Major General Cunningham in his office and come at once to the White House. Mrs. Stanley went to arrange with the cook for the fried chicken and hot biscuits, that none might leave. Brownell sent to the Executive Offices for new developments on the day's problems. Lewis Wardell phoned Chief Skinner that he might not return before midnight and that Skinner should continue with full authority. Oliver arrived, and soon after was followed by Attorney-General Davis, who had spent the afternoon at his own office on matters that would not wait. They discussed the generals. Oliver informed them that he had instructed Cunningham to establish contact immediately with all officers in the neighborhood from the rank of captain up, and report results to the White House.

At half-past seven Theodore Schick came in. He closed the library door behind him; his polished heels clicked on the parquet and then were muffled on the thick rug. They looked at him in surprise. Wardell, with nothing much left in him but nerves, blurted:

"Schick. Do we want Schick here?"

Schick bowed and smiled. "As you please, madam and gentlemen. I will go, of course, if you prefer. But do not regard me as an enemy; I haven't the temperament for it."

Liggett said, "What do you want?"

Schick was smiling. "Well. This is a Cabinet meeting."

"It has been, all day."

"True. But you haven't needed me, and I can't go even half a day, in a time of stress, without highballs."

Davis waved an impatient hand at a vacant chair. "Sit down, Theodore. I know you. We need a jester anyhow."

But before Schick could start for the seat Mrs. Stanley interposed by herself rising. Schick jumped to pull her chair back for her. She twisted to nod him thanks, but it was perfunctory far beyond the wont of her liveliness, though her tired and worried face did manage the hint of a smile. She said, "It is time to eat, gentlemen.—I know what brought you, Mr. Schick, in spite of the absence of highballs; you smelled my fried chicken. Wherever you may have been."

Schick bowed. "To look for discernment, Mrs. Stanley, is to find you. May I?"

She took his arm. The others were up, and followed.

At the meal, by agreement, they discussed and decided domestic and foreign matters of lesser weight which had been neglected in the afternoon. Wardell chafed; if the word might be used with regard to a Cabinet officer approaching a breakdown through the failure of his efforts at direction in a major national crisis, it could be said that he was petulant. He snapped at Brownell, was rude to Mrs. Stanley, and insulted all of them. The others were not much better. Mrs. Stanley, who loved a well-eaten meal, was resigned to no hope for this one and hurried it up. She said to Schick, "We talk and eat and move in a nightmare. It's horrible."

At half-past eight they were back in the library. They completed consideration of the contraband list and agreed that it should be extended by Liggett at his own discretion. At a quarter to nine a report came from Major General Cunningham. Many officers had not yet been found, but that was to be expected. Some absences, however, were being looked into, especially that of Colonel Graham, aide to Major General Hedges, who had received a note by messenger at his home and had immediately left without informing his wife of his destination. Oliver said, "I know Graham. He's a good officer, but he belongs to Hedges."

The door of the library opened, and a footman entered. He crossed to the large table where they were seated, and stood hesitating. They looked at him. Before Mrs. Stanley could speak, Wardell snapped:

"Well, what is it?"

The servant seemed relieved to know whom to look at. "The Vice-President, sir. He's outside."

There were glances. Wardell said, "Well, I suppose he's still Vice-President. Why doesn't he come in?"

"Yes, sir. He told me to say he was there."

"Ask him to come in."

The servant went. They looked around at each other.

Billings grunted to Liggett, "I thought the fat pig had his feet in another trough." Theodore Schick murmured to Mrs. Stanley, "If Achilles sulks in his tent, he should be aroused before an unworthy hand snatches his sword and shield." She, quick-witted, shot him a sharp and startled glance, then half closed her eyes and nodded vaguely. Schick smiled, not maliciously. They all looked at the door.

Molleson entered. He crossed over to them, to the table, and stood. No one said anything. His face looked flushed, his necktie was not straight, and the bottom button of his vest was undone. He stood straight, and blinked at them. Schick murmured to Mrs. Stanley, "The Vice-President has had more highballs than I have."

That was all Molleson needed, a little something to shoot at. He was, after all, an old campaigner, and had seen plenty of rough-and-tumble. He grunted, "Huh, Schick. I haven't seen you since yesterday at Grinnell's, when you were giving George Milton a tip."

Schick waved the insinuation away, but he lost a little color. He said, "Ouch. Don't count on a diversion from me, Molleson, I'd rather watch."

Billings spoke. "There's your chair, Bob."

"The hell it is." Molleson blinked at Mrs. Stanley, and said, "I beg your pardon." He looked at Brownell. "So you're here. More of Wardell's comedy." He took in the group. "If you think you are making history, boys, it's damned poor history." He inclined his head to Mrs. Stanley. "I beg your pardon."

They looked at him. Oliver said, "Sit down, Molleson. We want to ask you a few things."

They waited. Molleson hesitated, then went to the vacant chair, the only one left, pulled it back and got into it. He was directly across the table from Mrs. Stanley, with the Secretary of Labor on his right and Billings on his left. There was no chair at the end, where the President always sat; Mrs. Stanley had refused to occupy it. Davis was whispering something to Liggett and Liggett was nodding.

Oliver said, "Don't misunderstand us, Molleson. You were one of us. You left us. That's the fact. We are doing our best in an impossible situation. It will remain impossible until the President is found. You are making it harder for us. We resent that, and we demand an explanation of it."

Molleson said, "I didn't come here to make explanations."

Davis observed quietly, "You must have come for something."

Liggett spoke. "Whether you came for explanations or not, they'll come first if you don't mind."

"I came for something." Molleson put his hand to his mouth; his chest jerked in and out; he took his hand down. "I have nothing to explain. Except one thing perhaps. In this room on Tuesday afternoon the Secretary of Commerce suggested that in the absence of the President the leadership of the Administration was the natural and constitutional duty of the Vice-President. I declined it—no, I did not decline it; I failed to support the suggestion." Molleson threw his head up. "I was wrong, I was cowardly to evade the constitutional responsibility of my office. When a man permits himself to be *elected* to an office, he must hold himself ready for the burdens of its more unlikely contingencies as well as its routine demands. The responsibilities of an *elective* office are peculiarly and especially not to be evaded. You gentlemen of course have no reason to feel that, that sacred duty. Your first obligation is naturally to the President, to the man who appointed you. Mine is to the country, to the American people. I should have realized that and accepted the leadership when it was offered. I do realize it now. I am ready to accept it now."

He kept his head up, and looked around. Brownell: "It was never offered to you." Billings: "Did you think that up all alone, Bob?" Schick: "I believe I made the suggestion, but it was unanimously unsupported." Liggett: "Do you mean you want Wardell's job?" Davis: "We chose no leader; we delegated to Wardell the task of finding the President. I imagine it was thought that you would be engaged at the Capitol, and needed there, as one of us."

"I'm not asking for apologies." Molleson's face was redder; he pulled a handkerchief from his pocket and wiped his forehead.

Wardell snapped, "And you're not getting any. Come to the point. This is interfering with important business. What do you want?"

"It isn't a question of what I want." Molleson laid a fist on the table. "It is what the Constitution requires and the country expects."

"I have noticed," Theodore Schick offered, "that sooner or later everyone falls in love with the Constitution."

Wardell disregarded him: "And what does it require?"

"That the office of President of the United States be not

156

vacant. Consult the Attorney-General. Davis? Can there be any other interpretation?"

"Certainly not."

"Well?"

"It is irrelevant. The office is not vacant."

"No? We have a President? Where is he?"

There was a chorus of reproaches. Davis held up his hand. He was smooth and quiet. "Listen, Molleson. Don't try to start that argument. There's no sense in quibbling. We all know how it is. The Constitution says, *In case of the removal of the President from office, or of his death, resignation, or inability to discharge the powers and duties of the said office, the same shall devolve upon the Vice-President*. It all depends upon what is meant by *inability to discharge;* the question has arisen before. The Constitution does not define it and does not say who shall. In the present instance we, the Cabinet, the heads of the administrative departments, are defining it; certainly we have as good a right as anyone. We say the office of President is not vacant."

Molleson's fist, on the table, tightened. "I don't."

"What do you say?"

"I say that since Wednesday morning I have been, and I now am, President of the United States."

He glared around. Schick murmured, "Ah, we have it." Billings said: "But you see, Bob, you're outvoted."

"I recognize no right to vote. You can't vote down the Constitution. Would you attempt—"

Liggett broke in: "It wouldn't hurt to have a vote on record. Would it?" He looked around; there were nods. "If you don't mind, Mrs. Stanley, and Brownell, we'll confine it to the official members. The understanding is that this Cabinet agrees that the office of President is not vacant and that therefore the provision of the Constitution for succession is without relevance. Ayes, please?"

They were grunted and murmured.

"No's?"

Silence.

Davis said, "Come, Molleson, make it unanimous." Billings: "Forget it, Bob, it's no use. Be with us."

Molleson stood up, shoving his chair back so that it nearly toppled over. His face had gone suddenly pale, a startling change from its florid habit; he looked sick. "Gentlemen." His voice trembled; not for calculated effect as it so often had in his Senate fights before his elevation to the rostrum; this tremble was from a heart pumping desperately to supply the demand for courage. "Members of the Cabinet. I demand, immediately, occupancy of the Executive Office and custody of the Seal. I demand this in furtherance of the duties of my office and under the Constitution of the United States."

Billings shook his head. "Too bad, Bob. Too damn bad."

Davis said, "You're a fool, Molleson. You're next door to treason."

"Is it treason to adhere to the Constitution? Gentlemen, you have heard my demands. I advise you, I plead with you, do not plunge the country—"

He stopped. They all looked at him. Schick said softly, "Yes. Go on. Plunge the country—"

Molleson, with compressed lips, his face red again, shook his head. He backed off, into his chair, turned to shove it, and turned again. "My demands, gentlemen?"

Liggett said, "Don't be an ass."

"You refuse. Whatever happens, the fault is not mine. I tell you, it is a grave responsibility . . . the fault . . . whatever happens . . ." He was sputtering. He turned and started away.

Brownell had looked at Oliver, Oliver had nodded, and the two had left their chairs and passed around the group into the line of the door. Molleson, seeing them, swerved. Brownell caught at him. Oliver went to the door and stood with his back against it. The others, around the table, except Schick and Mrs. Stanley, were on their feet. Davis started toward the door.

Molleson jerked away from Brownell. "What's this?"

Oliver said, from the door, "You can see what it is. Do you think we're such fools as to let you out of here?"

Molleson glared. "I think I'm going out. Get away from the door."

Oliver and Davis were against it, side by side. Molleson started towards them. Davis said, "There's ten of us, Molleson. You might as well go back and sit down."

Brownell put in, "We don't want him in here. Unless you think he might tell us who's been interpreting the Constitution for him. I don't."

Schick's suggestion came from the table; he hadn't bothered to get up. "Lock him in the President's study. Put a bed in there for him. He can't kick on that."

Molleson's face had gone white again, and again his voice

158

trembled. "Davis... Brownell... you damn fools... has it occurred to you... what if Stanley's dead?... I'm President, you damn fools... this is treason...."

"Ease up, Molleson." Oliver walked to him. "You've heard of the fortunes of war. We're under martial law, and I'm the Secretary of War. You're under arrest, and you'll stay that way until President Stanley is back where he belongs. And if it should turn out, God forbid, that he's dead, you'll stay that way until you explain how the idea happened to be in your head at this curious moment."

Vice-President Molleson stared at him, not defiantly.

# 10

That night, Thursday night, at three hours after midnight, more than a score of army officers of various ranks were gathered in the office of the Secretary of War. All were in uniform. Some of them were busy around a table on which were arranged stacks of Manila filing folders; others were seated or stood around; one, a brigadier general, was in low-toned conversation with the Secretary at his desk. All faces were tense, and weary with distaste; they were engaged in a business fraught with a particularly nasty danger and offering no glory whatever by way of compensation. Major General Cunningham, in an armchair in the center of the room not far from the table, was fingering one of the Manila folders, glancing through its contents. Two orderlies stood at the door.

Cunningham spoke to an officer who had turned from the table to face him: "All right, send in this Captain Farrell."

The officer spoke to one of the orderlies, and the orderly turned and left the room. In a few moments he was back, preceded by a youngish man in mufti. The officer beckoned this latter over, and he came and stood before Cunningham and saluted. Cunningham looked him over, then spoke sharply:

"Captain Farrell. Colonel Arthur Hamlin visited you last evening around ten o'clock?"

The other was erect and stiff, holding himself together. "Yes, sir."

"He took you to the Chesapeake Club, to a room where other officers were present?"

"Yes, sir."

"Was Major General Kittering there?"

"Yes, sir."

"What was said?"

Captain Farrell tightened his lips, and breathed.

"Well? What was said?"

"I can't tell you, sir."

"Do you mean you didn't hear it? Were you deaf?"

"No, sir. I heard part of it. After about half an hour I left."

"Tell me what you heard."

The captain looked unhappy. His fingers, at his sides, were rubbing against each other. He pleaded: "I beg you, sir. I left as soon as I fully realized what was being suggested. I am not in any way culpable. I beg you, sir, do not compel me—"

"When you left, where did you go?"

"I returned to my quarters."

"Did you report the matter to Colonel Salmon of your regiment?"

"No, sir."

"You didn't. Having information of a mutinous plot, you did not report it to your superior, and you now wish to withhold it from me."

"No, sir." The captain went on hastily: "I mean, as I heard it, it was not a question of mutiny. It was a question of authority—"

"Nonsense. The definition of mutiny is not your affair, the Regulations attend to that. I can waste no more time with you. Your human obligations to your brother officers do not exist when they are in conflict with your plain duty. You know that. Will you tell me what you heard at that meeting? Yes or no."

The captain's shoulders sank a sixteenth of an inch. He pulled them up again. "Yes, sir."

Cunningham nodded. "Good." He turned and called, "Colonel Nash!" An officer hastened up. "Captain Farrell has a statement to make. Go across the hall with him and take it down. You may question him.—Captain, I want it complete."

"Yes, sir."

The two saluted, turned and went. An officer came from the table. Cunningham handed him the folder and took from him a fresh one, and flipped it open. He glanced at it.

"Captain James Foster. Who's this?"

160

The officer told him "Company Y, Hundred and Thirteenth. Up from Fort Corliss. At the Capitol. Colonel Blaine."

"Oh yes." Cunningham nodded. "Send him in."

Again an orderly was sent out, and returned, this time with a captain in uniform who was short, dark, and looked sleepy.

Cunningham said to him: "Colonel Blaine is under arrest. Colonel Atwood has your regiment."

"Yes, sir. So I understand."

"What have you been doing since six o'clock last evening?"

The captain grimaced; he had to keep his mouth shut against a yawn before he could answer. "I was on duty until nine o'clock. Then I turned in and went to sleep."

"What do you know of the affair Colonel Blaine was concerned in? I don't mean rumor; what do you know?"

"Nothing, sir. The man you sent for me woke me up. I didn't know Colonel Blaine had been relieved until after I entered this building."

Before the next question got out there was an interruption: Cunningham's name was called by the Secretary of War. The general grunted, "Wait here," got up and passed around the group of officers at the table. Oliver, with the brigadier general at his desk, waited to speak until Cunningham was close.

"About the guard for the White House. Barlett says that Hobbs is a good sensible officer, and reliable."

Cunningham nodded. "I have no doubt of it."

"Then do we leave him there?"

"We can. If you wish. You said there was a special reason for having the White House and the Executive Offices protected by men—which in this case means their officers—absolutely above question both in loyalty and in ability."

"There is. I repeat it, emphatically. The reason is—well—a Cabinet secret, but I assure you it exists."

"Is it up to me?"

"Yes."

"Good." Cunningham turned to the brigadier general. "Put Hobbs's regiment somewhere else, and send the Thirty-ninth, Colonel Wright, to the White House. Get Wright there before Hobbs leaves, I should say by seven o'clock." To the Secretary: "Is that all?"

"That's all."

Cunningham went back to his chair. The short dark captain was there waiting for him, and the general, unexpectedly

161

looking up as he sat down, got a good view of a hastily covered yawn. The captain blushed. Cunningham said, "I don't know how good an officer you are, but you're too damned sleepy to be an intriguer. Go back and go to bed."

He beckoned an officer from the table and handed out the folder. "Here, take this. What's the next one?"

# FRIDAY—CURTAIN

# 1

Around eight o'clock Friday morning it began to rain. That was as it should be; it was in the mood of things; it rained seriously and steadily on a stalemated capital, a stalemated Congress, a stalemated Cabinet, a stalemated coup d'état. The capital, like the country, was stalemated by confusion and exasperation: filled with wild and incredible rumors, impotent against an outrage of which the nature and the perpetrators remained undiscoverable, offering to explode at each false spark; balked again, retreating perforce to its murmuring of futile ferocity. The Congress was caught between two opposing and deadly threats, one from the men who owned the country and the other from those who did the voting in it; the only act it desired to perform, it did not dare to attempt; so it quit. The Cabinet was stalemated by its ridiculous and utter failure to solve the problem of the disappearance of the Chief Executive; it was even losing the anxious sympathy which had urged it on for two days and three nights; Friday morning the press and the people were howling with derision at what they had enthusiastically applauded the day before, the prompt and energetic dispatch of the cruisers to overhaul and search the *Richard Cranmer*. And the coup d'état was stalemated because, as its leaders discovered to their enraged dismay Thursday around midnight, the Vice-President had got lost or someone had stolen him. That was one of the very few poor guesses that D. L. Voorman ever made; Voorman guessed that Molleson had got too impossibly scared and had simply run off to hide. The enterprise might in any event have been frustrated by the prompt and energetic measures of Oliver and Cunningham, but the desertion of Molleson—poor Molleson did not deserve that from his old friend Voorman—made chaos of their arrangements and reduced Daniel Cullen to an imbecile fury.

It rained, steadily from low leaden skies, on a stalemated country.

## 2

During all the tense, vigilant, unforgettable hours of those three days and nights, Chick Moffat had only one piece of bad luck, and that didn't amount to much. He had known from the beginning that for this amazing enterprise he would need not only ingenuity, audacity, a quick wit and a cool head, but also plenty of luck. He admitted that he had had it; but at ten o'clock Friday morning, walking down a corridor of the White House, he thought it had deserted him when he saw the Chief of the Secret Service coming towards him, not twenty feet away. It was impossible to turn, to avoid an encounter. Chick went on, and without slowing down tried nodding a casual good morning.

Skinner stopped him. "What the hell are you doing here? I thought I tied you to Lincoln Lee's tail."

Chick nodded. "Sure. Sam Carr has him. We lost him once yesterday afternoon, but I picked him up again. I'm going home now for a phone call from Sam."

"Yeah. I suppose you came here to breakfast with the Cabinet. What's the idea?"

The quick wit had been trying, but could think of nothing better than the truth. "Mrs. Stanley sent for me. A personal errand. She's got the habit the three years I've been here."

"No doubt." The gray eyes disagreed with that. "I'd like to pay my respects to her. Wardell sent me over here to see the Cabinet. I suppose she's with them."

"She may be by now. I just left her."

"Yeah. We'll see. Come along."

Chick went, inwardly cursing his luck. Not that he had any misgivings as to Mrs. Stanley's wit; but it was at least undesirable, if not dangerous, that Skinner should know he had been at the White House for any purpose whatever; and if ever there should be no minute's delay it was now, the last and most difficult and perilous hour of all. He followed Skinner and cursed his back.

Upstairs, a Secret Service man stood outside the door of the library. Upon Skinner's instruction to ask Mrs. Stanley please to come out for a moment, he went in. After a short wait she appeared. She nodded to the Chief and looked at Chick with surprise, and stood sagging. She was pale, there were dark puffs under her eyes, and her wonted brightness was gone.

Skinner said, "Excuse me for bothering you, Mrs. Stanley. I ran into Moffat down in the hall, which surprised me because I thought he was on a job I gave him. He said something about an errand for you. I just wondered if it was important."

Chick, knowing how keen the Chief's eyes were when they seemed most casual, was busy looking indifferent. He couldn't blame Mrs. Stanley for hesitating an instant, but he hoped she would manage her voice. She did, extremely well; to his ear there was nothing in it but annoyance.

"Important? Not terribly, no. A private matter. If there was any reason . . . really, I'm sorry if I have interfered . . ."

"Not at all." Skinner was apologetic. "I just wondered what he was doing here. Considering everything, there was even a chance he was lying."

"Chick Moffat?" The ghost of her well-known smile flitted across Mrs. Stanley's face. "There are so many others it is so much easier to suspect."

The Chief nodded. "It's a good idea to have enough suspicion to go around, no matter who it is. But you must excuse me for bothering you. The Secretary of the Interior sent me here to the Cabinet. Do I go in now?"

"I'll see. If you'll just wait here." The man at the door opened it, and she went in.

Skinner said to Chick, "All right, get along."

"Yes, sir. I'll be back on Lee in less than an hour."

"Yeah. Beat it."

Downstairs in the anteroom, where he stopped for his hat and raincoat, Chick looked at his watch. It said a quarter past ten. Outside, it was raining harder than ever. Leaving the grounds and getting through the entrance, he was stopped four times by soldiers, the last time by one in the uniform of a captain, demanding to see his pass. He showed it to them— written on Executive Offices stationery and signed by Harry Brownell, Secretary to the President.

# 3

Fifteen minutes later, at half-past ten, Chick was driving his little black sedan through the rain down the dismal and doubtful street where six years previously he had found the apartment which suited him for a home whether its locality suited the ideas of his superiors or not. He rolled up to the curb in front of the entrance to that building, stopped, and got out. Pedestrians passed: a man and woman under an umbrella. Nearly a block off to the north a soldier stood huddled under his rubber cape; in the other direction, south, there was one much closer, a dozen yards or so. Chick let himself into the building with his key and ran up the flight of stairs to his apartment.

# 4

In another fifteen minutes, at a quarter to eleven, Chick came out again. From the sidewalk he looked right and left; he was keeping one eye shut and holding his head cocked at an angle as he squinted out of the other one. Keeping his eye shut was the prologue to the carefully considered program which he had just communicated to his collaborator, in minute detail, upstairs. As he paused a moment before the entrance his heart was pounding out a violent and rhythmic invocation to the lords of luck; there had to be luck now. Though his life, by the nature of his occupation, had known many moments of stress and two or three of deadly danger, this was the first time he had ever felt his heart beat; he noted it without wonder, for upstairs a man had just said to him, "I needn't remind you, Chick, that our slightest misstep will cut the thread of life for a million men." Chick had grinned with confidence: "Yes, sir."

Now, feeling his heart beat, he sent another glance right and left up and down the street, with his open eye, and turned with quick decision to the right. The rain had let up a little. He walked south down the sidewalk a dozen paces to where the soldier stood, and accosted him. The soldier greeted him as an acquaintance; in preparation for this contingency, Chick had made occasion for conversations with him the day before.

Chick said, "How are you on operations? I've got something in my eye and it feels like an oak tree."

The soldier said, "I'm not much good. Here, get under this awning. Got a handkerchief?"

Chick pulled one out. He had maneuvered to face north, which got the soldier's back where he wanted it. He could see the entrance he had just left, and the sidewalk for nearly a block; no one was passing. He let the soldier pry his left eye open, the lower lid down, then the upper lid up, and peer at it this way and that way, and dab at it with the twisted corner of the handkerchief. It was being done with more than ordinary clumsiness, but Chick didn't notice. He was using his right eye, and with it saw a figure emerge, to the sidewalk, from the entrance to the building of his apartment. It could be seen that it was a man, from the bottom twelve inches of his trouser legs, but the voluminous rain-cape and the hat with the brim turned down all around concealed all other details.

The soldier said, "Hell, I can't see anything."

"Try the upper lid again. It feels like it was up there."

The figure in the rain-cape had slowly and deliberately crossed the sidewalk and opened the rear door of Chick's sedan. Chick's right eye was straining to see. The figure was bending, was on the running-board, was inside. A hand came out and the door swung shut.

The soldier said, "There's a drug store down two blocks. You'd better go there. I'll blind you if I keep this up."

Chick blinked his eyes rapidly several times. He took the handkerchief and wiped the tears away from them. He could feel his heart thumping, plump, plump, plump, against his ribs. He said, "I believe you got it."

"Got hell. I've just made it numb so you can't feel with it."

"Anyway, much obliged. I'm in a hurry. If I feel it again I'll stop in a drug store."

The soldier nodded. "You'd better. Driving in the rain with one eye ain't so hot."

Chick thanked him again, held the handkerchief to his eye, went down the sidewalk without too much haste to the sedan, and got into the driver's seat. He did not look at the back. He started the engine, pulled the gear in, and rolled off.

At the first corner he turned right. Since eight o'clock the evening before, when the destination of that ride had first been definitely decided, he had over and over again considered each block and turn of the itinerary, and had finally determined on Eighth Street, Massachusetts Avenue, Tenth Street, and then Maryland Avenue to the garage. That gave him only two left turns, and at pretty good corners. He had figured that if he drove inconspicuously, not too slowly and certainly not too fast, it would take about twelve minutes, and it would seem like about twelve hundred years. As a matter of fact, it did not. His time-consciousness, instead of being elongated, ceased to operate at all. That drive was out of time. There was a remarkably keen vividness about all phenomena: cars approaching, cars passing, rain falling, pavements glistening, pedestrians crossing at corners, but in the forefront of his mind throughout was distributor points. A month previously, when out with Alma, the car had suddenly started bucking, stopping, starting, halting, and bucking again. A man at a garage had said it was the distributor points and had done something to them. Now, Chick thought, this whole thing, this whole cockeyed shebang, depends on a bunch of damned distributor points, and I don't even know what they are. He steered, swerved a little to the curb as a car whizzed by, sloshing over the wet pavement.

As he waited at a traffic light, the second and last one he would encounter, he glanced back at the tonneau. The back seat was empty; but huddled on the floor in front of it was a great long lump covered by the folds of the rain-cape.

Chick did not know whether the Maryland Avenue Garage was still under surveillance, but that did not much concern him, since in any event they would not be attempting to stop all entering cars. He had the collar of his raincoat turned up and the brim of his hat pulled down, and even if one in the Service who knew him was posted there, it was highly improbable that he would be recognized. What there was of risk in it could not be helped. As, down Maryland Avenue at last, he slowed up for the garage entrance, he kept his eyes working the corners, but saw no one that looked questionable. He swung in through the wide door. Two or three attendants and loiterers were there, but without halting he headed for the ramp. He went into second and roared up, around the swing on the second floor and up again, past the third and still up. On the top floor, he turned sharp right and rolled down the center lane toward the front of the building. He could see no one, as he passed by, except the floorman, who looked up, stopped rubbing at a fender on a car, and walked down the lane. Chick, at the far end, before he stopped and got out, turned his car around so that it was headed back the way he had come.

The floorman, approaching, said, "Hello."

Chick nodded. "Telephone company." He opened the front right door of the sedan and pulled out a little black box by its handle. "Where's that phone up here?" He was hoping that would work. It appeared that there was no one else on the floor, and the man did not look formidable, but it would be a trick to knock him out without a chance of an outcry.

The man asked, "What do you want to do with it?"

Chick was abrupt. "My boss told me to say that we have orders on that phone from the Department of Justice."

"Yeah." The man looked sour. "I suppose so. Come along."

He led the way. They squeezed between cars where there was little light, crossed a space, and the man fumbled at a door and opened it. Chick waited, hearing him shuffling inside in the dark, then an electric light went on. Chick entered.

"It's there on the table."

"Okay."

The man stood a moment, watching Chick open the box and take out a screwdriver, then turned and went out, leaving the door open. Chick looked at the telephone, the wires running along the ceiling, the connection-box fastened to the wall. Then he ran his eyes around the room, the cork-lined walls, the chairs, the table, the coat-hooks along one side. It was as he had pictured it, from a description given him by one of his friends who had participated in the Wednesday morning raid on the garage. He surveyed it, and nodded. He put the black box on the table, lifted out the tray of tools and looked inside; there were pieces of stout cord, neatly coiled, and a little bundle of white cloth. Chick put the tray back and tiptoed to the door of the room. There he stood to listen; there was no sound. He went out, crossed the space, found an alley between the cars, and went to the sedan and opened the rear door. He leaned inside and whispered:

"If you can hear me nod your head."

There was a movement beneath his eyes; he continued, "When I stop speaking begin to count. In ten seconds, go. Take it easy but don't waste any time. The light's on and the door's open."

He turned and started down the lane, briskly. The floorman was nowhere in sight; but when nearly to the ramp Chick spied him between a couple of cars, rubbing a fender, Chick went over to him:

"Has that phone got any connection with your garage phones, or just outside?"

The man didn't trouble to look up. "Can't you tell from the wires?"

"I'm asking you."

"Yeah. I heard you. So far as I know, it's just outside."

"Much obliged." Chick turned and went back down the lane; through the alley again, across the space, and into the cork-lined room. He was moving fast now, as he closed the door and wedged a chair against it with the top of the chair-back firm beneath the knob.

# 5

At twenty minutes past eleven Chick, in the sedan, rolled out of the garage and turned left. He went out Maryland Avenue at decent speed. At Tenth Street he turned right, and right again into Massachusetts Avenue. Two blocks down he stopped in front of a drug store and went in and entered a phone booth. He gave the operator a number, and he felt that his hand holding the receiver was trembling violently. He made no effort to stop it.

"Hello."

"Hello, is this the Maryland Avenue Garage?—This is the telephone man. Telephone man. I was just there for a phone on the top floor—get that, the cork-lined room on the top floor—and I forgot to turn the light off. Well, the man up there will explain. I thought you might want to turn the light off."

# 6

Ed Grier, manager and part owner of the Maryland Avenue
Garage, sat at his desk in the office, ground floor front, trying
to check over some repair sheets. Ordinarily he was fast and
accurate at that; today he was fussy and laborious. The fact
that he was there at all was a tribute to his toughness, for any
common man would have been in bed with the hundred
bruises, the aching bandaged back, the wrenched shoulder-
blade, the ribs that protested against every breath, which
were mementoes of the six hours he had spent Tuesday night
in a basement room of the Department of Justice building.
Added to these purely physical difficulties and to his worri-
ment over the calamitous loss of patronage the garage had
suffered through the publicity of the past two days, was a
slighter but more recent irritation. Five minutes ago someone had called on the phone to say that he had just been
upstairs to the cork-lined room to take the phone out, and
had left the light turned on. Grier had thought sarcastically,
damned polite of him, and had called on the inside house
phone to tell the floorman to attend to the light. Anything
that happened to remind him of the cork-lined room was
certainly irritating enough to impair his efficiency at checking
repair sheets. He moved to pull over another file of sheets,
and groaned.

Behind him, he heard the door of the office opening, and
footsteps. It took too much twisting to glance around; he
waited for the newcomer to announce himself. But the voice
made him twist:

"Grier."

Grier, incredulous, shoved his chair back and got around.
He rose to his feet, gaping. "My God . . . you . . . Good God."

The voice snapped, "Well, Grier?"

Grier said, "Union."

"Union." Lincoln Lee nodded. "Why shouldn't you? I
expected it. You're a man, Grier. I knew it."

Grier flushed with pleasure. In view of everything, that
was unbelievable, and it was a considerable tribute to the
force and fascination of Lincoln Lee. He flushed with pleas-

ure, and said, "I'm only one. There's plenty of us. But, Chief, you shouldn't be here. You mustn't. It's your own order: any risk that has meaning, none without. Bennett told me this morning you had gone north."

"I'm leaving in an hour. There's nothing I can do in Washington at present." Lee's eyes were clear and dominating; he stood straight and alert; he was freshly shaven; drops of rainwater gathered and fell from the brim of his felt hat; where his slicker flapped open it could be seen that he had not relinquished his gray shirt. He continued: "This city, which should be the greatest capital in the world, is now nothing but a stinking nuisance. Wardell's terriers are yapping at my heels; I will not waste my time eluding them. One of them has followed me here. Why not? I came to tell you I am going, that Bennett has the lists, and that Fallon is your captain as before. I was with Fallon yesterday—"

At the sound of the door opening behind him, and at the look on Grier's face, Lee stopped. He did not turn. He heard the shutting of the door, but no footsteps. Grier, looking beyond Lee, said sharply:

"Well?"

There was no answer. Grier spoke again:

"Well? What's the matter with you?"

Lee wheeled around. A man stood there with his back against the closed door, his face white, his lips working. Grier said:

"What the hell's the matter with you? Do you see the Leader? Well?"

But the man, the floorman from the top floor, was apparently in no condition to furnish the prescribed "Union." He did at length get out:

"Up in the room. Come up and see."

Grier was exasperated. "For God's sake, what is it now? What's the matter?"

The floorman did not reply. Instead, to the amazement of the two watching him, all at once he turned, flung the door open and dashed out, flew across the concrete and through the wide entrance, and started off down the sidewalk in the rain as if running for his life.

Lee raised his brows at Grier. Grier said, "That's funny. Joe's no coward, he must be crazy. I'll go up and see what it is."

"I'll come along."

"You'd better not lose the time. You'd better go."

"I'll come along. Through here?"

173

Grier led the way, outside the office and around to the corner where the stairs were. They had three flights to go, with turns, and dark and narrow. They winded up, Grier clumping and compressing his lips not to groan, Lincoln Lee light on the balls of his feet. At the top it brought them out at the edge of the open space behind the alley through the cars, not twenty feet from the door of the cork-lined room. The door was open and light was flooding out. Grier went in ahead, with Lee right behind him.

Grier stopped dead. There was silence. Grier stared at the man gagged and tied to the chair at the end of the table. Silence. Grier said:

"God bless me."

Lincoln Lee said nothing. Grier took a step toward the table, then stopped and turned square around with his back to it, facing Lee. He said:

"It's him. You see it's him?"

Lee nodded. Grier saw the tightening of the muscles of his face, the terrible concentration gathering in his eyes. Grier said:

"By God, it's him. Listen. We'd better turn off the light and go outside and shut the door and do some deciding." He started toward the table, to reach the light; Lee's voice stopped him:

"No. We can't leave here. Who's the man that ran away?"

"Joe Danners. He's one of us, but that don't mean anything now." Grier, again facing Lee, had himself become quite awful to look at, with his pumping blood swelling and empurpling his bruises. "Listen. If we only had time we might do something. We haven't. We've got to think fast and act fast. The guy that came to take the phone, he brought him. He called me up. Who else did he call up? God knows. They'll be here any minute. And Joe's run out on us. We're stuck, Chief. We can't move. We're stuck. Listen. There's only one thing we can do, phone Secret Service and tell them he's here, and we'd better do it damn quick. They'll try to hang it on us anyway, they'll say we got cold feet—Chief! No! Good God, no!"

No doubt Lincoln Lee's quicker and fiercer mind had darted through the situation a dozen times before Grier had finished with it once; and Grier's frantic exclamation of dismay was caused as much by the blazing lunatic fury he saw in Lee's eyes as by the slow precise deliberate action that was its culmination. Lee had raised his right hand and inserted it inside the slicker, inside his coat; it had come out again, still slowly and inexorably, grasping the butt of a blued steel automatic.

Grier yelled now, "Drop it!"

Lee was bringing the pistol up, carefully and deliberately, to its aim at the breast of the man in the chair.

Grier, getting what spring he could from his bruised and battered muscles, leaped for him.


# 7


Chick Moffat phoned nowhere but the Maryland Avenue Garage. At a couple of minutes after eleven-thirty he was back at his apartment. After parking his car in front he entered and ran upstairs, unlocked the door with his key, and went in, closing the door behind him.

Alma Cronin had jumped up from the red leather chair over near the desk and the telephone. She had been dreading to hear that telephone. She cried, not loud:

"Chick! Well?"

"He's there. Tied and gagged. The telephone is still connected. There was a cord binding the receiver down. I cut it loose and put the phone close to him, thinking he could at least knock the receiver off with his head for a contingency. I'd give my hope of happiness if I could call the phone company and tell them if there is a signal from that number to send the army."

"Chick, you shouldn't have taken him there. You shouldn't have left him. You shouldn't have let him persuade—"

"Shut up. You know what I mean, just shut up." Chick had taken off his hat and raincoat and put them on a chair; he went across to Alma and stood in front of her. "Listen, Alma. At this exact moment, and in view of what I've been through the past three days, including socking you in the jaw, I'm in no mood to deal with criticism like a gentleman. I'm not a gentleman anyway. I argued against taking him there. You heard me. I suggested a dozen other possibilities, some of which might have worked, and you heard him turn them down. Finally I gave in to him, for two reasons: because he

175

was being a good sport and deserved a little coöperation, and because his plan was the best and soundest of the lot."

"And the most dangerous."

"Sure. Has Sam Carr telephoned?"

"No. I've been praying the phone wouldn't ring, for fear it might be you . . . an accident or something . . . discovered . . ."

"Not this trip. And, Alma—" Chick grinned at her, but it could have been a better one. "It's not as dangerous as it sounds. That man Grier is essentially what he thinks he is, a good citizen. He's just got confused about things. The floor-man will go in to turn out the light, and he'll run down and tell Grier, and Grier will run up and take a look, and his first move will be to phone the Department. You'll see. It'll all be over thirty minutes from now."

"Then what are you sweating about?"

Chick put his fingers to his forehead and felt the moisture. "That's not sweat, it's rain."

"It doesn't look like it to me." Alma glanced around, saw her handkerchief on the desk, got it and returned to Chick. "May I?"

"I don't see why not."

She reached up and passed the handkerchief across his forehead, back and forth, and over his eyes. He said, "It smells good." He tried grinning at her again, gave it up, jerked away and went to the window and looked out: gray streaks of rain, a deserted street, his sedan right below. He looked at his watch: it was eleven-thirty-eight. He turned and started back towards Alma. "God, it was all right as long as I was doing something—"

He jumped as if shot. The telephone was ringing. He leaped to it and grabbed the receiver.

It was only Sam Carr.

"Chick? I've still got him. Hope I didn't wake you up. He's on to me again, but he don't seem to mind. I thought what the hell and got on the same street car."

"Why not?" Chick tried to bring himself, and his voice, to the subject. "Play backgammon with him if you want to. Listen Sam, will you do something for me? How about hanging on for another hour and phone me again? Would you mind?"

"Sure. Anything you say. I don't ever run down. You can eat first, huh? I'll wait till you take him over. I'm sitting pretty here now, in a cigar store right across the street from

176

the garage entrance where he went in. Unless he decides to cache himself in a truck coming out—"

"What! What garage?"

"Maryland Avenue."

"Good—" Chick caught himself, steadied himself. "I see. He's got a nerve. How long ago did he get there?"

"Just now, a couple of minutes ago."

"He did. I don't like that. I'm coming. Get on the sidewalk in front and keep your eyes open."

"What's the idea, there's no rush—"

But Chick had banged the receiver down and was headed for the door. Alma started after him.

"Chick! What is it?"

"Of all the dirty rotten luck—Lincoln Lee at the garage—"

He was gone. She stared at the open door and Chick's hat and raincoat on the chair. When she spoke there was a sob in her voice for the first time in years, since she had become a real intellectual: "Dear God... don't let anything happen..."

# 8

This time, on the same itinerary, Chick made no concessions to minor contingencies. At crossings pedestrians scooted, calling curses; no cars sloshed past; the little sedan circled around stopped street cars without halting, oblivious to maledictions. At Tenth and Massachusetts a policeman yelled; Chick did not hear him. At the acute left turn into Maryland Avenue he skidded, touched the curb, got traction again, and went on. Only three more blocks.

As Chick stopped and got out he saw Sam Carr standing in the wide entrance talking to a man in overalls. Chick walked over, making himself not run. Sam greeted him:

"Good lord, has that bus got wings on it?"

Chick grinned. "Is he still here?"

Sam Carr nodded. "A crazy man busted out of the office a minute ago and hotfooted it down the street, but it wasn't Lee. Lee left the office with another guy and I guess he went upstairs. Anyway he hasn't come out. No cars have left. This gentleman says he doesn't know Lee by sight."

"Yeah." Chick looked at the man in overalls. "Where's the stairs?"

The man jerked a thumb. "Over yonder."

Sam Carr asked, "What's all the uproar? Who stole your hat? I'm hanging onto him. You might as well have had another plate of caviar."

"I don't like it. I don't like his coming here. I'm going upstairs. You wait here. Don't let any cars out. Don't let anyone leave."

"All right, if you've got all that curiosity—"

Chick was gone. Inside, to the right as the man had indicated, and to the corner where he found the stairs. As he went up, fast and faster, two steps at a time, he left urgency to his muscles and listened to his brain: *This brings me into it, damn it, but surely by a good trail. God, I hope I'm seeing this right, I hope I'm not blowing the whole thing up.* The last flight; he took it on the bound. At the top he did not need to halt for a glance to get his bearings; there was the light streaming from the open door; and there was a yell from someone inside, "Drop it!" At the yell Chick leaped for the door, and as he did so whipped his pistol from his pocket. From the threshold he saw Lincoln Lee's arm out horizontal, steady, and Grier starting to jump him, late. There was no time for the nicety of popping a wrist or a shoulder. With the muzzle pointed at the middle of Lincoln Lee's back, Chick pulled the trigger twice.

Lee sagged, went down, and was still. There had been no report from his automatic; it dropped from his hand and clattered on the floor. Grier staggered back, bumped into the table and hung there with his rump on its edge. Chick, advancing, said, "Stick 'em up," but Grier didn't move. Chick reached him and felt over his chest, his belt, his hips, and said, "Just hold that. Don't move."

With his left hand Chick pulled the telephone over and took off the receiver; he was thinking grimly, *By God, we'll just end this little comedy right now.* He gave the operator a number; and in the moment of waiting, seeing that there was nothing to fear from Grier, he performed the only act of pure bravado that he was ever guilty of. He looked at the man gagged and tied in the chair not five feet away, and stuck his tongue out at him.

"Hello."

"Hello, Secret Service? This is Moffat. Yeah. I've got a

message for Secretary Wardell.—All right, then Chief Skinner.—Sure, I know that, didn't I say I have a message? Tell him to send a car and a couple of men to the Maryland Avenue Garage, top floor. I've found the President here. —I'm talking English.—Yeah, the President of the United States of America."

# 9

Chief Skinner sat at his desk in his private office in the Bureau of Secret Service. It was six o'clock Friday afternoon. A bottle of bourbon, nearly empty, and a whiskey glass were handy at his elbow on the desk. The whites surrounding the doubting gray irises of his eyes were bloodshot, his hair was a good deal of a mess, and he needed a shave. It had stopped raining around two o'clock, and a shift in the wind had herded the clouds across Maryland and Delaware into the ocean; now the late afternoon sun was shining, slanting in through the windows onto the desk, the bourbon and the glass, and passing there into the face of Chick Moffat who sat in a chair facing the Chief.

Chick was saying, "All right, but I'd like to go home and wash up. I have a date for dinner, and I want to be back home again by nine o'clock, in time for the radio."

Skinner blinked at him. "Then how about tomorrow morning? I'm drunk now anyway."

Chick grinned. "I'll be on duty at the White House. I've got to guard the President."

"Yeah. I see. Look here, Moffat. You may be a hero, but I'm going to have a little conversation with you anyhow."

"I thought we'd already had one. And I've written my report."

The Chief nodded, but the nod was interrupted by an idea occurring to him. He turned to the desk and picked up the bottle of bourbon, filled the glass and upped it and swallowed it. He cleared his throat, twice, slid back into his chair, and regarded Chick more doubtfully than ever.

"Moffat. I'm too old and too drunk to take any fooling. I hate to be fooled even when I'm sober. Here's the situation; let us recap—let's go over it. Two hours ago Secretary

179

Wardell called me to the White House and took me to see the President, who was lying on a couch in his study drinking tea. The President tells me that he doesn't wish to show any vindictiveness, and he doesn't want me to. Vindictiveness is out. If I find that floorman from the top floor of the garage, I'm just to straighten his necktie and give him a bag of candy. Grier is not to be prosecuted, he's to be thanked for being so anxious to save the President's life. And so on and so on. The only thing he didn't tell me was to bury Lincoln Lee at Arlington and put a marble slab over him. The Unknown Kidnapper."

"That would be nice."

The Chief cleared his throat and blinked. "Sure it would. The idea is that tolerance is the best weapon with disaffected minorities. That's what he said, unless they commit an overt act. He doesn't want to consider the kidnapping an overt act, since he got back safe and sound. He said that in spite of my great ability it would probably be impossible—what'd you say?"

"Nothing, sir."

"No. I mean yeah. He said that in spite of my great ability it would probably be impossible to fasten the guilt where it really belongs. He said that he would inform the Cabinet of the details of the affair so far as he knows them, but that for the Secret Service to attempt an investigation of the few clues he could furnish would only lead to this and that. In short, Moffat, let's see if you can take this without choking: President Stanley does not intend to tell me a single solitary teeny-weeny thing about how he was kidnapped. He will inform the Cabinet of the details of the affair so far as he knows them! He will inform Secretary Brownell, and Brownell will cook up a nice little dish for the newspapers."

Chick said, "I've got that down all right."

"Sure you have." The Chief turned to the desk, poured another glass of bourbon, and drank it. He cleared his throat and turned back to Chick; frowned, moved his brows up and down a couple of times, and frowned again. "I'm getting drunk only because I desire to let you know that nobody is going to make a fool of me."

"I already know that, Chief. I'd like to go home and wash up."

"You may. In a moment. Moffat, you're a low double-faced

blackguard. You're a slippery atrocious liar. You're a treacherous unprincipled viper."

"Yes, sir."

"You know you are. I've asked Sam Carr a couple of questions. This morning you drove through traffic over two miles in four minutes to get to the Maryland Avenue Garage. You had a White House pass signed Thursday by Secretary Brownell, who bought chloroform Monday night. In working on this case I've run across eight or nine things that I couldn't account for unless I wanted to suppose that instead of being kidnapped by violence the President had just decided that he needed a holiday. Well, in that case who did he visit? Now try making a fool of me."

Chick did not appear amused. He looked at the bottle of bourbon and back at Skinner. He finally said, "Look here, Chief. Let's say you're sick. Just for the sake of argument, let's say you're pretty damn sick. How many other people do you think have got the same disease?"

Skinner nodded approvingly. "That's more like it, Moffat. As long as we understand each other. Nobody."

"You're sure of that?"

"I am. Good and sure."

"Wardell?"

"Hell, no. He's so mixed up he still suspects the Japs."

"How drunk are you?"

"Don't worry about me. I'm just as drunk as I want to be. I'm going home and eat five beefsteaks and sleep five days and nights."

"Aren't you going to hear the President on the radio?"

"I can read it in the morning.—Good night, Moffat. Of course I could have just kept my mouth shut, but I'm not a national hero like you, I'm just a detective."

# 10

The clock said eight-fifty, the one on the mantel of the living-room of the Delling home, which was just across a vacant lot from the drugstore, but the correct time was two minutes till nine. Viola Delling knew that, she knew her clock was eight minutes slow, so she had the radio already on.

*...are listening to a program sponsored by the Olympus Chemical Corporation, makers of Nightcharm, the fruit laxative with candy in it, loved by children and good for father and moth ...*

"I hope no one is late." Viola Delling was offering a plate of cookies around the group; the colored girl was refilling glasses with grape juice. "I hope there are no interruptions; this is an historic occasion, whatever we may think—I mean, it is a moment crucial to our great nation, particularly to me, since I may say that it was permitted to me to glance behind the curtain screening the great events..."

Harriet Green snickered. "You mean you got arrested."

Viola Delling smiled at her complacently, but it was noticed that the plate of cookies got tipped at such an angle that two or three of them slid off to the floor. "I was detained as an important witness."

"Sure. That's why detectives came around to all of us asking funny questions about you."

*...this is the Federal Broadcasting System. We wish to thank the Piedmont Tobacco Company, makers of Buckingham cigarettes, for relinquishing their radio time at this hour in order to permit us ...*

Mrs. Orcutt, plump and beaming, had stuffed the rest of her cookie in her mouth in order to pinch Harriet Green's arm. "Hold your tongue, Harriet. Of course she was arrested, but aren't you a guest in her home drinking her grape juice? My boy, Val, wasn't arrested at all. They just kept him in the hospital until this afternoon on account of his head. He's gone down..."

*...will talk to you from his study in the White House in Washington, and in a moment now you will hear him ...*

"S-s-s-sh." "Here he is." "Be quiet." The admonitions were chiefly directed at Mrs. Orcutt, who nodded complacently and reached for another cookie. Viola Delling put the plate down, breathed, "An historic occasion," and sat.

*Citizens of the United States, my friends.*

The voice was conversational, pleasant, unforced. Marion Vawter coughed and everyone glared at her.

*I hope you will not think that I take advantage too frequently of the opportunity which this modern invention, the radio, offers for talking to you. I know that you all have your own personal affairs and problems pressing upon you, and that I am one among many public servants whom you hire to*

*manage the routine and direct the policies of your govern-
ment. As the executive head of that government, I try constantly
not only to exert my own powers and abilities in what I
conceive to be its best interests, but also to lead it in the
direction of your own conceptions of right and justice. So
long as you know pretty well what I am trying to do, and I
know pretty well what you think of it, it will work all right
that way; but it sometimes happens that complications develop which fill me with an uneasy conviction that we no longer
perfectly understand each other, and I need to make sure that
my intentions and purposes are clear in your minds, so that
you may in turn inform me and others of your public servants
of your opinions in the matter. The radio offers the simplest
and quickest means to that end.*

*I wish to talk to you this evening about war. Most of the
great nations, of Europe and Asia, who are linked with us
and our sister countries in this hemisphere in the complexities
of what we call modern civilization, have been engaged for
more than a year in a fierce and cruel and deadly conflict.
Even if it were proper for me to do so, I could not comment
intelligently on the problems of right and wrong, the questions of aggression and defense, which the conflict has raised:
or, if I might manage a sensible comment, I certainly could
not furnish an intelligent decision. I cannot answer the
query, who started the war and who is responsible for it? It is
sure only that they are fighting.*

There was a crash, and a gasp of dismay. Mrs. Orcutt,
nodding, had dropped her glass half full of grape juice. She
exclaimed, "Oh, I *beg* your pardon. I . . ."

"S-s-s-s-s-sh." She subsided, muttering.

*That is the fact. They are fighting, and the vibrations from
that gigantic collision are shaking the world—our world too,
for part of it is ours. We are part of the structure, political
and economic, to which the impulse has been applied, and
inevitably we feel it. Wherever on the surface of the earth
cannon shots are fired and bombs are dropped from air-
planes, something owned by an American citizen will be
destroyed; wherever a ship is sunk American property will be
engulfed; wherever a government crumbles and falls American investments are endangered.*

Senator Corcoran cried, "By God, he's gone war!"

Senator Reid, host in that enormous and ornate living-room, puffed his cigar and said nothing. Bronson Tilney, not too old either for truth or for beauty, was passing the tips of his fingers absent-mindedly back and forth across the pretty wrist of Mrs. Wilcox, who had her forearm on the arm of his chair. Others were around, all seated, all post-prandial, all looking uncomfortably here or there or nowhere because it was too impossibly silly to sit and look at the radio, even the Louis Seize cabinet of Senator and Mrs. Reid.

Senator Sterling said to Corcoran, "Grab a straw, Jim, and take it down with you."

*What is worse, my friends, American citizens will be killed. Not many, but one is too many. More than eight hundred of them have been killed since the beginning of the war. Of these, some seven hundred had crossed the ocean and volunteered for the conflict on one side or the other; they were combatants; the others, chiefly passengers on ships, have been the victims of submarines or aerial bombs.*

*American citizens have lent colossal sums to belligerent nations and will probably lose their money if their debtors lose the war. As for our liberty of movement, there are citizens old enough to vote who have never even heard the ancient phrase, freedom of the seas; and we enjoy freedom of the air only because we have so much of it all to ourselves, immune by distance from the dangers of their deadly incursions. Our relatives and friends abroad are in peril of their lives, and we cannot communicate with them or they with us; our foreign trade is utterly destroyed, for those who would buy are prohibited from doing so by the blockades of their enemies; the conveniences and ornaments we have been accustomed to receive from overseas are forbidden to us by the arbitrary mandates of foreign and unfriendly powers.*

*For some months a New York newspaper has been carrying on its front page a box with the prominent headline, Let's Look at the Record, and filling it with the details of the injustices, restraints, and affronts which I have just summa-*

184

*rized for you in general terms. That is the record, I know it. I daresay that I am as painfully familiar with it as the editor or the owner of the New York paper, or anyone else. The paper cites the record, and says, over and over again, we must declare war. Many other papers and organs of opinion say we must declare war. Many thousands of citizens, and among them eminent leaders, say we must declare war. As for myself, I have on various occasions made my attitude apparent, but it is evident that I must now state my position unequivocally and with no possibility of a misunderstanding. I say, my friends, that we must not declare war.*

Senator Sterling jumped to his feet. "Ha! What about his liver now, Jim? What about your own?"

Corcoran didn't even glance at him. Bronson Tilney, in the armchair, stroked Susan Wilcox's wrist.

# 12

Martin Drew grunted, "Here's where he starts his swansong."

He was in the most comfortable chair in the Grinnell library, with his leg resting outstretched on a cushioned stool and a pair of crutches handy on the floor. Old white George Milton was lying on the sofa, Voorman stood over by a window, and Daniel Cullen and Caleb Reiner were in chairs. The radio could not be seen; Mrs. Hartley Grinnell, George Milton's daughter, had had it concealed behind a grille in the bookshelves.

At Martin Drew's observation Voorman shook his head, turned to knock ashes from his cigarette into a tray, and turned back to the window.

*That is my position: we must not declare war. I would like to defend it, or assert it, in two ways. First, those who demand war, for various reasons and with various arguments, deserve answers. I would like to reply to them, but I shall make my replies very brief.*

*There are those who say that Japan started the war, that it is immoral to start war, and that she should be punished for it. I have already answered that. I am certain that twenty years from now historians will be quarreling about who started this war. I am not willing to enter upon a moral*

185

*crusade where even the facts are questionable, let alone the morality.*

*There are those who say that American citizens are being wantonly murdered. I reply, of course they are; and I hope that the hardness of my reply will not be taken to prove me devoid of compassion. The point is that in this respect compassion is all that is left to us. What if a peaceful citizen of a neutral country had gone strolling about Waterloo during the height of that famous battle? Would he probably have been killed? Yes. Would his government have protested against the outrage? Certainly not; he was on a battlefield during an engagement; the risk was his. But Waterloo was more than a hundred and twenty years ago. In the fourth decade of the twentieth century a battlefield is no longer a hill and a stretch of valley and a bend in a river; a battlefield is a continent, a hemisphere, the oceans, and the skies. When the nations of Europe are at war and an American citizen embarks on a ship to cross the ocean, he is venturing on a battlefield in precisely the same sense as the hypothetical stroller at Waterloo. The plain fact is that modern methods of warfare have stretched the confines of the field of battle to include the entire land and water surface of the earth, stopping only at the borders of neutral countries who may be depended upon to defend their neutrality; and however violently we may protest against this expansion of the domain of war, whatever we may do or say, we cannot alter that fact. We may fight, if we choose, to lick an enemy; but to fight in an attempt again to confine the hazards of war within the neat corral of a nineteenth century battlefield would be quixotic nonsense. American citizens have ventured upon a battlefield and been killed; I deplore it and I grieve with those who loved them. You all do, my friends.*

*There are those who say—some openly, some by indirection— that we must enter the war to protect our foreign trade, our investments in alien lands, and the vast sums that have been lent to certain belligerents. I believe that to some of you that position appears reasonable. To me it seems so insupportable that it is difficult for me to reply to it with patience and restraint. Would our entering the war have the effect desired? What about the last war we entered? On that occasion, too, we had lent enormous sums. We entered the war, and lent additional billions; and we and our allies won. Splendid; we had protected our loans and investments and foreign trade,*

*and it had only cost us a paltry three hundred and fifty
thousand American young men killed and wounded. Splendid! But, did we then collect our loans? Have we collected
them? Will we ever collect them? No. It was too bad, but it
didn't work that way. But that is not my real reply. It is, I
believe, a pretty good one, but to my mind there is still a
better one. Even if it were likely that our entering the war
would safeguard our foreign loans and investments, I would
still say, no! When a man, be he American or British or
Hottentot, lends or invests money in an alien country he
should know, and in fact does know, that one of his risks is
the chance that that country will become involved in war. It is
his risk; it is his gain if he gains; let it be his loss if he loses. I
tell you, my friends, I have done my very best to think clear
to the bottom of this; I have done so to my own satisfaction,
and I can only say that so long as I remain in the position of
the executive head of your government, not one American
boy carrying gun and bomb and the expectation of death will
be sent to foreign soil to leave his blood there as security for
your loans. No loan on earth deserves that sort of collateral.*

Martin Drew grunted as he shifted the position of his leg
on the stool, and muttered savagely, "The clever, clever
bastard." Daniel Cullen and Caleb Reiner, like a team of
comedians responding with humorous simultaneity to a cue,
chewed on their cigars. D. L. Voorman tossed the butt of his
cigarette through the open window, turned and stepped
silently across to the sofa where old white George Milton lay,
and stood looking down at him.

George Milton was snoring.

# 13

Chick Moffat said, "The old boy's going good. Do you realize
that you're sitting at the desk where he wrote that?"

Alma Cronin said, "Be quiet."

Chick went over to the radio and touched a knob to make it
a shade louder. Against the radio, at its angle with the wall, a
heavy walking stick was leaning. Chick grinned at it. He
would probably keep that as a souvenir. He couldn't very well

have taken it along to the Maryland Avenue Garage, and the President had plenty more anyway.

There are those who say our sovereignty has been challenged and we must assert it. That I flatly deny. Our territory and borders and possessions are undisturbed, and none of our truly sovereign rights have been violated. I have already spoken of the vast extension of the theater of war caused by modern methods of fighting. That is a fact which no victory we might gain could alter. For that reason some rights which were formerly thought sovereign to a nation no longer exist; but since they are not vital and could not in any event be recovered by any nation whatever, we shall, with no great privation I am sure, manage quite well without them.

There are those who say our national honor has been impugned. Well, conception of the demands of honor is a highly personal and highly variable quantity. For those who really and honestly feel that way and are not merely seeking the last refuge of a scoundrel, I feel in my heart a warm and sincere sympathy, but I do not feel as they do. I can only say that I do not feel myself dishonored, I do not feel my office dishonored, I do not feel my country dishonored. Do you? Honestly, do you? Has anything happened in connection with this war, has anyone done anything or have we done or failed to do anything, that would make you ashamed to look a German or an Englishman or a Russian or a Japanese in the face and say, "I am an American"? That is what a sense of national dishonor would mean. I can only say that I would not be ashamed, and I hope you would not.

I said that I would like to defend my position, or assert it, in two ways. I have finished with the first. Now for the second.

I am not what is popularly called—and frequently sneered at—a pacifist. I do not agree with them that violence never decides anything. If an insane man attacks me and I—or someone else—shoot him, that act of violence has certainly decided that I am not going to die—at least not on that occasion. If a choice is unescapable between my life and that of the insane man, or even for that matter a sane one, I shall not hesitate. Similarly, should any foreign power attack our true and vital rights, or our means of livelihood, or the land we live on, or our existence as a united people, I shall be proud that my position as Commander-in-Chief of our Army and Navy places me in control of the necessary violence to

188

repel, suppress, and annihilate. I believe that if the use of violence becomes unavoidable, it should be employed with vigor, dispatch, and ruthlessness. I am sure, my friends, that you will have nothing to complain of me on that score if the occasion should arise, which God forbid.

What I say is that the occasion has not arisen. Not yet. I hope and believe it will not, if the nations at war understand that we will not shed our blood to assert rights problematical at best and certainly not vital, to protect or salvage property unluckily caught in the path of their cyclone of jealousy and hatred, to defend our honor when we have no reason to feel it betrayed; and if they also understand that we are prepared to deal swiftly and surely with any assault on our lands, our livelihood, or our basic human and national rights. It is a sad commentary on the shortcomings of human intelligence that the contemplation of violence, and adequate preparation for it, should be necessary at all; but we shall have to leave that comment for our philosophic moments, and in our practical hours make sure that we are ready for violence, both in body and in spirit, if and when it becomes inevitable.

And to make equally sure of another thing: that we use it only when no other feasible and honorable course is left to us. Not at the behest of the selfish and rapacious among us, not through false pride and a too easily inflamed sense of injury, not through mere resentment at interference with some of the things we would like to keep on doing here and there over the surface of this amazing globe. After all, it is not all ours; we know where our country is, our beautiful and beloved country. We are not cramped in it, as some others are in theirs; there is plenty of room for us here, plenty of things to do, plenty to eat. We have, God knows, a job here at home difficult enough to engage all our intelligence and energy: so to arrange our affairs that plenty may be enjoyed by all of us. That is a job worthy of our genius and offering a reward beyond the limits of our hope.

That, my friends, is all I shall say to you about war. I trust and believe that you will agree with me. I would like, here at the end, to say a word of thanks to the thousands from whom I have received messages of sympathy and goodwill since my return to the White House this noon. I thank you with all my heart. There is no need for me to comment on the experience I have been through except to say that I am happy to be back

189

*again and I am glad I didn't get hurt. Thank you again for your many welcome messages.*

*...This is the Federal Broadcasting System. You have been listening to a talk, from the study in the White House in Washington, D. C., by...*

Chick walked over and turned it off. He picked up the walking stick and, twirling it, crossed to the desk where Alma was and sat on its edge. Alma, her fingers interlaced on her lap, was not looking at him. At length she sighed, and said:

"It was a great speech. It really was."

Chick grinned. "It ought to be. He wrote it on my desk."

"Don't you think it was great, Chick?"

"Yeah. I guess I do. I'm no judge of speeches. I never heard one yet that didn't sound like hooey."

"That one didn't."

"I admit that one didn't. It was all right. Anyway, it certainly did the job it was meant for, and that's all you can expect of a speech or a beefsteak or a poker hand or anything else."

"Chick, I believe you're pro-war."

"I'm not. Even if I had been I wouldn't be now. A war would be a tame show after these three days. In the space of three little days I've shot a billionaire in the leg, bound and gagged a President of the United States, and socked a beautiful woman in the jaw."

"And killed a man."

"Yeah. I couldn't help that."

"It's still swollen."

Chick bent over and looked carefully at her face, her cheeks and chin. He shook his head. "Not a sign of it. If anything, you're better looking than you were before."

"Thanks. How much do I owe you? If you lose your job at the White House you can start a beauty salon. Special unique treatment. Chick, will that speech keep us out of war?"

"Sure it will. I don't know how long, but for a few minutes anyhow. It all depends."

"Wouldn't it have had the same effect if he had said it to Congress on Tuesday? Or on the radio Monday night?"

"I don't know. I know he thought it wouldn't. He was sure the cards were stacked against him and he didn't stand a chance. So he shuffled the deck." Chick grinned. "It certainly was some shuffle. Another three days like that would kill me. The nicest little stomach-ache I got was hearing that Lincoln

Lee was in the garage. That was swell. That, and the wrist-watch. But the wristwatch was my own fault, I was a magnified fool ever to have it in my pocket."

"You couldn't help it. Mrs. Stanley made you."

"Of course I could have helped it. If she was fool enough to think her husband would lose his appetite because he had left his watch at home, that was no reason for me to give in to her. I should never have had it on me. I was responsible; it was up to me, and I should have told her nothing doing."

"Well, I'm glad you didn't."

"You're glad?" Chick raised his brows at her. "I thought you didn't approve of cave-man techniques."

"I don't. But if it hadn't been for the watch you wouldn't have had to bring me here where the President was, and I would never have known anything about it. You would never have told me, would you?"

"Sure I would. On our Golden Wedding Anniversary."

"Oh." Alma passed that. "Well, I'm not going to wait that long for you to tell me what really happened."

"You know what happened."

"I do not. What happened Tuesday morning. You might as well tell me, why not?"

Chick grinned. "I guess I'll make you coax me."

"I don't know how to coax. But if you don't tell me I'll ensnare you. You know; I'll set my cap for you."

"Oh my God. In that case—here's what happened Tuesday morning: I woke around ten and the butler drew the curtains and brought my tea—"

"Don't be smart, Chick. Please tell me."

"All right, then I'll make something up. Like this: at nine o'clock Tuesday morning Val Orcutt put the empty baskets in his truck at the White House. The President came up and they looked around to be sure no one was looking, and the President got in the back of the truck. As Val approached the entrance going out he slowed down and picked out a moment when the sentry had his head turned and then went through. That wasn't so important. He drove to a side street and stopped alongside my sedan where I had it parked. We had to wait to make the transfer, trying to make sure it wasn't noticed. The President got out of the truck and into the sedan, and I got in the truck. The President drove to this address and let himself into his apartment with my key.

"In the back of the truck I fixed up my face a little and put on an old cap, and took the driver's seat and drove over by the park. Val and I picked the right moment and got into the middle of a thick clump of bushes. I took this walking stick—you can see the place on it here—and cracked Val on the side of the head. I had to grit my teeth to do that, and you should have seen the look on his face when he knew I was going to hit him—of course it had all been arranged— that boy is a lad. He's a lad clear through. I left him there on the ground and again picked my moment to go back to the truck. I forgot to say that we had stopped at a cigar store and Val had phoned his boss that he had hurt his ankle and would put the truck up and wouldn't be back.

"I drove around some, out Southeast, looking for a good spot. Finally I found one, in front of an empty house on Fifteenth Street. I waited again for a clear coast, got out of the truck, went through the yard of the empty house to an alley and up that to another street, got on a street car and came here and ate sandwiches with the President. And do you know something? Would you believe it? I came within an ace of forgetting to wipe Val's fingerprints off the President's penknife which we left in the back of the truck. Wouldn't that have been just absolutely sweet?"

"What about your own fingerprints?"

"I had gloves. I wasn't leaving any of my spoor anywhere around that truck at all, thank you."

Alma looked at him. The admiration in her eyes was frank, tender, faintly possessive, and just a shade fearful. She said, finally, "And you knocked Val Orcutt down with that stick, in cold blood, deliberately. That was much worse than hitting me, you just hit me on the spur of the moment. Of course I understand you had to do something with him, but . . . B-r-r-r-rh! I don't see how you could do that. Why didn't you use choloroform on him?"

"I'm no anesthetist. With chloroform I might have killed him. Anyway, he needed the mark of a good wallop to show how honest he was."

"Who put the chloroformed handkerchief on the lawn?"

"Oh, Brownell did that when he went out to look for the President. He had it in his pocket all the time."

"Well." Alma sighed, looked at him, and let her eyes wander around the room. "It's too bad no one will ever know about this—this apartment. It deserves to be turned into a historical museum. It's a nice room, Chick. You've made it very attractive."

"Yeah. I kind of like it."

"I should think you would hate to think of giving it up."

"I do, a little. Not because it might be a historical museum. It will be one of my fond memories because it's the place where my wife and I lived together in secrecy and obscurity before we got married."

"Huh." Alma snickered. "I suppose that's blackmail. Anyhow, you'll have to agree that there wasn't anything obscure about our chaperon."

# 14

Around nine-thirty Saturday evening four people were walking down a hall on the second floor of the White House. They had met by appointment in a room down stairs. They passed an open door on the left, and a closed one on the right, and then came to a closed one on the left—the door of Mrs. Stanley's sittingroom. They stopped, and Harry Brownell knocked on the door. The voice of Mrs. Stanley came through to them: "Come in." They entered, and Chick Moffat, through last, shut the door.

Mrs. Stanley stood by a table, trying to make a rose hold its head up in a vase. In a chair nearby, at ease, doing nothing, sat the President. He looked tired and a little worn, but there was light in his eyes to greet the visitors, and a genial smile.

"Well." He smiled at each in turn. "Alma. Harry. Chick. Val. Come and shake hands with me."

They crossed to him. Mrs. Stanley joined them. She invited them to sit down. Brownell said he thought they shouldn't, that the President was badly in need of rest, but that was waved aside and Chick and Brownell pushed chairs up. Val Orcutt watched Chick and seeing that he got right back in his chair and made himself comfortable, did the same.

The President said, "How's your head, Val?"

Val put his hand to it. "It's all right. It's a little sore, but it's all right. I'm going back to work Monday."

"Good." The President looked around at them, and said again, "Alma. Chick. Harry. Val. Though I shall see you, and

193

you will see me, frequently, I think it was a happy idea for us to make this gesture and have this brief meeting." He smiled at his wife. "Thank you for it, Lillian,—I don't know whether to try to thank the rest of you or not. I've learned from experience that when I have unusually deep and warm feelings it is better for me not to try to put them into words, and certainly my feelings have never been deeper and warmer than they are to you four people now. So if you'll just take the thanks for granted..."

They nodded. Alma said, "You don't need to try to thank me, Mr. President, for I haven't done anything anyway. But since you've asked Val Orcutt how his head is, you might just inquire about my jaw."

Mrs. Stanley laughed. Chick grinned. The President smiled, and shook his head. "I'm sorry, Alma, but it's too obvious that it's perfectly all right. But it's false modesty for you to say you haven't done anything; I can shut my eyes and still taste your mushroom omelet.—But though I shan't try to thank you, I should like to offer each of you a gesture that will be a little more lasting than this little meeting. A memento, a favor for each of you... Mrs. Stanley and I have discussed this. She thought I should make each of you a little gift, but that is only because she loves to choose gifts for people. I outtalked her; I would rather you would choose your own. That is the last favor I shall ask of you—this week." He smiled. "Alma?"

Alma smiled back at him. "This is wonderful, Mr. President. I was hoping—anyway, it's wonderful. I have no father and no family. I want you to give me away at my wedding."

"Ah! Soon?"

"Well..." Alma blushed, and they laughed at her. She defied them: "Yes, indeed. As soon as possible."

"Good. That will be a great pleasure, and nothing shall interfere with it.—Harry?"

Brownell folded his arms and stared at the roses, thinking. Finally he said, "I can think of only one thing that would be adequate. I want permission to cut off Vice-President Molleson's nose."

"Ha! So do I, Harry. But it can't be done. Something else."

"Very well, sir. I need a wristwatch."

"You shall have it. Mrs. Stanley will select it for you. —And, by Jove, that reminds me." He turned to Chick. "My watch has stopped running again. Something must have broken when you dropped it."

"Yes, sir. I have no doubt."

"I hope it can be fixed. It was a gift." He smiled at his wife. "And now, Val, what will you permit me to do for you?"

Val Orcutt swallowed. He was not at all overawed; he had of course spoken to the President before; but this seemed to be different. And in fact it was different, as he proceeded to explain.

"You see, Mr. President, on my way here tonight I kept saying to myself that this was the chance of a lifetime. Of course I didn't know if you was going to ask us what we wanted, but there was no reason I shouldn't mention it anyway. You see, I had reason to know that what I had done was really worth something, or at least what I knew about. Because day before yesterday in the hospital a man came to me and offered to give me five hundred thousand dollars if I would tell him what I knew about you being kidnapped."

They stared at him. Brownell asked, "Who was it?" The President said, "Indeed, Val. That's a lot of money."

"Yes, sir. That's what I told him. Naturally I told him I didn't know anything."

"Naturally for you, Val. I made no mistake about you. It's too bad that every man and woman in the country won't have a chance to be proud of you for it."

"Yes, sir." Val nodded. "I don't know who he was, but he said the money would come from George Milton."

The President nodded, and looked thoughtful. Brownell observed, "I tell you, after George Milton has been ten years in his grave, he will still be just a little shrewder than anyone else.—Anyway, we here are proud of you, Val."

"Yes, sir. So that showed that what I knew was certainly worth something, and this was the chance of a lifetime, and I thought it over, and I decided that I would ask you for three things."

"All right, Val. If they are within my power."

"Oh, they are. There's no trouble about that. The first thing is that I would like to have a big photograph of you, and you write on it, *To my faithful subject, Valentine Orcutt*, and sign it."

There were no laughs, but the smiles could not be stopped in time. Mrs. Stanley and Alma bit theirs off; the President's, friendly, could not offend.

"But you're not my subject, Val. Only kings have subjects. This is a republic."

"Yes, sir, I know all that. But that's what I want on it."

"Then, by Jove, that's what you'll get on it. And your next one?"

"Thank you, sir. The second one is about the arrangements in the basement. There ought to be more shelves. Half the time when I make a delivery I find my empties piled there on the concrete, and they're covered with dust and then I have to clean them off, and even then they're nothing to brag about. There ought to be some shelves there on the left as you go in, back of the two wheelbarrows."

This time there were no smiles. Alma looked at Mrs. Stanley and saw the tears standing in her eyes, and looked away to hold her own back.

The President said, "All right, Val. It seems to me that a man who has just turned down half a million dollars ought to be entitled to a few shelves. All right, Val."

"Thank you, sir." Val swallowed. "This last one is a little different. I may not have the education for it, but maybe you could manage it without too much trouble. Of course maybe we won't go into the war after all, but if we do I'd like to be an officer instead of a private. Could you manage that?"

They all, even the President, exploded with laughter. Alma's tears came now, gaily trickling down her cheeks. But the President became sober:

"Are you pro-war, Val? Do you think we should enter the war?"

Val looked wise. "I don't know, sir. I suppose it's just that I wouldn't mind getting into one."

"Yes. I suppose that's it." The President nodded. He looked around at the others. "That's their strength, damn them. They use boys like Val for their strength." He lifted his shoulders. "Well, we'll see who is stronger; and we won't let them ruin this little meeting. If we enter the war, Val, you shall be an officer, and you'll be a good one."

"Yes, sir. Thank you very much. That's all for me."

"I wish it were more. Perhaps I shan't be able to restrain Mrs. Stanley from choosing a little gift for you.—Your turn, Chick."

Chick was all ready. He said promptly, "Mine is this, Mr. President. I'd like you to be best man at my wedding."

The President looked at him; at his grin, and then at Alma's smile. The President smiled too, broadly and with great friendliness. "I'm afraid I'll have to refuse that, Chick. I am already engaged for that occasion. I'm not an acrobat, so I couldn't very well give away the bride and act as best man at the same wedding."

## ABOUT THE AUTHOR

REX STOUT was born in Noblesville, Indiana, in 1886, the sixth of nine children of John and Lucetta Todhunter Stout, both Quakers. Shortly after his birth, the family moved to Wakarusa, Kansas. He was educated in a country school, but, by the age of nine, was recognized throughout the state as a prodigy in arithmetic. Mr. Stout briefly attended the University of Kansas, but left to enlist in the Navy, and spent the next two years as a warrant officer on board President Theodore Roosevelt's yacht. When he left the Navy in 1908, Rex Stout began to write freelance articles, worked as a sightseeing guide and as an itinerant bookkeeper. Later he devised and implemented a school banking system which was installed in four hundred cities and towns throughout the country. In 1927 Mr. Stout retired from the world of finance and, with the proceeds of his banking scheme, left for Paris to write serious fiction. He wrote three novels that received favorable reviews before turning to detective fiction. His first Nero Wolfe novel, *Fer-de-Lance*, appeared in 1934. It was followed by many others, among them, *Too Many Cooks, The Silent Speaker, If Death Ever Slept, The Doorbell Rang* and *Please Pass the Guilt*, which established Nero Wolfe as a leading character on a par with Erle Stanley Gardner's famous protagonist, Perry Mason. During World War II, Rex Stout waged a personal campaign against Nazism as chairman of the War Writers' Board, master of ceremonies of the radio program "Speaking of Liberty" and as a member of several national committees. After the war, he turned his attention to mobilizing public opinion against the wartime use of thermonuclear devices, was an active leader in the Authors' Guild and resumed writing his Nero Wolfe novels. All together, his Nero Wolfe novels have been translated into twenty-two languages and have sold more than forty-five million copies. Rex Stout died in 1975 at the age of eighty-eight. A month before his death, he published his forty-sixth Nero Wolfe novel, *A Family Affair*.

# "THE BEST POPULAR NOVEL TO BE PUBLISHED IN AMERICA SINCE *THE GODFATHER.*"
—Stephen King

# RED DRAGON

## by Thomas Harris, author of BLACK SUNDAY

If you never thought a book could make you quake with fear, prepare yourself for RED DRAGON. For in its pages, you will meet a human monster, a tortured being driven by a force he cannot contain, who pleasures in viciously murdering happy families. When you discover how he chooses his victims, you will never feel safe again.

Buy this book at your local bookstore or use this handy coupon for ordering:

## THE CHILDREN

They look so innocent with their angelic faces,
their blue schoolboy blazers.
But behind their shining eyes lurks a plan
for cold, brutal murder.

## THE CHILDREN

You might meet them anywhere. In the subway.
On a plane . . . In your bedroom.

## THE CHILDREN

They are waiting. For you.

## THE CHILDREN

A horrifying novel of the new generation of evil
by Charles Robertson
author of *The Elijah Conspiracy*

# WHODUNIT?

**Bantam did! By bringing you these masterful tales of murder, suspense and mystery!**

# Masters
## *of*
# Mystery

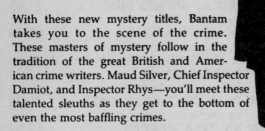

With these new mystery titles, Bantam takes you to the scene of the crime. These masters of mystery follow in the tradition of the great British and American crime writers. Maud Silver, Chief Inspector Damiot, and Inspector Rhys—you'll meet these talented sleuths as they get to the bottom of even the most baffling crimes.

| | | | |
|---|---|---|---|
| ☐ | 22702 | MURDER GOES MUMMING A. Craig | $2.25 |
| ☐ | 22826 | THE FAMILY AT TAMMERTON M. Erskine | $2.25 |
| ☐ | 22827 | NO. 9 BELMONT M. Erskine | $2.25 |
| ☐ | 22828 | CAST FOR DEATH M. Yorke | $2.25 |
| ☐ | 22858 | DEAD IN THE MORNING M. Yorke | $2.25 |
| ☐ | 22829 | DEATH ON DOOMSDAY E. Lemarchand | $2.25 |
| ☐ | 22830 | BURIED IN THE PAST E. Lemarchand | $2.25 |
| ☐ | 20675 | A MOST CONTAGIOUS GAME Catherine Aird | $2.25 |
| ☐ | 20567 | EXPERIMENT WITH DEATH E. X. Ferrars | $2.25 |
| ☐ | 20040 | FROG IN THE THROAT E. X. Ferrars | $1.95 |
| ☐ | 20304 | HENRIETTA WHO Catherine Aird | $2.25 |
| ☐ | 14338 | SOME DIE ELOQUENT Catherine Aird | $2.25 |
| ☐ | 14434 | SHE CAME BACK Patricia Wentworth | $2.25 |

**Buy them at your local bookstore or use this handy coupon for ordering:**